The Portuguese Fragment

Also by Owen Sela

THE BEARER PLOT

THE KIRIOV TAPES

The Portuguese Fragment

OWEN SELA

HODDER AND STOUGHTON
LONDON SYDNEY AUCKLAND TORONTO

for
BUDDY
for all the leap years

Over 2500 years of history and legend, Ceylon has been known by many names. The Macedonians knew it as Taprobane. Ptolemy called it Sila-Diva, later corrupted into Serendib. It has also been known as Zeilan, Sailan, Ceylon and on the 22nd of May 1972, it formally reverted to the ancient Sanskrit name of Sri Lanka—the resplendent isle. Throughout this book, however, I have referred to this beautiful island as Ceylon, the name by which it is most familiar to me, and I believe, to most readers.

 First printed 1973. First printed in the United Kingdom 1974. ISBN 0 340 17961 9. *Printed in Great Britain for Hodder and Stoughton Limited, St. Paul's House, Warwick Lane, London EC4P 4AH by The Garden City Press Ltd., Letchworth, Herts., SG6 1JS.*

1

I WAS BEHIND THE BAR when he came in, moving quickly with the panic stricken air of a squirrel being chased by a large dog. There was sweat on the flesh beside the crew-cut sandy hair and the white nylon shirt stuck to his body in pink blazonry. Outside it was winter.

I poured out a Martini and plopped two cherries into it. When I looked up he was standing across the counter from me, blinking round blue eyes behind the rimless glasses.

"Hello Elmer," I said.

Elmer was trailing a vivid check jacket like a flag of defeat. His check trousers were creased and rumpled. His Adam's apple bobbed as he said, "Hello, Nicholas." With a shy smile he picked up the glass and drank. "That's civil," he said, putting the glass back on the bar. "That's most civil."

Elmer was worried. He'd even left the cherries untasted. I reached behind the counter, refilled the glass and left the bottle where he could get it.

"You aren't drinking?" he enquired.

I shook my head. "Rules," I said. "When you're surrounded by the stuff, you've got to have rules." I flared a black Sobranie into life.

"Smoking's bad for you," Elmer said. "Gives you cancer."

I smiled. Elmer hadn't come all the way from Spain because he was worried about my health. "How's the Marquesa?" I ventured.

Elmer drank. Slower this time, the tension sagging visibly,

like a cut power line. "As well as can be expected, sir," he said and looked down at his glass.

"And you?"

He didn't look at me. "There have been a few problems," he admitted.

Problems weren't anything new. Ever since I'd met Elmer three years ago, there had been problems. Three years ago I'd been working for a two bit air freight outfit called Air Chartel. Its fleet consisted mainly of two superannuated Daks, a converted DC6 and an early 680 series Aero Commander. Air Chartel's offices were wherever there was someone broke enough or desperate enough to want to use their aircraft.

Most of the time we flew ordinary cargo, ground nuts from Nigeria, oil drilling equipment into Kuwait, that kind of thing. Other times we flew goods that were very different, the sort of cargo you didn't enter on a plane's manifest. Altogether, flying with Air Chartel made for an exciting kind of life. You were never far away from jail or close enough to your next meal.

Three years ago Elmer Robey had been looking after the legal affairs of Air Chartel. Then, Elmer had been glad to have the help of someone who, as he put it, gave him the story without frills and left him to worry about what legal subterfuges were necessary. The last time I had seen Elmer, he had been running an airline of his own, operating from the vast and secluded estate of the Marquesa de Maerez in southern Spain.

"How's the flying business?" I asked.

He smiled sadly. "Could be better, if we had the pilots. We always need pilots." He looked at me. "You were a damn good pilot," he said. "The best."

I grinned. "You're still a damn shrewd lawyer," and broke the rule about not drinking before nine o'clock and sloshed Chivas Regal into a glass.

"What's your problem?"

"It isn't," Elmer said, "what you'd call a problem. Not really a problem."

Over the next Martini, he told me. The air freight business wasn't good. The Spanish were unhelpfully arbitrary and he had been forced to fly legal cargoes, shipments of engineering and medical supplies, an occasional extrovert film director and that was it. There wasn't enough work to go round and, Elmer admitted, the profit had gone from the flying business. Ask any of the big carriers. They'd soon tell you. He stopped and looked around the bar. "How're you doing with this place?" he asked.

I looked round the bar. There wasn't much to see. It was like any other bar in Tangier, any other bar in the world. That is to say it was small and dim-lit, with tattered Coca-Cola calendars on the wall and hookers spilling their tits on the counter.

"It's doing alright," I said.

I'd bought the bar from the relict of a cirrhosis-ridden Englishman named Custer. Custer's Bar had cost me all of three thousand pounds and that included the stock Custer had not been able to drink, an assortment of fixtures and fittings, a reputation (we still had the odd American visitor looking for the Western Ranch Bar) and the relict.

The relict was called Abbas. He was good looking, twenty-five and because of a stupid regulation precluding tourists from owning property, technically the owner of the bar. "You won't be sorry, Nicky." Abbas had said when I'd given him the cash "I promise you that you won't be sorry. Look you've got to see it when there's a ship in. It's full. Packed." I remember how his eyes had gleamed, but it was not, as I later discovered, at the thought of profit.

There was a ship in tonight. All the Royal Navy had been able to muster were two callow eighteen year olds, who sat nervously in a corner, and sipped beer while trying to decide whether getting laid was worth the risk of clap.

"And how is Abbas?" Elmer asked.

"Abbas is fine," I said. He was probably down at the Dante, with the rest of the Royal Navy. Abbas loved the British Navy. Very, bloody patriotic.

Elmer leaned across the bar and said, "I've got a deal."

I didn't say anything.

Elmer said, "Played right, sir, we can both be rich."

I drummed fingers on the counter. All I had left from the de Maerez affair was a few hundred quid. Three thousand pounds had gone on the bar, and believing Abbas, I'd treated myself to a spanking new BMW. The bar just paid for itself. But my visa was running out and there was a seedy looking Englishman called Ponsonby who'd been asking about the five thousand pounds the Department had paid me some time ago. Ponsonby told me I lacked foresight. I should have realised that the Department would want the money back, especially as I'd botched the job.

"Tell me," I said, "How we are going to be rich."

Elmer sighed, and unstuck his eyes from Dolores to look at me. "It's your scene," he said. "It was just made for you."

Which meant that it was probably ill considered, underpaid and illegal.

"Art," Elmer said.

I shook my head. Pornography was risky at the best of times and ever since the Scandinavians had begun performing in public, the market had crashed.

"Paintings," Elmer said. "Statues, sarcophagi, stellae, bronzes, manuscripts, vases." He paused and looked down at his drink. "I tried to export a Velazquez drawing," he said, "and two El Greco's."

A Velazquez drawing was notching one hundred and fifty thousand pounds and the El Greco's were probably worth a million.

"Genuine?" I asked.

Elmer shook his head and looked sheepish. "It doesn't make any difference. I can't go back to Spain for a bit."

I poured myself another scotch in sympathy.

Elmer said, "I've got a customer, sir. The British Museum, no less."

"And what about Velazquez?"

"They aren't interested in Velazquez. They're interested in ancient art. Prehistoric art. To be precise, sir, they are interested in an Etruscan vase."

I put my drink down slow. Etruscan vases were all the rage these days. No self respecting museum could afford to be without one. And with fashion had come vast profits and the *tombaroli*, the professional tomb robbers who operated around ancient Etruscan sites near Rome.

"Why come to me?" I asked. "I know nothing about Etruscan art."

Elmer looked up at me and blinked. It was an honest blink. "For a start," he said, "there's Ponsonby."

2

Two hours later, there was still Ponsonby, with his tired RAF moustache drooping around a fourth glass of my whisky and his brown, dish-plate eyes unfocused on the row of bottles above my head. He brought me into vision obliquely. "I've cleared it with McGregor," he said. "He was positive you'd do it."

"McGregor was positive I'd do what?" McGregor was the new head of the Department. Like most other Air Chartel pilots, I had been a part-time employee of the Department. At least part-time was what they had called it, because they hadn't wanted to stamp our National Insurance cards. The truth was we worked for the Department, any time, any place, anyhow. The Department knew too much about Air Chartel and too much about each of us. Working for it had never been a question of choice. You did exactly what you were told, especially if you wanted to keep flying. Three years ago I'd wanted to keep flying.

I'd never worked for McGregor before. All my work for the Department had been done for a waspish, paranoid, establishment bastard called Carruthers, who in the end, turned out to be a double agent. After that, I'd hoped they'd think of me as a security risk, and never ask me to work for the Department again.

Except the Department said I owed them five thousand pounds. And there was Ponsonby.

Ponsonby said, "McGregor is sure you'd like to help. Need

you, old boy. Mother country and all that."

"My mother comes from Amsterdam," I said.

Ponsonby sighed, twisting his lips to reveal large, yellow teeth. "We've paid them off," he said. "The Department, you know. Paid them the five thousand pounds you owed."

"You're a bloody fool," I said.

"We paid," Ponsonby said. "To get you."

It was as crude as that. Christ: Even professional footballers had to consent to a transfer *and* they got a percentage of the fee. Who did McGregor think he was? And what did he think I was? A slave to be sold to the highest bidder? Well I had news for McGregor. "Who the hell are you?" I asked Ponsonby.

Ponsonby looked down at the whisky glass revolving slowly in the long white-worm fingers, with dirt-grimed nails. "Actually," Ponsonby said, "as a matter of fact, I work for the British Museum."

Actually, as a matter of fact, he was lying. The shiny, electric blue suit was wrong for the British Museum. The vivid choker of a tie was wrong. Even his manner, with its combination of minor public school, the armed forces and decaying gentility was wrong. I couldn't imagine Ponsonby in the museum, not even as an exhibit.

Elmer said, "It isn't much to do, sir. It's really quite simple."

I turned and glared at him. He swallowed a cherry hurriedly. "What's your involvement in this, you little twit?"

"Velazquez," he said choking on the cherry. "Velazquez." It sounded like a cough.

"We're arranging for Robey to return to Spain," Ponsonby said hurriedly, and added, "If all goes well." He placed the empty glass on the table with a suggestive thump.

I let him do his own pouring. "What do I have to do?" I asked cautiously.

"Well," Ponsonby said, "It's like this. I buy pieces for the British Museum, you see."

I did. Clearly. Ponsonby worked for the British Museum in the same way that a currency forger worked for the British Treasury.

"And there was this vase," Elmer said. "An Etruscan vase."

"Not Etruscan. Attic. Sixth century B.C. An exquisite piece. Red figure, you know, signed by the painter of Pan."

"Signed where?" I asked.

"We paid fifty thousand pounds for it," Ponsonby said, again identifying himself with the Museum.

"And somehow," I said, "you cocked it up."

Ponsonby flushed. "The seller welshed," he said, "He welshed, like any common or garden bookie."

"We want to get the vase back," Elmer said. "That's all. It's quite simple and very nearly legal."

"Why not send a solicitor's letter?" I asked.

Ponsonby sighed. "There are complications."

I nodded. With someone like Ponsonby there were always complications. Like the vase had been illegally acquired in the first place, and Ponsonby had gone to a great deal of trouble to give it a provenance, complete with affidavits from private collectors stating they had owned it for the past twenty years. Except now there was no vase. Unless I could get it back.

"It's not a vase," Ponsonby was saying. "It's a *krater*."

"Still a vase," Elmer said firmly. "Whatever fancy name you call it."

"What do I get out of it?" I demanded.

"We've cleared you with the Department," Ponsonby said. "I did, out of my commission."

I stared at him.

"Perhaps a hundred pounds," Ponsonby said.

And perhaps Elmer could go back to Spain and live happily ever after. And I could return to England any time I chose. I didn't believe in benevolence, but there was no harm in asking. "Where's the vase now?"

"Here," Ponsonby said. "Right here in Tangier."

"It's with Stavros Dirkian," Elmer said, "the art dealer."

And smuggler. Stavros Dirkian who had a winter residence on the hill overlooking Tangier bay complete with security system and two armed guards. Stavros Dirkian who was rumoured to be in with the Corsicans operating out of Marseilles, who had a diving business in Turkey, and who was not only rich enough to live in the better part of Tangier, but rich enough to leave a Rolls Royce Corniche there for his use during the short and infrequent visits he made. Stavros Dirkian was big time. Big trouble. No thank you.

"McGregor wanted me to tell you that I knew." Ponsonby waved a flaccid hand. "About this place and a few other things."

So Ponsonby could get me thrown out of Tangier. So he knew about the file with Interpol. I supposed McGregor called it cost efficiency, counting with Gaelic glee the five thousand pounds he'd never expected to see again. I would have been far better off being a professional footballer.

"Dirkian was no gentleman," Ponsonby said.

"Few of us are," I said and left the rest of Chivas untouched. "If we are going to hit Dirkian," I said, "we do it tonight. Now."

"Tonight?"

I stood up. There was no way I could convey to Ponsonby that Barney Goldman had already told me about the vase. More than that. Barney had already given me the entire plan of Dirkian's house.

3

I'D KNOWN BARNEY GOLDMAN SINCE the old Air Chartel days. Then he had been involved with one of those fringe outfits smuggling Czechoslovak weapons into Africa. With East European guns you didn't always need end-use certificates, and if the damn things subsequently exploded in the face of some kaffir, that was just too bad. Profits were what wars were all about. Ask Neville Chamberlain or old Moishe Tshombe.

After Biafra, things had gone rather quiet for Barney. The Angolan rebels could look after themselves, thank you, and if Tanzania ever thumped Uganda, it would be with second-hand British weaponry. For a while Barney had run an antique shop in Camden Town before discovering it lacked both profit and excitement. One day Barney had disappeared.

There had been rumours that he'd married a South American heiress and lived in the Argentine, that he had become an art dealer in New York, that he was in Paris running a gentlemen's film club, that more improbably, he'd been recruited by the Israeli Secret Service and was spying on Palestinian guerrillas in Syria.

Whatever he was doing Barney Goldman had been ten days in Tangier before he contacted me.

He charged into the bar one afternoon, all big and bearded, a grin like a row of white kerb-stones splitting his sun bronzed face, and crying, "Nicholas man! Good to see you!" and pumping my hand as if he wanted to wring oil from it.

"Barney," I'd said and reached for the gin. Barney was one

of those mercurial gin and tonic people, yarpily hearty and all over you one minute, suicidally paranoid the next. He was about six foot two with dark curly hair and dark shiny eyes, whose whites looked as if they had been bleached in Daz. With his thick beard and flapping khaki bush jacket he looked like a hunter newly returned from safari, and there was the kind of purity about him that you only get from eating free range eggs.

Barney was still talking loudly. "It was only last night that I heard you were in this dump! How are you, man! I mean, how are you?"

"Well Barney, very well." There was no point in telling him about my problems in getting back to England. "You?"

I'd heard rumours of trouble in the Atlas Mountains, and that the Moroccans were buying arms. I couldn't believe they would be foolish enough to deal with the likes of Barney. So that couldn't be why he was in Tangier.

"I'm on top of the world," Barney crowed. "Yes Nicky baby, I'm really on top of the world."

I made his drink a long one, two-thirds Gordons, one-third Schweppes, ice and lemon. "What brings you to Tangier?"

"Business," Barney said, "Business, and," he pushed his dark head across the bar at me, "revenge. Someone in Tangier owes me a bloody fortune."

"Been buying lottery tickets then, have you?"

Barney moistened the edge of his beard with gin. "Stavros Dirkian owes me money." There was an ugly ring to his voice.

I whistled softly to show that I realised Dirkian was big time.

"He sold some clobber for me," Barney said, "and kept back more of the proceeds than he should have."

"I didn't know Dirkian was into gun-running."

Barney looked annoyed. "Guns man! Ach! Who wants with guns these days! Dirkian owes me money for some statues." Barney lowered his voice. "They were just the teeniest bit hot."

"How teeny?" I asked. "And where from?"

"The fact is," Barney said, "the people to whom the statues belonged are very annoyed with Dirkian. He was supposed to sell them on a commission, not keep half the proceeds."

"And they've asked you to get the money back. Even if I say so myself, they couldn't have found anyone better."

"The only thing I need is a good safe-man," Barney said and looked at me.

I said "You won't find one here. The best safe men are in Europe or the States."

"We were buying in Rome when we heard that Dirkian had got himself a marvellous Greek vase. Fifty thousand pounds worth of Greek vase." He kept his gaze on me to be sure that last fact registered.

"Is that what Dirkian owes you?"

"There's a couple of thousand in it for you, Nicholas."

"Not for me, Barney," I said, quietly. "I like running this bar. I like living in Tangier. I don't need two grand's worth of complications. Use someone else."

Barney said, "It isn't big enough to import someone, and I couldn't trust a local, especially if something went wrong."

"You'll have to get someone else."

"There are no complications," Barney said. "It'll be quite a simple job. Three times a week, Tuesday, Thursday and Saturday, Dirkian goes down to the casino. He doesn't get back until about four."

"How boringly predictable."

"The house is wired," Barney said, "But that won't be difficult. The alarm can be looped out."

"That's good," I said.

"There's the safe," Barney said. "I don't know about that."

I didn't say anything.

Barney fidgeted with his drink. "Aw, come on, Nicky baby. Say you'll do it."

I kept my mouth shut.

"There's two grand in it for you, clear. What's the matter? Isn't it enough?"

"It isn't the money," I said.

Barney said, "We could make it more, and there will be other things, afterwards."

"Sorry Barney," I'd said firmly. "Nothing doing. I like my life the way it is."

And now I was doing the same job for a measly hundred quid. Well, perhaps it was more than a hundred quid, especially if you counted being able to get back to England, and not being booted out of Tangier. I suppose it amounted to more than a hundred quid if you counted letting Elmer get back to Spain and repaying my so-called debt to the Department. Christ! The things one had to do in order to be left alone.

* * *

While I got the equipment sorted out, Ponsonby paced about my bedroom and smoked menthol tipped cigarettes, looking, with his long, spindly legs and paunchy body rather like a pregnant ostrich. Occasionally he would peer at his watch, wind it, and mutter to himself each time he discovered the watch was already fully wound.

Abruptly he stopped and looked at the array of tools on the bed. "Aren't we going to use any metal cutting equipment like, you know, oxy something . . ."

"We're not," I said firmly. "Oxyacetylene equipment is too bulky and we won't need it. If the safe is the very latest kind, then it's going to take too long to cut through it with a torch. If it's an old model, then we run the risk of baking the vase into a shape your Etruscans never dreamed of."

"It's not Etruscan," Ponsonby said sharply. "It's Greek."

"Sure," I said, "Sure. It's Greek, sixth century B.C., by the painter of Pan."

The last thing I wanted was to get into an argument about his bloody vase. I busied myself with checking that all the gear I needed was there. Drill, masonry and metal bits, extension plugs and sockets, stethoscope in case Dirkian's safe was one of those really old-fashioned combination efforts where you could actually hear the tumblers click, hammers, rope, a coil of insulated wire, tape, two hacksaws and a set of spare blades, jack, two pairs of steel rollers, two pairs of insulated pliers, chisels, gimlet, rasps, and crow-bar. That was all there was to it, except for the pieces of angled steel that slotted together to form a light and strong eight-foot ladder.

I smiled. Every single item of equipment so far was perfectly innocuous. Even together they comprised little more than a master plumber's tool kit. I packed them away neatly into a framed leather carrying case. Then I changed into a thin, black turtle-neck sweater and tight fitting black pants, without cuffs. I took out a dark blue jerkin and slipped into its pocket a pen-light, a pair of cotton gloves, a chisel with a wooden blade, and the zap gun. The zap gun was one of my choicest possessions. It had been invented by a well-known American burglar, Harry Zap, and had been given to me by a former policeman named Quimper. Quimper would never have believed that I ever intended to use it seriously.

Ponsonby looked at his watch and asked, "Where on earth is Elmer?"

"Still getting the car." I poured out a small Chivas and lit cigarette. "He shouldn't be long."

"I'm tired of waiting."

"You've got a few more hours to wait, George." I pointed to the Chivas and the bed. "Make yourself comfortable."

Ponsonby's hand stopped the cigarette halfway to his mouth. "I'm coming with you, Nicholas," he said and drew tightly at the cigarette with a hissing sound.

"Like hell you are."

He let out smoke through clenched teeth. "I'm afraid I am, old boy." He paused and said hesitantly, "It should be jolly good fun."

I scratched my cheek with the edge of my thumb. "You done anything like this before?"

"As a matter of fact, no."

"Then let me tell you something, George. It's rather different from raiding the college tuck shop. You can get hurt doing this. You can even get sent to jail."

"I realise the risks," Ponsonby said, "But it's unfair, dash it, it's unfair that only you should be exposed to such dangers."

"That's the way you set it up," I said. "Don't let your conscience stop you now."

"I'm afraid it does, in a way, rather." Ponsonby did his best to look conscience-striken.

I sipped the Chivas. What was worrying Ponsonby was not his conscience, but the fact that I would be alone with his precious vase for a couple of hours. And then I would, I could, return the vase to the museum myself. That way I could make sure both the museum and the Department saw me right.

Caesar had once wanted to know who would guard the guards themselves. I could tell him the answer for nothing. It wouldn't be Ponsonby.

4

STAVROS DIRKIAN LIVED SOME KILOMETRES outside Tangier, preferring proximity to the airport to the Edwardian elegance of somewhere like Le Montagne. I suppose the way he did business, the capacity for instantaneous flight was preferable to a fashionable address.

The house was situated in splendid isolation, half way up a gentle folding hill which overlooked the narrow road to the airport. A small, unmade track led from the road, over a field, up the side of the hill, past Dirkian's house. The house itself was built in an old Moorish style, square, with shuttered wooden windows set into arches, a low flat roof, a large ornate door under a trefoil arch. Its freshly-painted white walls were in marked contrast to the green of the hill and the rusted tin shacks of the herdsmen in the fields below. Taxi drivers bringing passengers from the airport were apt to point it out as a building of importance. That night all I could see were the pot-holes under the waving yellow beam of the Renault TS that Elmer had borrowed.

We drove slowly past the house and reversed off the track beside the wall on the further side. The gate was certain to be alarmed or controlled by a photoelectrical device. The safer way was over the wall. Elmer turned off the engine and the parking lights. Silence and darkness enveloped us.

I took out my case and set off, walking uphill, beside the wall. Ponsonby followed, carrying the collapsible steel ladder. The grass felt tough and springy under my feet and after a few yards, the Renault merged into the night. It was just like Elmer to have picked a black car.

I stopped after a few yards, slotted the ladder together and leant it against the side of the wall. Taking care not to touch the wall, I went up. Apart from the light over the main entrance, the house was in darkness, the fast shut windows and thick walls making it look like a fortress. Or perhaps that was only my state of mind.

The light over the entrance washed along a gravel drive that ran in a straight line from the gate and expanded out in front of the house into a rectangular parking area. From the parking area the drive extended towards me and an open, empty garage. Between me and the house was about thirty yards of well kept lawn, flower-beds and thin trees. There was absolutely no cover.

I unclipped the penlight from my pocket and ran it low over the wall. Dirkian was not relying on anything as crude as bits of broken glass embedded in masonry. Stretched out along the top of the wall were two wires, about six inches apart, connected to twin rows of insulators and running over the entire circumference of the wall. The wires were so placed that it was impossible to get a hand or a foot over the wall without touching one of them. Both wires were undoubtedly live and undoubtedly connected in such a way that cutting them would only sound off the alarm.

I went down the ladder again, opened my bag and took out the reel of insulated wire and a pair of pliers. Then I told Ponsonby exactly what he had to do when he came over and went up again. Carefully I twisted one end of the reel and fixed it to the insulator furthest away from me. Then I let the reel out in a long loop that fell on the far side of the wall, cut it and fastened the free end to the parallel insulator. I did the same with the second set of insulators, looping the wire on my side of the wall. Now having provided an alternative pathway for the current, all I had to do was cut the original wires. And wait.

I waited. No harsh jangle of alarm bells, no rapid turning on of lights. I placed a foot across the severed wire, braced myself and jumped. I landed lightly rolling forward into a flower-bed to absorb the shock of the fall. By the time I spat out a mouthful of earth and removed flowers from my hair, Ponsonby was balancing precariously on top of the wall, waving my case.

He let the case drop and sat astride the wall to haul the ladder up after him. I stood beneath and prayed that he wouldn't fall over, or that he wouldn't trip the loops with the ladder or his flailing feet. I helped him fix the ladder and then he came down, breathing heavily and smelling acidic.

"If anything goes wrong," I whispered, "run like hell. Get up the ladder and get over the wall. Don't worry about the alarm system, and don't worry about me."

Ponsonby said he wouldn't worry about me. I led the way along the edge of the drive, towards the house. From time to time I looked back to try and memorize the place where the ladder was. In that darkness it was difficult to see anything. I hoped like hell we wouldn't have to make a hurried exit.

I left Ponsonby beyond the pool of light by the front door, pulled on my cotton gloves, and went up the steps alone. The door was a big one, solid, built of six inch thick wood, banded with iron. It was three hundred years old and built to resist a battering-ram.

The lock was three hundred years old too, large and ornate, requiring a key about a foot long. It was about as secure as the coin box on a pay phone. Using the wire on my Roman finger-key-ring, it took me all of thirty seconds to open it.

Beckoning Ponsonby to follow, I stepped in. I stood on a wide, tiled patio, whose gentle arches surrounded a square, open courtyard. The courtyard was tiled too, and an ornamental fountain stood in its centre. The fountain wasn't playing.

Doors led off three sides of the patio to the interior of the house. I went to the left, the side opposite to where we had left the Renault. By working backwards from the furthest point, the later it got, the nearer we'd be to our escape route.

The door leading into the house was as massive and as old as the front door. It had the same lock. It seemed that Dirkian had believed that once he had protected the perimeter, he was impregnable.

We crowded into a narrow corridor, made even narrower with gilt and leather upholstered furniture, with hassocks, the stuffed heads of animals and assorted statuary. The roof was low arched, and the corridor seemed to extend the length of the house, with cave-like rooms leading off it.

I went along the corridor trying doors. If Dirkian had any resident servants, they were in all probability locked away from the main residence at night. La Montagne vibrated with tales of the duplicity of Moroccan servants and few of them were allowed to remain in an unoccupied house for any length of time. At a wage of under 10p an hour only the more foolish expected honesty.

When I came to a door that was locked, I stopped. A quick flash of the penlight. Enough to show that this lock was different, modern, incapable of being opened with hope and a little piece of wire. I took out the zap gun and placed its barrel against the keyhole. Very gently I squeezed the trigger.

There was no sound. That was as it should have been. The gun was filled with little wire rods and moist thread. Slowly the wire fed the thread into the lock, jamming it tight against the tumblers. In about five minutes the lock was full. All I had to do then was insert the wooden chisel into the keyhole and twist. Voilà! We were in Dirkian's study.

Dirkian's study was large, with a window opening out onto the garden. A Moroccan sofa in Regency style stood by the window, beside an inlaid, Amboyna-wood table. Bookshelves covered the rear wall, extending in short L's along the sides. A row of club armchairs stood around a thin reading lamp, and slightly off centre, at an angle to the window, was a leather topped desk and three chairs. The floor was covered with Oriental rugs and the walls were covered with gilt framed, Victorian paintings of a singular lifelessness.

The safe was wedged into a bookcase beside the desk and framed with a rosewood veneer. Rosewood veneer was very pretty but it didn't do much for security. I stood on an Oriental carpet in the centre of the room and stared at the safe.

It wasn't, thank God, a straight-from-the-forge modern one. It was formed from a single metal plate, bent over at the back to form four flanges. There was an impressive looking Royal Warrant in the centre of the door, but it did not say to whom the manufacturer had been appointed, or what for. That was hopeful.

Because safes look solid and heavy, few people doubt them. In that sense, they are like car safety belts. You never know how strong they are, till you crash. Because the numbers of people being burgled are always fewer than those who are not, there is no great emphasis on keeping up with the latest developments in safe-making or safe-breaking. After all, safes never ever wear out, do they?

"We're going to have to work fast," I said. "I can't tell if the safe is bugged or not. We'll have to assume that it is."

"Won't the alarm go off?" Ponsonby asked.

"Not if it's connected directly to a police station."

I moved Dirkian's desk to the centre of the room, took the crow-bar and smashed the false rosewood panelling. Ponsonby looked horrified. For that I made him clear the bookshelf around the safe. They were mostly coffee table art books, a few works on porcelain, and a few on underwater salvage. I remembered that Dirkian had a diving business in Turkey.

I fitted the jack onto its rollers, made Ponsonby tilt the safe and slid the jack underneath. Once I'd got the safe clear of the ground, I used the jack lever to tow jack, safe and all into the middle of the room. There I yanked the safe round so that the back faced me. I dropped the jack and stowed it away, and using the chisel cut a deep gash along the edge.

There was no time for finesse now. I gave Ponsonby the spare hammer and chisel and together we attacked the safe. The noise of our hammering filled the room. Fortunately it did not take many blows to cut into the casing and peel the edge back far enough. Ferromanganese filling spilled over the carpet. I looked through the gap we had made. The back of the safe had been screwed, from the inside.

I connected up the drill and jabbed the bit fiercely into the screws. Press, the shriek of metal cutting into metal, press, screech, press, screech, the drill cutting through metal as if it were nylon.

When I'd got enough of the screws away, I prised the safe open, with crow-bar and chisels. It was a hundred times more brutal and about a hundred times more difficult as opening a sardine tin.

Inside the safe stood the vase, a black shallow cup with

handles, decorated with a red horse being led by figures in flowing Greek robes. That's what it was like at Troy, I thought and eased the vase out and placed it on top of the safe.

From above me Ponsonby breathed, "My God, it's beautiful!"

I reached into the safe for the wad of paper that had lain beside the vase. As Ponsonby cooed over the vase, I slipped the paper into my case.

I reached along the floor to unplug the drill. There was a slam of a door opening and a level voice saying "Keep very still both of you."

I looked up at the stubby grey-haired figure of Stavros Dirkian. Behind him were two swarthy Corsicans. They were all in evening dress and they all carried guns. The guns were pointing at Ponsonby and at me.

5

I LAY AT FULL LENGTH on the floor and thought, what a ridiculous situation. There were only two ways out of the room. The door and the window. The window was shut and Dirkian's men stood by the door, with guns.

Ponsonby towered above me, holding the vase to his chest, staring uncomprehendingly at Dirkian. Dirkian stared meanly back.

I said, "George, whatever you do, don't put that vase down."

Dirkian shifted his mean look to me. He was a little man with a lot of fat, a lot of solidity. The face with its sharp nose and deep-set eyes was nearly handsome, spoilt only by the loose-lipped mouth and the good-living jowls.

Ponsonby said, "Stavros, put that gun away."

Dirkian kept looking at me. In one of those brown cigarette voices he asked, "Who are you?"

It wasn't really the time for exchanging calling cards. I said, "Why don't you do what George wants and put those guns away."

Ponsonby said, "Let's not be silly about this. I've paid for this vase, you know." I thought his voice quavered.

I moved into a squatting position and very slowly, very obviously so that they could see I wasn't trying anything, drew my case to me. "If you won't put those guns away, you could try shooting George," I said.

Ponsonby said, "Nicholas, now look here—"

I kept my eyes fixed on Dirkian. "Of course if you do shoot

George," I said, "he'll drop the vase. That's one way of kissing fifty thousand pounds goodbye."

Dirkian didn't like that idea at all. He said, "I could shoot him in the leg."

"He'll still fall, won't you, George?"

Ponsonby spluttered.

I unplugged the drill from the wall socket and began to wind the lead slowly around the handle. You got more insulation that way. "Tell you what, Stavros, why don't you let George and the vase go. That way you'll have an evens chance of getting it back. It's much better than shooting him and losing everything."

Dirkian turned to Ponsonby. "Put the vase down," he said.

Ponsonby gave him a twitchy smile. "No."

I said, "You see, Stavros, you'll have to do it my way. Go on George, get moving." I hoped Ponsonby would have the nous to keep the vase between him and the guns. I looked at the Corsicans. "Go on boys, give him a bit of room. That vase is pretty damned valuable. Ask Stavros."

Stavros spoke to them in Italian and they moved away from the door as George approached.

"You too, Stavros. He needs a lot of room."

Ponsonby approached them, holding the vase outstretched before him. It was obvious even to the Corsicans that it was so lightly held that any move would cause it to fall and shatter. Of course the bits could be put together, but then it would never again be worth fifty thousand pounds. As Ponsonby approached the door, he turned and backed towards it, the vase still between the men and his body.

"If you hear anyone coming after you," I said, "just drop the vase. OK?"

Ponsonby was pale and sweating. There were dark shadows under his eyes and his skin had a peculiar desiccated look. "What about you?" he asked.

"I'm staying with Stavros," I said.

He turned to look at me.

"Keep your eyes on them, George."

He jerked his head away. One hand on the door, he asked, "Will you be alright?"

"Sure," I said, "Don't worry about a thing."

* * *

The door shut after George, the sound of his footfalls faded along the corridor. Stavros Dirkian looked at me and said, "I'm going to kill you."

"I wouldn't," I said. "George knows where I am, and how could you ever explain away my body."

Dirkian said, "I'm going to kill you, anyway."

I squatted and waited. Go on, George. Hurry up, George and George, for Heaven's sake, don't lose your way.

Dirkian said, "For what you do this? The vase is mine. You understand. Mine. And you helped that man steal it. Why? I ask you, why?"

"Simple," I said. "How much are you going to pay me, to steal the vase back?"

Dirkian thought hard about that. Then he began to look even meaner. "You making funny of me. I don't like that."

He started to move across the room towards me, the Corsicans following in a tight knot. I was pretty certain Dirkian wasn't going to kill me, but there was a lot of damage that he and his thugs could do that stopped short of killing. Besides with George and the vase gone, they didn't owe anyone explanations. I was an ordinary intruder and they could have a lot of fun with me, before calling the police.

"Let's be reasonable about this," I said to Dirkian.

Dirkian wasn't going to be reasonable. At an order from him, they put away their guns. There were three of them and one of me and guns were not necessary for what they had in mind.

I let them come half way across the room towards me. Then gripping the drill with its insulated handle and the coils of its insulated wire wrapped round it, I jabbed it into the live socket of the plug.

There was a muffled explosion, a yellow-white flash, and the lights went out.

Outside, the alarm bells clanged like tin barrels bouncing along concrete. I hurled myself sideways as someone fired. Still sliding, I lifted up my case and hurled it at the window.

Twelve pounds of case and a hundred and sixty pounds of effort smashed through the wooden shutters as if they were only glass. The room exploded with gun fire and bright pin-points of light as the Corsicans loosed off. I picked up the crow-bar and hurled it where I'd last seen the flashes.

A heavy-sounding whir. Thump. A shriek of pain. I dived at floor level for the window, placed my hands on the sill, and vaulted through the broken shutters.

I nearly broke my neck.

For the second time that night I landed in a flower-bed. Thank Heaven for flower-beds. Thank Heaven Dirkian didn't fancy roses.

I picked up the case and began to run. There was a shout behind me, the crack of a pistol shot. I weaved and turned, discerning shadowy figures crowding at the window. Then a yellow flash and the whizz of a bullet high above me. I hurled myself to the ground.

From the window behind me, they fired half a dozen exploratory shots at the wall. Someone flashed a torch. Then the wall began firing back.

There was a piercing cry and the firing from the house stopped. Crouching low, still dragging the case I sprinted for the corner of the house and the drive.

I ran madly along the drive, reached the gate, threw the case over and climbed up after it. My feet were running when they hit the road and I sprinted along the outside of the wall aware of nothing but the track under my pounding feet and a white wall that seemed to go on forever and ever.

I came around the corner of the wall and nearly ran into the black Renault. I ran up to the driver's window. "Where's George?" I panted.

"Not here yet," Elmer said.

I thrust the case at him and ran up the hill, along the wall, to where we had left the ladder. About twenty yards up, a shadowy figure balanced precariously astride the wall, trying to manoeuvre the ladder and the vase at the same time.

"Jump," I cried, "For God's sake man, jump!"

Ponsonby said, "What about the vase?"

"Hold it tight and jump."

Ponsonby got his left leg over and sat, looking down. If he sat there long enough, he'd never make up his mind to jump. I reached up and pulled at his legs. With a startled "yolk!" he came collapsing onto the springy grass, rolling onto his back, holding the vase up and away from him.

I tried to pull the vase from him, but he wouldn't let go. He got to his feet and we ran in the darkness, back towards the car. There was no sound of gunfire now, but faint and far away I could hear the distinct wail of police sirens.

I turned and looked back, "Hurry up man," listening to Ponsonby plodding behind me.

"I'm coming," he panted, and then I ran into the back of the Renault. So did Ponsonby. So did the vase.

6

ELMER TOOK OFF LIKE A SCARED CAT, hurling the Renault onto the track in a wheel spinning slide. The car dipped, twisted, straightened in a series of seasick-making lurches. It shaved the wall of Dirkian's house. Dirkian's house was ablaze with light. Ahead of us another pair of headlamps flashed momentarily into the sky.

The car bucked and swayed, wallowing through the pot-holes. Dust poured from the wheels. Stones clattered against the body and the suspension set up a ceaseless thumping. The whole body began to rattle, louder after the tools in the rear broke free.

We went down the track like a runaway toboggan, bouncing, clattering, hurled against the doors and the roof, Elmer twisting furiously at the steering, keeping his foot hard down all the way. Once the car dipped and slid sideways with a horrible, metallic dragging noise. Once we leapt six foot over a bump before crashing solidly onto the rugged earth. At the long corner before the main road Elmer threw the car into a lunging drift, open throttle and thrashing front wheels pulling the car along, the rest of us following. The rear wheels smashed over a series of bumps, the car juddered, and I thought it would keel over. Then the moment passed and there was only the straight tarmac road rushing to meet us, with the evenly spaced row of flashing blue lights streaking across it, headlamps blazing. Elmer switched off our own lights as the Renault screeched sideways across the road, shredding chunks of rubber. We clipped the grass at the far end, lurched straight and settled along the smooth road to the airport in nearly complete darkness. Momentarily, the beam of police cars lit up the inside of the Renault. Then they were gone screaming up the track towards Dirkian's house.

Before we got too far away from danger, I thought I'd sort something out with Ponsonby. "We've kept our part of the deal," I said. "Let's be clear about that."

From behind me, Ponsonby said, "We've lost the vase."

"You lost the vase. I told you, you shouldn't have come."

Ponsonby asked, "What do I tell the British Museum?"

"Tell them they should insure their vases against breakage."

"Fifty thousand pounds," Ponsonby said. "That's what it cost."

"Plus five thousand. I did the job right. I got you the vase. You broke it."

Ponsonby went silent.

"Now I'm square with the Department. And Elmer gets back to Spain."

Ponsonby said, "I don't think I can fix Spain yet."

After a while he said, "I think you'd better drop me off at the embassy."

An hour later after we'd got back to Tangier, through Cap Spartel, we did just that.

* * *

We wiped the car as clean as we could, left it in a side street off the Boulevard Pasteur, and went back to my flat. I sloshed Chivas into two glasses, handed one to Elmer and flung myself across the bed, feet stuck up on the dressing-table. "I'm sorry Spain didn't work out for you," I said.

"Or the Department for you."

"I think the Department will be alright. McGregor will never give them the money back."

"And it looks as if Ponsonby won't even be buying picture postcards for some time."

"Right." We drank. Now that the excitement was over I was coming aware of pain and fatigue of a million different aches in all parts of my body. "The sofa in the living room is collapsible," I said. "Why don't you fix yourself a bed."

"What was all the shooting about?" Elmer asked.

I shrugged. "Dirkian's heavies were shooting at me. Then someone started firing at them, from beside the wall. For a moment I thought it was you."

"Don't carry a gun," Elmer said.

"Me neither."

We drank more of the Chivas. I lit a cigarette.

"Who could it have been?" Elmer asked.

"It could have been his own guards," I said, "startled by the shooting."

"That's one explanation."

I shrugged. "Remember Barney Goldman?" I asked.

Elmer nodded.

I told Elmer about Barney's proposition. "It could have been Barney," I said.

Elmer screwed up his face in doubt. "Don't think so," he said. "Barney was a gun-runner, not a gun-man."

"This time he had friends."

"True, sir. True. But the way Dirkian lived it could have been anybody. He double-crossed enough people to run a baseball team all by himself."

"Well we know it wasn't Ponsonby."

"It sure wasn't," Elmer said, finished his drink and put the glass down. "Where did you say the bed-clothes were?"

"Let me show you." I stood up and stretched and thought longingly of sleep. But it wasn't to be like that. As I stood up there was a loud, hurried knocking at the door.

* * *

I went through the living room and stood by the door. More knocking. More impatient. Louder. I stood hesitating. I could pretend I wasn't in. Then another knock. A voice. "Nicholas?"

I recognised the voice. Still I asked, "Who is it?"

"Me. Abbas."

I let Abbas in. He was dressed in his raver gear, ruffled silk shirt, skin-tight yellow pants, cowboy boots and studded belt. "Nicky," he said. "You've got to leave town."

"Why?"

3—TPF * *

"My uncle. He came to the club, looking for you."

Abbas' uncle was a policeman. Sometimes the Moroccan police had fits of morality and tried to clamp down on the brothels. Custers Bar wasn't a brothel, but still the police came, fired by a righteous sense of public duty, and a desire to see what the traffic would bear.

I said, "I've explained to your uncle about this before. There's nothing I can do about the girls using the place. As long as they're prepared to pay for their drinks, I've got to treat them like any other customers."

"It isn't the girls, Nicky. It's you!"

"Me?"

"They want to talk to you. About the murder of Stavros Dirkian!"

I felt as if someone had hit me with a sackful of Etruscan vases. At last I manged, "Why me?"

"One of his bodyguards recognised you from the bar."

"Oh Jesus!" I said.

If I waited to be questioned by the Moroccan police, it wouldn't do me much good. They had a positive identification, and all they would be interested in was who my associates were. They'd never believe I didn't know that.

"You've got to get out," Abbas repeated.

"Sure," I agreed. "How?"

"Don't worry about a thing," Abbas said. "I'll look after the bar for you."

"How the hell do I get out of Morocco?" I asked.

Abbas' face clouded. "You can't leave from Tangier," he said. "There are no planes until the morning, and they'll be watching the airport."

And they'd also know the number of my car. With a murder charge hanging over my head, stealing a car would be too dangerous.

Abbas said, "I have a car. Come, we go to Casa now."

Four hours later we were in Casablanca. The first plane out was a Swissair flight to Geneva and Zurich. We took that. There is an old proverb about beggars not being able to be choosers.

7

MALAGA WAS BAD. We had to wait there half an hour, sitting in the gleaming terminal building, trying to look as if we missed our families and the last of the winter sunshine. Elmer worried that a Spanish policeman would recognise him. I worried that the Moroccan police would have found out which flight I'd taken, and radioed the Spanish police to stop me.

Thirty-two thousand feet above France, I relaxed. Nothing but a hijack could divert the DC9 from Geneva. It was only then that I thought to see what I had taken from Dirkian's safe and took it out from my case.

At first sight it didn't look much. A yellowed scrap of paper whose ink had turned brown, a type-written essay entitled "The Pagode" (Trans. Doctor F. Cabraal), a holiday snapshot and the negative of that same snapshot and some bank payment advices.

The yellowed paper looked about two hundred years old, its edges browned with time, showing termite holes instead of full stops. The writing on it looked two hundred years old too, neat and legible, letters evenly formed, lines evenly spaced, a product of a time when penmanship was an art form. It was written in Spanish or Portuguese or some Latin language.

The typescript appeared to be a translation.

The photograph was more interesting. It was a typical holiday snapshot, one of those pictures where someone sets the shutter to delayed action, and runs to join the group. It showed Dirkian and two friends on a beach. They all wore bathing costumes, and diving masks strung around their necks. The group consisted of Dirkian, a young man and a girl. I looked at the girl.

She was in her early twenties, slim bodied, with small breasts and heavy thighs. A narrow bikini stretched across right-sized hips and she was smiling at the camera, a right size smile with a right-shaped mouth. She had an arm around each of the men and a marvellously sexy face, high flat cheekbones, large angled eyes, a head so full of dark curly hair that it seemed too weighty for the slender neck. I began to have other thoughts for the first time since I'd left Tangier.

The other man in the picture looked about twenty-eight or so, wiry, flat pectoralled with an intelligent, pointed face and a receding blonde hairline. In the picture he showed the beginnings of a beard and he had thrust one shoulder to the camera, as if protecting the girl from the photographer. He had thrown his head back and sideways in imitation toughness and his smile showed large friendly teeth. He looked the joker of the group.

Dirkian stood square to the camera, smiling slightly, a cloth cap pulled down over his eyes and looking just the slightest bit embarrassed and proprietary.

The bank slips were more puzzling than either the manuscript or the photograph. There was one slip clipped to each of the documents I had taken from Dirkian's safe, and they were all duplicates, evidencing payments made to a numbered account at the Union Banque Suisse in Zurich. The slip attached to the negative was for twenty thousand Swiss francs, that to the print, ten thousand. The manuscript and the translation were worth ten thousand francs each.

So Dirkian had paid forty thousand francs for these documents, over four thousand pounds. A lot of money.

I dumped the lot onto Elmer's lap, stretched and listened to the keening whistle of the engine. We were still pointed for Switzerland. I thought about girls. I think about girls at the oddest moments. I thought it was nearly three weeks since Penelope left me.

"Blackmail," Elmer said at last.

"No. She didn't like Arabs."

"Blackmail," Elmer repeated looking at me in surprise.

"Dirkian was being blackmailed."

"Oh" I said. "Who would blackmail Dirkian? And what about?"

Elmer frowned. "The man and the girl in the photograph. They look as if they were good friends, and Dirkian looks something of an outsider."

"You mean some kind of sexual thing?"

Elmer shrugged. "Maybe Dirkian was AC/DC, who knows?"

"Even if he was, what difference would it make? Dirkian wasn't married and he wasn't in the kind of job where he'd have to pretend he'd never heard of sex."

"Perhaps she was under statutory age."

"Elmer," I said, "look at that body." I took another look at that body too. "That's no fifteen year old."

"Alright," Elmer said, "you tell me."

"It couldn't be a sexual thing. If Dirkian was being blackmailed, what's the manuscript got to do with it?"

"Read" Elmer said, "and learn."

I started to read the translation. I can't say that I learned very much.

THE PAGODE

(Trans. Doctor F. Cabraal)

THE PAGODE THOUGH NOT of great size was very beautifully and finely wrought. In structure it resembled a pavilion after the fashion of the Cherins. On account of the magnificence of the Pagode and what I have afterwards received from the inhabitants themselves and known to be true amongst them, this Pagode was formed by the Cherin. In a city two leagues or so distant, there resides a lord who is a Chin, and ruler of all the coast on the further side, but this last I have not verified with my own eyes.

From afar the Pagode appeared as stately as a galleon, so exquisitely was it constructed and so perfectly proportioned. The roof of the Pagode was formed of tile, in the shape of small Pagodes and all richly decorated with fine figures of warriors, bearing bows and spears, but no other instruments of war. The roof was in three storeys and from the lowermost level there were projections formed in gold, in the shape of that snake that is called graspers, which is not longer than one and a half ells and which lives in trees. It was this roof that covered the inner courtyard of the Pagode and there were like projectures on the roof which was on the second storey, which covered the interior of the Pagode itself.

The third storey was more like a tower and stood in the middle of the Pagode. It was more sumptuously decorated than the other two and on the four sides there were golden sculptures of bulls. According to their religion the people are forbidden the eating of meat at all times and the bull they hold sacred and they allow to wander hither and thither without molestation.

The principal gateway was from the west under an ornamented tower whose workmanship was not so fine as the Pagode itself, but of good quality, nevertheless. A path led from this gateway to a wide flight of stone steps for the Pagode was set inside a high wall surrounded by a garden of flowers and palm trees.

At the top of the steps was a wide stone platform, eight cubits wide, of regular shape, being levelled all over and longer than it was wide. The entrance to the platform was flanked by stone carvings of two royal tygers and over these there was erected like an umbrella of stone, the hood of a snake that was of such dimension that it contained within it seven other snakes also with upraised hoods. This snake is called cobra and about a fathom long and when angered it rears itself upwards and throws out a hood surrounding its head. It possesses a strong venom that is dangerous to man, for if a man receive a bite and if an antidote be not immediately applied, he will surely die. This snake too they hold sacred for it is supposed to protect their god.

At regular spaces around the platform they had constructed pairs of stones in the form of this snake, being smaller in size than those by the steps and joined with rope, serving to prevent worshippers falling by accident to the path below, when they had great crowds.

There was a covered pathway at the top of the steps its

roof supported by four stone pillars on which many carvings were carefully wrought with great skill and artistry. Each pillar was twelve cubits high and constructed from a single stone, with a squared top in the shape of a lion on whose back the roof seemed to rest. All had a carving beneath of a peacock, and the remainder of the stone was covered with carvings of men and other designs in careful patterns. The pathway led to the inner courtyard which was open to the side so that the more worshippers could gather and pay reverence to their Pagode. The inner courtyard was covered by the lowest roof which was supported on pillars of carved wood, painted in divers colours and of such beauty that it was impossible for me to cast my eye upon them and not feel uplifted. In all there were sixteen such pillars and the outside of them was shaped like prancing horses and their bearers also, who were but boys.

On either side of the Pagode, joined by stairs were the cells and store houses, wherein lived the priests and custodians of the Pagode, and also the women dedicated to the service of the Pagode. The pathway is on the outside of the platform decorated with flower-pots of many colours and was exceedingly comforting to look at.

From the courtyard entrance was obtained to the inner Pagode by three doors constructed of dark polished wood and banded with copper. The floor of this inner Pagode was decorated in polished tile bearing the design of a trident, which is their god's coat of arms, being a god of war, unlike our own Saviour who laid down His life for His love of sinners. The tiles I have described were set throughout the floor of the inner Pagode and into the wall of the Pagode also, up to the height of a man's knee. Above that the walls were decorated with carvings of plaster and wood, in four galleries all the way even to the roof. Set into niches in the wall were statues of a hundred idols, made of gold and silver and copper, some of which had inset in them precious stones as are found in the country. At various places around this part of the Pagode they had placed flower-pots with delicate flowers and fragrant herbs so that their Pagode might thus enjoy himself.

In the middle of the floor were four stone pillars and it was these that supported the square roof of the highest storey. They were joined by a stone frieze and had two central doors made of mahogany and which were of great size, facing the gate which was the main entrance. These doors were highly ornamented by designs of flowers and tendrils surrounding in a regular pattern the figures of men wearing naught but loin cloths and carved with great passion and exactitude. Behind these doors rested their Holy of Holies, which being heathen and idolatrous they hold sacred above all, a large and beautiful phallus.

The phallus was formed out of a single piece of jade, about a cubit high and thick as the neck of a man. It was set about with seven bands of silver which were only half and joined to seven bands of gold which themselves were only half. Each band was studded on opposite sides with blue sapphire and coral. The whole idol rested on a base of solid silver on which were carved representations of their god, and his attendant warriors, and whose weight was such that four men could scarcely move it.

To the rear of this hateful idol there stood a chapel protected by ornamental doors carved of ebony and again much decorated. Within the chapel there were a figure of their god who dances, as big as a man and all covered with gilt. At the rear of the Pagode there was another like chapel dedicated to the woman whom they say their god took to wife, for it is not allowed to them to worship a god unless he have a wife, and not virgins of any kind. This chapel too was shielded by ebony doors and the woman's form within it was exceedingly beautiful, and covered with gilt.

It is the duty of an escrivao to make a record and I write of these things as I saw them so that in words at least the prophecy cast in stone may be broken. I do not write to glorify a heathen and idolatrous faith but in the hope that one day my writings will be read in a manner of compensation, and that those who read will the more fully understand that without love of God and love of one's fellow man, there is no God. If I have sinned, Jesu forgive me.

Iesus Salvator Orientalium indicarum

I finished and looked across at Elmer. He'd finished reading the original. Show-off.

"Doesn't help with the blackmail," he said, "But for your elucidation, it's Portuguese, about sixteenth or seventeenth century."

"What's it worth?"

"Well, I'd say about seven hundred and fifty dollars. More if it was part of something else."

"Dirkian paid a thousand pounds for it." I thought about it. "Perhaps the temple really exists."

"Possible, sir, but unlikely," Elmer said and stared thoughtfully out of the window. "You don't suppose it's merely coincidence. That he simply kept the bank slips with these documents?"

"They were clipped together," I said. "If they were clipped together, then they were clipped together deliberately."

Elmer asked, "Why don't we go to the Union Banque Suisse and try to find out to whom the account belongs?"

"You're joking," I said. "We're in enough trouble already. In Switzerland it's a crime to even *try* to find out about someone else's bank account."

"What are we going to do in Zurich, then?"

I thought about that while the plane descended 2000 feet. Finally I said, "We move on."

By now the Moroccan police must have found out we'd left on flight SR 227. All they had to do was get in touch with the Swiss police and ask them to hold us till they could come over and ask questions. I had no doubt that on a matter of murder, the Swiss police would co-operate wholeheartedly.

"We're going to fly on to Turkey," I said.

"Why Turkey?"

"It's another country. And that's where Dirkian started operating. He's still got a salvage business in Bodrum."

Elmer said, "I don't know if we should go that far."

"Look," I said, "We've got nowhere to go. You and me, both. And we've got to find Dirkian's killer."

"You want to start at the beginning?"

"It's as good a place as any," I said. It was also over three thousand miles from Tangier.

8

ZURICH WAS GREY, CALVINIST, COLD, the runways at Kloten lined with ribs of grimy snow. We drank coffee mixed with kirsch in the Quick Airport Restaurant, the cheaper one that was on a level with the airfield, and watched the big jets taxi in. We took off, over a city whose steepled roofs were blotted out by darkness. From above, the sprinkling of lights could have been any city in the world.

Istanbul sweltered behind Byzantine walls. Minarets punctured the night sky, the mosques of Suleiman and Mehmet Fahti and Rustem Pasha. We took a Dillinger-style taxi to the Hilton and a similar one back to Yeskiloy Airport the next morning and picked up a flight to Izmir. From Izmir we drove to Bodrum. It took nearly ten hours.

Bodrum lay along a shallow bay, a cluster of rectangular, whitish buildings dominated by the square tower of an old castle. Beyond it lay the deep blue of the Aegean and a hazy outline of islands.

The Dirkian Deep Sea Salvage Company, like most of the businesses of Bodrum, was situated near the waterfront. The sign had peeled more than most and the door was locked, with a yellowed message pinned to it in Turkish. Dust and sand lay in equal proportions about the doorway and the office had that abandoned look about it, as if it had not been used for some time.

Elmer and I went out into the sunlit street again, thinking of a ten hour drive and a thousand and fifty dollar airfare, all gone for nothing. A crowd of children played about the rented

Camaro and pressed around us, not begging, but open to alms, wide eyed, curious. I picked the one with the brightest face and indicated that I would like to talk to someone in the building. The boy kept pointing to the harbour and the cafe, speaking rapidly. He kept repeating one word, Osman.

We decided to see Osman.

The boy led us into the cafe, a shabby building with a group of straight, armless wooden chairs arranged in the shade of a tree, a few amphora and men with unshaven faces and baggy trousers, wearing floppy caps. They stared at us with sullen curiosity as we came by, and the boy twitteringly shouted for Osman. Osman sat at a wooden table inside, in front of a glass of milky *raki* and a plate of black olives. He was about sixty with a weather beaten face and a skin like stretched leather. The forehead and the flesh around the eyes was creased like folds in old parchment, and there was a keen, far-away look in the eyes, the eyes of a sailor looking for land. Osman's body was still pronouncedly muscular and he had thick wrists and large, scarred fingers. He wore a white skull-cap over close-cropped white hair and despite the heat, wore a faded green jersey.

I noticed the white cane by the chair and asked, "How many fathoms, uncle?"

He looked at me piercingly, as if he was trying to see my thoughts. "Thirty-five, off Cesme."

There were men like Osman in every town where there were divers. Men who had gone down too deep and come up too quickly with nitrogen bubbling through their blood. The little bubbles blocked capillaries and arteries, caused paralysis and all too often, death.

"I want to talk to you about Stavros Dirkian."

Osman appeared not to have heard.

I grasped the back of the chair and indicated I would like to sit.

"*Lütfen.*" The open palmed gesture gracious, nearly aristocratic.

"I'm from a newspaper. I want to talk about Stavros Dirkian."

"I heard you. Dirkian is so famous?"

"We want to write about him."

"What you want to know? That he was a good diver? Yes,

he was a good diver."

The cafe owner poured raki for all of us. I asked him to leave the bottle. Osman and he exchanged pleasantries and I caught the name Stavros mentioned twice.

I pointed down the road to the building which housed the remnants of the Deep Sea Salvage Company. "I want to know about that."

"Ah," Osman said.

"We will pay you for what you tell us."

Osman stared deeply at me. I placed two hundred Turkish pounds on the table and sipped raki. After a while Osman put the money away. "That is Dirkian's office," he said. "I am no more with Dirkian."

"But you were with him?"

"Yes. That is true. I teach Stavros to dive. He was a good boy. He learned fast. But he was not like the people here. He was more Greek than Turkish, you understand. More concerned with money." Osman rubbed his thumb and middle finger together in a simulated shuffling of notes.

"Dirkian did not come from here, you know. But he lived in Bodrum two years. And he knew how to dive and went out with the men—the sponge divers. But he did not like diving much and let others do it for him. He bought his own boat but always he talks of money. I used his boat the first time. One day Stavros says to me, 'Osman, I make you very rich so you don't have to worry about a thing'." Osman looked at the cane and grinned ruefully.

I poured out more raki. We lit cigarettes.

"He began with taking sponges to Karabaglar. Smuggling, you know. Not good. And I tell him one day the customs sink his boat and leave him to drown. But he says it is the only way to make money from diving and he still buys sponges and takes them to Karabaglar."

"I remember, after a few months, Stavros goes away. I have his boat and collect money for him. Then he comes back and says we are going to do business, him and me. Not much diving and not diving too deep. That summer people came to Bodrum. Tourists." Osman smiled at me. "*American* and we showed them the sponge beds. You dive?"

I nodded. The eyes raked me. "The soft way huh! With mask and tank?"

I smiled. "Yes. The soft way."

Osman leaned forward. "You have re-compression tables? You think . . ."

Slowly I shook my head. Re-compression only worked if the diver went back immediately. If it didn't work then, it was too late afterwards. Forever.

Osman said, "Never mind. Sometimes . . . I think I would like to dive again."

I left him with the thought and sat silently, watching the sea rolling against the sloop-rigged sponge boats.

"The tourists do not bring enough money for Dirkian, so I look after tourists and Dirkian goes to Istanbul. It is my work that summer and the next. We go looking at wrecks and they collect broken pots. From time to time Dirkian comes back, but not for the tourists." Osman leaned across the table again. "You understand what I mean? He came to use the boat."

I passed cigarettes round.

"After that summer, the tourists stopped too. I went back to the sponges and got this."

"Did Dirkian know what happened?"

"Yes. He tells me to close the office. I say to him the office has been closed for three months. And then, for the first time I ask him about money. All the time I work for him he gives me money. Not much. I make more from diving for sponges but Dirkian says to me, I keep the money for you and when there is enough I will give it to you to buy an orchard. I think he is a wise man and knows about these things, but when I ask him he will not give me any money."

"When did you last see Dirkian?"

"About a year, fifteen months ago. That is when I ask him for the money to buy the orchard. He throws me out and he tells me I am too old and he takes the boat and gives it to Kemal. That is right because I cannot dive any more, but he does not give me the money. In the winter he sends Claude to work with Kemal and learn diving. Claude is nice boy. From Italy. He talks to me sometimes because he likes to talk about diving and he was unsure, you know what I mean? He tells me Dirkian is going on a big trip, to dive for a temple underneath the sea. He take Claude with him."

"Where?" I asked.

"Claude told me. A place called Zeylan."

*   *   *

"Ceylon," Elmer said musingly. "It fits, doesn't it?"

I looked at him and raised my eyebrows.

"The Portuguese manuscript. It must come from Ceylon. The Portuguese occupied Ceylon three hundred years ago."

"And the temple?"

Elmer nodded. "Dirkian didn't find it. If he had, the manuscript wouldn't have been in his safe."

"If the temple's still there, maybe we should go to Ceylon and look." We couldn't remain in Turkey indefinitely. Perhaps in Ceylon we would find the reason for Dirkian's death, perhaps also find the temple. If we found the temple, it would solve a number of problems. For a start, both Elmer and I would be rich.

I said, "We haven't enough money."

Elmer's face took on a tuned-in look. "There are ways, sir," he said. "There are ways."

"What devious scheme do you have in mind?"

Elmer persevered looking tuned-in. "Ceylon," he said, "thirty miles south-east of India, a lush tropical island, the Buddhist vatican, strongly influenced by Hinduism, the centre of a pre-Christian civilization as remarkable as that of Egypt." Elmer blinked his eyes open to stare mildly at me. "There's money to be made there, sir. There's money to be made."

"How?"

"Past greatness and present penury. That's how."

"I freaked out of college," I said. "Please explain slowly, clearly and very, very simply."

Elmer asked, "Remember Velazquez?"

I nodded.

"Well the people I was setting up to buy it, were the Reede Museum of Art, in New York."

"I'm not going to forge any pictures," I said, firmly. Being wanted for murder as well as fraud could make the world a very small place.

"I wasn't thinking of forgery," Elmer snapped. "I was thinking that the Reede Museum's curator is crazy for Oriental art. Papyri, pottery, sarcophagi, bronzes—especially bronzes."

"Go on," I said. The drive to and from Bodrum and the flight back to Istanbul had left me worn out. Now I was beginning to feel stupid.

Elmer said, "Western art is pretty well catalogued, right?"

I nodded. Western art was so full of experts that you couldn't buy or sell anything these days without a provenance, a certificate of authority, a letter from the artist's dealer, a forensic test, scrapings of the artist's dandruff. Oriental art was quite another story. Experts were few and far between and it had not been investigated with the precision of Western art. The field, as they say, was wide open. Even so, I couldn't see what it had to do with us.

"If we buy a bronze," Elmer said, "there aren't many people around who'd know its real worth. What's going to be important is if the buyer likes it and whether he can pay for it. As the buyer will not see the bronze until after he has bought it, it is also important that the buyer trusts me."

"And the Reede Museum will trust you?"

"With bronzes, yes."

"So we traipse off to Ceylon, buy a few bronzes, flog them to the Reede Museum and live happily ever after. Is that it?"

"In a nutshell, sir, yes."

"There's one thing," I said. "We haven't the money to do it."

"We've got credit cards, haven't we?"

"Right. But you can't buy bronzes with credit cards."

"But you can buy air tickets. I've got about fifteen hundred dollars. What have you got?"

"About the same. About six hundred pounds."

"Fine. Then let's go to Ceylon. With the right mark-up we should clear at least twelve thousand dollars on the bronzes. And that will give us the time, the opportunity and the funds to find the temple."

"And Dirkian's killers," I said. "You forgot them."

"Alright, we'll find them too."

"Tell me again, how we're going to make twelve thousand dollars." I was still feeling stupid.

"For a start," Elmer said. "We're going to double our capital, by flying through Dubai."

9

LATE, THE NEXT AFTERNOON, WE WERE in Dubai, sprawling in the back of a large Mercedes as it squawked its way beside the three mile long creek that divided the city. The furled sails of Arab dhows jammed the skyline like television masts, and white djellabaed guards stood outside the British Bank of the Middle East, carrying rifles. Heat haze reflected off the high white buildings and outside the air conditioned Merc, it was a damn sight hotter than Tangier or Istanbul and devastatingly humid.

Our business was transacted in an air conditioned executive suite at the northern end of the water-front. It all went smoothly and took hardly an hour. Afterwards, we had enough time for a leisurely dinner before getting back to the airport and our connecting flight to Ceylon.

* * *

Ten hours later Ceylon spread out below us, thick with foliage, a gorgeous tapestry of irregular fields coloured green and brown. The engines went silent, and we hovered in the brilliant sunshine, banking slightly.

Pain filled my ears. I swallowed. The plane edged away from the land, white wing tip angling over an azure bay shafted with silver. Thin yellow beaches, fringed with leaning palm trees, snaked into heat haze.

The engines screeched into whining life. Six bars of canned music brayed over the intercom, stopped and picked up again

4—TPF * *

with a grating noise. We slid smoothly over the palms and landed with a gentle thump.

The engines shrieked in reverse thrust. The awareness of speed heightened as the flat landscape blurred. Then the brakes bit and we slowed to a clicking of seat belts and the jolting of wheels bouncing along the joins in the concrete.

Flags snapped tightly over the flat roof of Bandaranaike International Airport. A balcony below the flags was crammed full of Ceylonese, sun-dark, smiling, waving with indiscriminate frenzy.

I stood at the top of the gangway and sweated. It was two o'clock in the afternoon and the heat radiated off the tarmac like a transparent wall. My clothes clung to my body with humidity and my briefcase stuck to my fingers, as if pressed there with surgical plaster. The fact that I was wearing a worsted Jaeger suit didn't help one bit.

From behind me Elmer said, "I think I'm going to faint."

His small round face had turned cherry red. Large blotches of sweat stood out on his forehead, darkening the short, sandy hair. In his glen check and spotted bow tie, he looked as if he were going ratting.

"Not now," I said. "For God's sake don't faint now. It'll be cooler inside the building."

"It isn't the heat," Elmer said tightly and followed me across the tarmac.

A pleasant-looking, sari-clad girl met us at the entrance to the terminal building. With modestly averted eyes she handed me a booklet. "Welcome to Ceylon," it said, "The Republic of Sri Lanka." The customs regulations were on page four. Page nine informed me that the water conformed to the highest standard of the World Health Organisation and page two that the export of antiques over a hundred years old was prohibited. So much for bronzes.

Another girl, with even more modestly averted eyes, handed me a D form. Ceylon, like its continental neighbour, India, was suffering from a chronic shortage of foreign exchange. In order to prevent tourists being tempted to sell their currency to touts and taxi drivers at three times the official rate, the government compelled all visitors to declare the currency they brought with them. Then the government, through banks and authorised dealers, offered to change it at twice the official rate. Very practical, I thought. That at least was encouraging.

I completed my D form scrupulously. Sixty pounds traveller's cheques, fifty US dollars, one Omega wrist watch, one Pentax 35mm. camera, one Philips cassette recorder, seven cassettes, no jewellery containing Ceylon precious stones, set or unset.

From behind me, Elmer asked, "What next?"

Next was a wizened old man in khaki who sat behind a counter marked "Health". After he had checked our vaccinations we went through to immigration. Elmer looked quite pale.

My heart was beginning to thump with a slow, pulsating motion that seemed to fill my chest cavity and dry my throat. The airport building was not air conditioned, but my reactions had little to do with the heat.

"It won't be long now," I said, my tongue feeling like cotton wool.

"I know sir," Elmer muttered despairingly and stood behind me in the queue.

Immigration was no problem. A brief look at our embarkation cards and D forms, a cursory look at our passports, how long are you staying? and plonk! We were stamped in for a month. Now all we had to worry about was customs.

Customs men rarely accord with national characteristics. They are the same the world over. Mean, nasty and suspicious. Our particular customs officer was a thin, sharp-featured man with a tight little moustache and eyes set too close together behind horn rimmed glasses. His hair was slicked back and his mouth was twisted in an expression of supercilious mistrust.

He was looking suspiciously at our winter suits. I became aware of the fact that though I was sweating profusely, none of it was coming through my clothes. "How long are you staying?" he asked.

"A month."

"Holiday or business?"

I gave him my grade one, twin set, platinum smile. It was supposed to look honest, sincere and candid, not necessarily in that order. "Holiday," I said, still smiling. "Visit your ruined cities, taste some of your fabulous shell-fish, do a bit of skin diving." It was, I thought, a superb blend of culture, gastronomy and healthy recreation. It was also difficult to talk through a twin set platinum smile.

The customs officer thumbed through my passport. He looked at the D form. "You haven't brought much money," he pointed out.

"Not for a month." There was something final about the way he snapped our passports shut.

"My friend and I left in rather a hurry," I said.

"Fleeing from the misery of an English winter," Elmer interjected.

The customs officer looked at each of us in turn. "You have just come from Istanbul," he reminded us.

"Not warm enough," I said quickly.

"Our bankers will forward us any money we need," Elmer said.

"And we've got credit cards." I held out Diners Club and American Express cards for his inspection.

He opened my passport. "You have any firearms? Or knives?"

"No."

"Spear-guns?"

"Diving equipment is too bulky," I said.

He returned my passport and looked searchingly at our cases. "Anything to declare?"

I took a deep breath. From this point on, there was no turning back. "No," I said.

He gave me the hard eye to eye look perfected by customs men all over the world. "You have whisky? Cigarettes?"

"Yes," I said quickly. "A bottle of whisky each and four hundred cigarettes."

The eyes raked us. Then with a deft movement of his wrist he chalked our bags. A porter seized them and jogged towards the exit. In the silence that followed, I could almost hear the tick of the watches underneath my shirt. They sounded louder than the pounding of my heart.

* * *

The crowd beyond the glass doors parted. Outside the customs, it was even hotter. I followed the swing hipped, stringy muscled porter anxiously. He had put Elmer's plaid case on his head and was using my Airlite like a bludgeon. I hurried after him. Quite often a precariously balanced, jogging case was the last sight an arriving passenger had of his luggage.

The girl was standing away from the crowd, partially obscuring an advertisement for Ceylon tea. Ordinarily I would have looked at her more than twice. This time I stopped. I even let our luggage go.

She was small and attractively built under the chocolate brown smock and blue cotton jeans. The last time I'd seen her, she'd been wearing a lot less and then she'd had one arm around Stavros Dirkian and the other around a diver, whom I presumed was named Claude.

I pushed through the crowd towards her. She looked better in the flesh. Much better. The eyes seemed larger, the cheek bones flatter, she had skin like newly polished marble. Her mouth was large and smooth and made to dream about.

I went up to her and said, "Hi! I'm Nicholas Maasten. I'm very affectionate."

She turned her head, startled. The eyes stopped searching the crowd and focused on me. There was a glint in them, half suspicious, half inviting, the kind of look you see on the face of dealers in second hand cars. She decided I was okay and gave me a half smile. She said, "I'm Cindy."

"You meeting someone special?"

"I brought some people here from Colombo," she said. "I was hoping to find a fare back."

"If you like," I said generously, "You can take me and my friend to Colombo."

10

WE WENT OUTSIDE THE TERMINAL into the blinding glare. A gaggle of taxis were huddled round the porch, looking like remnants of the retreat from Stalingrad. Crows darted along the roof, cawing loudly. The sun beat down like a hammer. By the time Cindy extracted her car from the parking lot, I had nearly dissolved.

She drove a cream Peugeot 404 with "TOURIST CAR" emblazoned on its doors. Our luggage was enthusiastically loaded, and we climbed in. The car felt like a steam bath and smelt of hot plastic.

"It'll be better once we're moving," Cindy said, as we drove away. She swerved round the barrels of a disused military checkpoint and I remembered that about fifteen months ago, there had been a rebellion in Ceylon. The checkpoint served to remind me that islands were difficult places to get out of.

We swept down a short, bumpy carriageway past hoardings advertising Air India, Pan Am and Aeroflot and turned onto the narrow, cambered road that led to Colombo. The air became blessedly cool and full of blaring car horns.

Wattle and daub huts with thatched roofs huddled by the roadside. Waif-like dogs dozed listlessly in flowerless gardens, people lazed on cool verandahs.

We travelled erratically, great rushes of speed alternating with harsh braking. Wooden carts with roofs of plaited coconut leaf, drawn by emaciated bullocks meandered somnolently in the centre of the road. Slower vehicles jogged firmly astride the camber. And there were cyclists everywhere, spreading happily in groups across the road, or wheeling spectacularly spider-like between the cars.

"You working your way through college?" I asked.

Cindy didn't take her eyes off the road. "What?"

"I mean are you a student, or do you do this for a living?"

She hesitated. "I work for American Express. This is an American Express car."

I let that pass. We edged slowly through the congested streets of a little town, jammed full of people and cars and bicycles, smelling of dust and dry fish, noisy with the screech of loud-speakers and radios tuned to a Hindi pop station.

With practised ease Cindy asked, "Is this your first time in Ceylon?"

We left the town. A Mercedes bus swooped round a blind corner, forced us to the edge of the road and passed with a rush of air and braying windtones.

"Bloody nationalised road-hog!" Cindy muttered.

I asked, "You been in this business long?"

"About two years." She gave a quiet, secret smile. "I could arrange some nice tours for you. You will see everything and it would be quite comfortable. We can go to the ruined cities and you can see the biggest dagoba in the world, and Sigiriya, the rock fortress with all the frescoes, where Kasyapa hid after murdering his father. Also Polonnaruva, the twelth century city with the large reservoir. You will like it." She reached across to the glove department and handed me four picture postcards.

I looked at the coloured pictures of the dagoba and the rock fortress. Magnificent. But not for me, yet.

"It will not be very expensive," Cindy said. "One thousand six hundred rupees for both of you. Only two hundred and fifty dollars, and you will see all of Ceylon."

"Does that include your services as a guide?"

She hesitated a moment, and said, "Yes."

"Great," I said. "You can start by guiding me to dinner tonight."

* * *

The only way I could be moderately comfortable was by wriggling. The problem was the waistcoat in which I had smuggled the watches was too closely wrapped around my torso, and I had been sweating steadily since we'd crossed the Arabian Sea seven hours ago. The straps of the waistcoat cut into my shoulders like bands of fire, and now I had started to itch."

Cindy asked, "Is the heat worrying you?"

"No," I said. "It's the mosquitos."

Cindy said, "There are no mosquitos in Colombo. It's the heat or something else. As soon as you get to your hotel, you should have a bath."

"Thank you very much," I said. "I would have you know I bathe regularly."

"In that case, you shouldn't itch." She darted a sideways glance. "Why are you wearing that suit?"

I couldn't tell her it was the only suit I had which wouldn't reveal that I had watches underneath my shirt. I said, "I like travelling properly dressed."

"Then you should get yourself some lightweight suits. I know a tailor who can make you some very quickly."

But not quickly enough to prevent me wriggling against the seat like a frustrated chimpanzee. I asked, "What happened to the mosquitos?"

"DDT," she said, "That's what happened to them." Another sideways glance. "Why don't you take off whatever is bothering you?"

"It'll keep," I said, "till I have my bath."

We entered Colombo over a narrow metal bridge behind a creaking bullock cart. It was a city of one and a half million people and they were all there, swarming over the pavements and across the road in a flutter of sarongs. We drove past shanties made of corrugated iron with cardboard boxes for windows, past rows of boutiques with jars of multi-coloured sweets and junkyards full of ruptured cars.

I wriggled and said, "You look the sort of girl who goes diving."

Cindy's expression didn't change. "You want to go skin-diving?"

"Yes."

"Okay. Leave it to me. We'll go when you return from your tour."

She took time off from the hard sell to point out an old Dutch church and to say that she would take us through the Fort. The Fort, as everyone called it, was built on the site of an old Portuguese fortress and was the economic heart of the country.

From behind us, Elmer said the glare had given him a headache and he was going to take an aspirin.

I said that should make him feel better and if it didn't, he could always have a look at the Fort.

Cindy said it was on the way and wouldn't really take long.

We drove between granaries and a high wall bordering the docks, over which cranes towered listlessly, petrified by the heat. The whole area smelt of dried fish and over-ripe fruit and there was fine gritty dust everywhere, creeping through the windows of the car and making me itch.

The Fort when we got to it was a neat arrangement of stolid buildings, built in a style that allied dullness with virtue, which meant that everything was thick, solid and artlessly functional. The shaded corridors around the buildings were shabby, covered with a melange of dirt, traffic grime and red betel-spit. Even the vivid mixture of saris and sarongs could not overcome the general sense of drabness, the heat and the dust.

Here in this gridwork of streets and solid buildings, amongst the people scrambling along the shaded corridors and over the unpainted kerbstones that directed an improbable traffic system, were tea-broking firms, banks, jewellers, ship-brokers, all housed in a colonial mausoleum, with windows stained with salt spray and terribly short of paint.

Once, Cindy informed us, the shops in the Fort had stocked English goods. Now there were only locally manufactured shirts and stationery and food, tastelessly displayed in crowded windows. Of course if one was very rich, or a foreigner, there was Chivers marmalade to be had, Nescafe, Australian lamb, Dunhill cigarettes and very dated long playing records.

Cindy showed us the stained white hulk of the Post and Telegraph office and stopped on an empty road flanking the sea, pointing out the harbour.

Outside the Fort were the Houses of Parliament, built in pale stone, looking like outbuildings of the Palace of Westminster. Armed policemen in khaki tunics and shorts stood outside the building, necessary, Cindy said, since the uprising.

After the Houses of Parliament came the nicest part of the drive, an esplanade of parched brown grass, flanking the sea. Beyond the esplanade was our hotel.

The Galle Face Hotel was impressive. Originally built to Victorian standards of munificence, a new façade had recently been erected in South-East Asian Temple style, with high pillars and intricately carved doors. The mixture worked well, and it was fronted by a spacious, gleaming verandah full of air and light and low, modern furniture.

Cindy stopped under the high, vaulted porch. A white clad porter scurried down the broad steps. Cindy turned to me and said, "That'll be sixty rupees."

I held out my American Express card. "Charge it," I said.

She ignored the card. "You can cash a traveller's cheque in the hotel. Or give me ten dollars."

Elmer dropped a ten dollar bill on the seat between us. "Let's get out of the heat," he said. "I feel ill."

Cindy climbed out of the car and opened the boot. I waited till the porter had taken our luggage and she had got in behind the wheel again. She asked, "Is the tour okay?"

"If the dinner's okay."

She brushed a bead of sweat from her upper lip with a thoughtful finger. "Alright," she said hesitantly. "I'll see you about eight."

"Right on," I said and climbed out of the car. I watched the Peugeot curve around the drive and disappear up the slip road. Then someone tapped my shoulder and a hearty voice, hardly six inches from my ear, cried, "Nicholas man, what are you doing here?"

I turned sharply and nearly smacked my nose into Barney Goldman's bearded, smiling face.

* * *

Barney flung his arms out and said, "Welcome to Ceylon,

Nicky baby!"

I said tightly, "What the hell are you doing here?"

"It's a free country, isn't it?"

I said, "I thought you were in Tangier."

"You too."

"Did you ever get that vase?" I asked.

Barney's eyes clouded. "No,"he said. "I hear someone went after it, shooting." And his eyes looked directly into mine.

"Did they hit or miss?"

"They hit all right, man. They got Dirkian."

"And you Barney? What did you get?"

"Ach man! Sweet fanny adam!"

"What are you doing here?"

Barney shrugged. "The same old game," he said.

With Barney that could mean anything. "Antiques or guns?"

"I suppose you could say antiques," Barney said. "And you?"

"Guns," I said tightly. "Especially the gun that killed Stavros Dirkian."

Barney said, "The best of luck man. Dirkian had enough enemies to fill a telephone directory."

"Then perhaps I should start with G."

Barney laughed and clapped me on the shoulder. "Nicholas, you know me. Why would I get involved in murder?"

Why indeed, I thought.

Then Barney said, "I've got to run now, Nicky baby. If you're around for a while, let's have a drink."

I watched him climb into a dusty jeep and pull away. I went up the steps to where Elmer was standing. "That was Barney Goldman," I said.

"I don't care if it was Babe Ruth himself," Elmer snapped. "I'm going to grab some sleep."

* * *

I went upstairs and took Cindy's advice and had a bath. Then I thought for a while about Barney Goldman. And for slightly longer about Cindy.

Barney had been involved in illegal deals from the time he was knee-high to a dingbat. But he had never been involved in murder. At least not as far as I knew. His involvement in Africa had always been a business one, and he'd never served with any of the mercenary groups even when he was down to his last rand. No, I had to admit, I couldn't see Barney as a killer. Not even for fifty thousand pounds worth of Etruscan vase.

The glimmerings of an answer lay with Cindy. Cindy was no fragile Eastern flower. She acted like, and thought like an Occidental. I remembered that the Ceylonese had a mixed culture, that nationalism was only a creature of the last twenty years, and that for three hundred years they had been schooled in the ways of the West.

On the surface at least, Cindy was as tough as nails. I could see her cope with someone like Dirkian, but not for long. The toughness did not penetrate very deep. There was a brittleness about it that was interesting. I thought I would love to see the Cindy behind the mask. In that at least, I was hopeful.

* * *

At precisely eight o'clock Cindy announced herself. I went down straightaway, stopping only to deposit the waistcoat with the watches under Elmer's bed.

Cindy was waiting in the lobby, mouth and eyes made up, wearing a white shirtwaister and pale pink jeans. She gave me a heart-tripping smile. "How's the itching?"

"All gone," I said truthfully.

"What would you like to do?"

"Eat," I said.

"Okay. Let's go to the Renuka. It isn't far from here and they serve European food."

She'd parked the Peugeot behind the wall that ran in front of the hotel. I followed her down the steps and along the drive. She walked quickly with short, brisk steps, narrow feet alive in gold strapped sandals. We reached the Peugeot. A dark thick set young man sat behind the wheel.

"This is Sunil," Cindy said, "He's my cousin-brother. He's coming with us."

11

CINDY WAS THE LAST PERSON I WOULD have expected to suffer from an attack of virginity. Cindy had made me only too acutely aware that it was over three weeks since Penelope had left me, tired of boiling her own drinking water and the way the Arabs had stared at her mini-skirted thighs. Penelope had splendid thighs, nurtured on years of free school meals and plenty of horse-riding. You didn't have to be Arab to stare at them, or to have zealous thoughts.

I sat alone in the rear of the Peugeot, cursed Cindy and her cousin-brother and had zealous thoughts.

Sunil stopped the car with a jerk that ended zealous thinking.

"This is a new hotel," Cindy informed me. "It will not be very full. The season hasn't started yet."

We marched across a smiling expanse of lobby above, into a swarm of smiling waiters in the dining room, below. There was a small bar, crowded with low tables and even lower chairs, full of male Ceylonese drinking bottled beer. The dining room was by comparison, empty.

"Don't drink scotch," Sunil warned. "It's expensive."

He was a dark, intense young man, with a large square head and a moustache so carefully cultivated that you could count each separate hair on the smooth skin above the too-full upper lip. Sunil was one of those few people who could wear white and still manage to look raffish. He wore a long sleeved white shirt and slim-jim tie, tapered slacks and a narrow crocodile skin belt. His eyes were curiously blank. They had a manner, not of looking through you, but past you, acknowledging your presence, but at the same time avoiding it. One thing I decided Sunil would be frightened of, was commitment.

"How are you liking Ceylon?" he asked pronouncing the words carefully.

I ordered our drinks, and wondered why, if the two of them worked together, Sunil hadn't been at the airport. If Cindy's present coyness was unforced, that would surely have been more usual. Unless of course someone had determined that we should meet. Who?

I offered cigarettes around and answered Sunil's question. "I like Ceylon very much." Every visitor says it.

"It is very nice at this time of the year," Sunil agreed. "At the beginning of the season it is not too hot." He lit our cigarettes with a gold plated Dunhill, a souvenir no doubt of a previous tourist season.

The waiter brought our drinks and took our orders. The gin was good, without the after taste of meths, common in so many foreign gins. "Tell me about American Express," I said. "How come you both work for them?"

Sunil's eyes sloped sideways. "They are big travel agents," he said, and began to study the menu carefully.

"But not in Ceylon," I said. "In Ceylon they only do banking. They are not in the car hire business."

"They asked us—" Cindy said and stopped. She laughed. "What do you do, Nicholas?"

"I buy art," I said. "Pictures, sculptures, bronzes, that kind of thing."

"And you have come to Ceylon to buy statues?"

"And other things. I am interested in all kinds of Oriental art —coins, manuscripts, jewellery—everything."

Cindy looked thoughtful. She looked very pretty, looking thoughtful. "You must be very rich," she said, "to come so far to buy all these things."

I let that go unanswered. You never know when a mistaken impression can be useful.

The waiters placed food before us and we began to eat. I looked directly across the veal escalope, at Cindy. "You're not from American Express," I said.

She looked back across the table at me, not eating, not saying anything.

"Your mistake was that you thought we were Americans, and that Americans rely on American Express the way Britishers rely on Entero-Vioform." I remembered Penelope hadn't cared much for Moroccan food, either.

Cindy leaned back in her chair and raised a cigarette held near the butt in slender, long-nailed fingers. Her mouth was beautifully moist. She puffed at the cigarette timorously, like a child playing trains. Her eyes crinkled with laughter. "You're right, Nicholas," she said using my first name with an easy familiarity, as if somehow, my discovery of their little scheme had turned me into a fellow conspirator. Still smiling, she asked, "What do you really do?" Adding inconsequentially, "For an Englishman you are very brown."

"I live in Tangier," I said, "and I travel a lot."

Cindy leaned forward and stubbed out the cigarette, dark curly head bent over the table. "Buying art?" There was the minutest trace of sarcasm in her voice.

"I travel enough to recognise the usual dodges," I said. I was beginning to worry about these two. Cindy was too perceptive for my liking, and I was beginning to think that Sunil's presence had little to do with preserving her chastity. There was a rip off somewhere. But how? And for whom?

Meeting Barney Goldman had made me suspicious. After all, the chances of meeting someone like that, even in a city as small as Colombo, were still a million and a half to one.

"You aren't from American Express," I said, "Two hundred and fifty dollars for your tour is too much. I could charter a helicopter for that." Sunil looked surprised.

"I suppose that's why you came up to the airport," I said to Cindy. "You're better-looking than him and you were hoping to get lucky."

Cindy looked up from her plate. "Yes," she said. "Right, first time."

As we ate, they told me. The travel agency belonged to their father, not to American Express. The government was encouraging tourism and running a travel agency had been one way of obtaining a foreign exchange permit to buy a new car. That was how it had started. Since establishing the agency, their father had retired from his job in the government service. The government, concerned at the rapid growth of the travel agency business, had insisted that travel agencies justify their expenditure of foreign currency. Then, they had discovered that being in the travel business gave them an opportunity to meet tourists and do deals.

Cindy explained that there were four brothers and a sister, all younger than her, all being educated in a haphazard way in a language that was not spoken beyond the sandy shores of Ceylon. For their sake, her father had decided that the family should emigrate.

"Where?" I asked.

"I'd like to go to England," Cindy said. "But that's difficult. We have applied to go to Australia."

She explained that Australian immigration rules were easier to comply with, and that perhaps, after a few years in Australia, she might be able to come to England. If only for a holiday.

The problem with emigration was the country's shortage of foreign exchange. Normal travel outside the country was banned, unless tickets could be paid for in foreign currency. Emigrants were allowed the cost of their passage and precious little else.

"So we have to do deals," Cindy explained. "We give rupees here and get sterling or dollars elsewhere."

"And sometimes we sell things," Sunil added.

Sunil said the deals were becoming more difficult. For a start, Ceylon was attracting the wrong kind of tourist, Germans and Scandinavians on package tours, who arrived at the airport in groups and were whisked away to one of the newly-built hotels along the coast in coach-loads. That didn't give an enterprising foreign exchange dealer much of a chance. His moustache drooped with disappointment.

Cindy said that most of the package tour operators only dealt with the larger travel agencies, so they were forced to rely on casual pick-ups.

Moodily Sunil enquired if I had declared all my foreign currency.

"Yes," I said. "Sorry."

"You have anything else you'd like to sell? Cameras?

Watches? Tape recorders?"

Cindy mentioned that I had a tape recorder.

"What kind?" Sunil asked.

"Philips," I said.

Sunil wrinkled his nose. "Could have got more for a Sony. These people like Japanese goods. But never mind. I get you a good price. Eight hundred rupees."

I shook my head.

Sunil, however, was not to be deterred. "Look," he said, "what you worry about? You pay how much for Philips cassette recorder in Tangier? Twenty pounds? Twenty-five pounds? Tangier is free port, no. Twenty pound is five hundred rupees at *feex* rate. So you make three hundred rupees for nothing." He flung out his hands in exasperation.

"No," I said. "I don't want to sell just now." I didn't think there was any point in telling Sunil that the tape recorder had already been declared, that Tangier was no longer a free port and that I did all my duty-free shopping in Gibraltar. I also didn't mention that if at the *feex* rate, which was the hundred per cent bonus the government gave you for bringing in foreign currency, the tape recorder was worth five hundred rupees, with duty and everything it would be worth at least twice that, not the eight hundred rupees Sunil had quoted.

Cindy asked what cassettes I'd bought.

I told her and stopped on the verge of inviting her back to the hotel to listen to them. She'd only bring Sunil back with her and there was no advantage in that.

"I like the Stones," Cindy said, "and hard rock. There's very little rock here. Most of the bands play straight. The last rock concert folded because no-one went to it."

Sunil enquired whether I wanted to buy any jewellery. "I have friend in jewellery business," he said. "He give you good price."

I told him that I didn't need to buy anything, or sell anything and if I did, he would be the first to know.

"But tomorrow, you need car," Sunil said. "Tomorrow we go and see the ruined cities?"

"No," I said, laughing. "Not tomorrow, Sunil."

He looked at me, amazed.

"My friend is ill," I explained. "Too much heat and too little sleep. He has to rest tomorrow. Besides you charge too much."

"We go the day after, then, promise. I fix special price." He held out his hand to be shaken in confirmation. Some British habits die hard.

I ignored his hand. "I'm not making any promises, Sunil. It all depends on whether Elmer feels better or not."

"Day after tomorrow will suit me fine," Sunil said. "Tomorrow I have an airport pick-up." He looked at his watch and stood up. "I go now. I have business to do. I see you day after tomorrow, OK."

"Goodnight Sunil," I said, not rising.

With a carefree wave he left us. I ordered coffee and French brandy.

"What do you want to do tomorrow?" Cindy asked.

"Let's talk about tonight," I said. "Let's talk about Stavros Dirkian."

* * *

"Who?"

"Stavros Dirkian, a fat, short art dealer who was diving in Ceylon about a year ago."

"I don't know who you mean," she said confusedly. "I don't remember."

"Of course you do, Cindy. You must do. You don't have that many diving clients."

"What do you mean diving? Who are you?"

"Nick Maasten. Art dealer, collector of manuscripts, and failed purloiner of Etruscan vases."

"I don't know what you're talking about," Cindy said. "Come, let's go. I must show you some Kandyan dancing."

"Tell me about Claude. Do you remember Claude?"

"I don't know anyone called Claude. I don't remember anyone you're talking about. What are you asking me these questions for? Can't you see I don't remember anything?"

She was getting hysterical and it was quite obvious that she wasn't going to remember. Not yet, anyway.

I stood up. "Let's go watch some Kandyan dancing, right."

12

She drove to a hotel, perched on a headland overlooking the sea, gleaming like polished bone in the moonlight. The batch of excited spectators hardly filled a large and splendid room whose doors opened out to the night and the sea. Romantic, I thought, momentarily forgetting all about Dirkian. If I could make her relax here, there was a possibility about Dirkian too.

We were hurried to tables. The waiters rushed to bring our drinks, scotch and soda, brandy and coke. I asked Cindy about her work. It was always a good question and she responded eagerly.

She'd been working ever since she'd left secretarial college, two years ago, and she loved it. She'd met some very nice people, some of whom still wrote to her and sent her cards at Christmas. Her face began to lose that shut in look. Animation crept behind the dark, slanted eyes. Then the dancing started.

The dancers bounded into the room, the pounding of their feet on the bare wooden floor captured and magnified by the mind-splitting beat of tom-toms. Flutes wailed piercingly. Bells tintinnabulated. The hard, primitive rhythm filled the whole room, making the entire building vibrate. The dancers whirled under their tinkling, pointed head-dresses. White pantaloons and coloured tassles flashed and spun. Bodies writhed and gleamed with sweat. The noise filled my head with wild, insensate music.

It was cultural no doubt, beautiful even, but it stopped conversation dead. It murdered strategy. Twice I tried to catch Cindy's eye, but each time she was absorbed in the dance or herself. Shut in.

The dancing ended as we finished our drinks. Applause rippled round the room, sounding feeble after the fulsome beat of the drums. A five piece combo wandered onto the band stand, middle-aged men in dinner suits, wearing flat early fifties hair-styles. They played flat early fifties music too, the kind you could hold your partner and dance to.

Cindy stood up and said we should go and see the fire walking. Still no word about Dirkian.

A short hurried drive. A glimpse of cool, emptying streets, a moon that was pale silver above unlit street lamps. A hall with about two dozen people, freckled-armed women and big, good-living men with Leicas and flash guns resting on comfortable stomachs, all sweating slightly. In the centre of the room an emaciated old man, body ceremonially marked with ash, white hair bound in a tight knot on the top of his head, walked over a pit of glowing embers. Flutes warbled, a sitar plucked anguished notes, a drum thumped woodenly.

Cindy told me I could fire walk too, if I had faith.

I said I had other problems. Like her and Dirkian.

Dirkian's name brought on the tightness. Her magnificent lips thinned into a straight line, and the sparkle left the large black eyes. Somewhere close by was hysteria.

I decided to cool it, at least for tonight. She was obviously unready to talk to me and I thought it would be easier after she'd lived with the idea for some time, after she fully comprehended that a stranger knew about her and Stavros Dirkian. It would be easier too if she'd had time to worry about it.

For the rest of the evening I decided, I'd concentrate on her.

"Where do we go next?"

"You want to go somewhere else?" Unable to keep the surprise out of her voice.

"Why not?"

She took me to see the snake charmers and after that the masked dancers. She became less wary as the performances progressed. Still I drew the line at an hour and a half of Sinhalese poetry.

"No culture," I said firmly, "Especially not in a language I don't understand."

"There isn't much else to do," she said. "You were lucky tonight. Normally these shows do not go on till so late. Tonight was the last night of the Folk Art Festival."

"Some luck," I said. "Tell you what we'll do. We'll go back to the hotel, have a drink and listen to my cassettes."

"I don't think that's a very good idea," she said.

"You mean listening to music?"

She smiled. "No. I mean—you know what I mean—trying to see if we can make each other and all that."

"What's the matter? You have a boyfriend?"

"No," she said. "No boyfriend."

"Something wrong with me then?"

She gave me a studied look. "Not specially." She smiled. "Except you itch." She traced a finger musingly along my cheek. "Why don't we just have a drink somewhere and I'll drop you back at the hotel. You must get some sleep, yes?"

"Yes," I said. And we did that. Mostly.

We drove back to the hotel more relaxed, more sleepy, talking of other things. She stopped the Peugeot away from the porch, where the omnipresent porter couldn't open the door and the pale yellow light did not wash over it.

I said, "It's been a nice evening."

Cindy patted her palm against the steering wheel. "Yes."

We sat in silence, listening to the sound of the sea and the soft sigh of the wind. I said, "Tell me about diving here. What's it like?"

"Good," she said, "You interested in spear fishing or what?"

"Just diving," I said. "You've dived a lot?"

"Enough," she said, the tattoo of her palms against the steering wheel growing faster.

"Perhaps we could go tomorrow or the day after."

"Not tomorrow," she said. "Tomorrow I've got a fare out of town. Sunil will see you, however."

"That'll be nice," I said.

"Where's the best place to dive?" I asked.

Cindy said, "At this season, perhaps the South. The reefs are still alive there."

"Great," I said.

Silence fell between us in a thick impenetrable blanket. I

fiddled with the ashtray. The Peugeot wasn't fitted with a radio and in any case Radio Ceylon packed up at eleven. Cindy's fingers tapped the steering wheel, softly.

I turned and kissed her. No strategy. Just a lunge. Her lips met mine, pliant, growing firmer to hard, unyielding. She jabbed me in the solar plexus. No strategy. Just a lunge.

It slammed my lungs right out of air. I doubled up in the seat sucking great gobfulls of air, my chest feeling as if it would burst.

"Christ!" I gasped. "That hurt."

From across the width of the car, Cindy said, "You kiss me only when I'm good and ready."

I sucked in more air. "Go screw yourself," forcing the words out in separate hiccups.

"Only when I'm good and ready."

I breathed more regularly now. Deep, slow breaths, fighting the sharp impelling pain in the centre of my rib cage. Cindy leaned back against her door, head tilted back in the moonlight. The light came off her thick lips, dark and liverish, throwing entrancing shadows under those slanted cheekbones. My breathing went all awry again.

I leaned across and brushed her lips with mine, gently prising them apart, moving my head over hers. Her hands clasped themselves round my neck, mouth parting slightly as I drew my head away and pressed my cheek against hers. I moved closer, fingers tracing a path up her flat stomach, underneath the smock. I snicked the gear lever into first before it did me a worse injury than Cindy's jab had done and kissed her again. Tongues touched, twisted, moved like live things, lubricous. Desire licked through my stiffening body. My fingers curled inside the tight brassière and started to caress a small, upraised nipple.

Then there was a noise. A flat, slamming noise, of something skidding across the roof. Cindy moaned, twisting her head away, thrusting her hands between us. I turned and stared. Outside the car it was still hot. However long we sat in that car, there would be no condensation, no fog on the glass. Because there was no fog, I could see right through the glass. And the gang of urchins crowding around the gate could see right into the car.

"Shit!" Cindy cried, twisting herself straight, coming upright behind the wheel.

"It'll be alright," I said, "I'll go and thump them."

She started the engine and roared up to the porch. "It wouldn't do much good," she said, "and it's late anyway. See you around."

"We could go somewhere else," I suggested, but as far as Cindy was concerned, the mood had gone. The porter was already opening my door. "See you around," she repeated.

"Sure," I said.

I watched her pull away, screaming down the drive, scattering the mob of urchins now spread across the slip-road. They ran into the darkness, laughing and screaming and I wondered what on earth they were doing out at that time of the night.

"Troublemakers," the porter beside me said. I wasn't sure whether he was referring to the urchins or us.

I went up to my room, feeling very second-hand. I felt even worse when I opened the door. My suitcase had been pulled askew and the drawers of my dressing table were open. I rushed in. Anxiously, I examined them. My passport and travellers cheques were there and heart trip-hammering with relief, I looked around the rest of the room. Only my tape recorder had been taken. That and three cassettes. Sunil, it appeared, had found better things to do that evening.

13

THE NEXT MORNING ELMER DECIDED he needed twelve hours more sleep. He also decided *I* should sell the watches. That way, if anything went wrong, there would only be one of us in a Ceylonese jail.

Me.

With its multitude of small jewellery shops crammed full of curios, wooden elephants and ornate bijouterie, the Fort seemed the obvious place to sell the watches. I bounced over to the Fort in a Morris Minor taxi, whose better days were so long ago they weren't even a memory. The driver let me out by a clocktower that was pale yellow, except it wasn't a clocktower but a lighthouse. The lens was still there, protected by wire mesh and it stood right in the heart of the city. The clock below it had stopped. An auspicious portent. Someone, somewhere was going to buy watches from me.

I walked around the Fort. The jewellery business was in a bad way. There were no big spending tourists nowadays, the P & O liners hardly called, and the International Airport was too far away. So the souvenirs of brass and tortoise-shell remained unsold together with the sapphire rings, the amethyst cufflinks and the wooden elephants. No-one was buying watches, either.

At eleven o'clock I went into the hotel, sweating and irritable, full of sweet, bubbly aerated water. Sunil was waiting for me, sipping beer and looking blankly across the verandah at the esplanade.

He saw me and waved. "Why you take taxi?" he enquired in

a hurt tone. "I tell you I come for you. I take you everywhere."

I took my steel capped Sheaffer ball-point out of the top pocket of my shirt and walked across to Sunil, holding the pen loosely in my left hand.

Sunil looked at his watch ostentatiously. "I waiting for you nearly two hours," he said and looked up and smiled. "But never mind."

"I'm terribly sorry about that," I said, and extended my right hand to shake his. Like an English gentleman.

Sunil's hand reached out for mine. I slipped the pen into the space between his outstretched second and third finger and jammed my right hand tightly around his. Hard.

"Ow! Man! What you doing?"

I tightened my grip and brought my face right up to his. "What the hell were you looking for in my room, last night?"

There were bright spurts of water from his eyes, and his face screwed up with pain. I closed my left hand over the right and jerked. His head flew back with the shock.

"This is a good way of breaking fingers," I said. "Very painful."

The colour drained out of Sunil's face, a thin trickle of saliva dribbled out of his gaping mouth. He gasped.

"Start rapping, you lovely bastard," I said. "Unless you want to end up left-handed."

"It was Cindy," Sunil gasped. "She wanted to see what you'd brought. Underneath your jacket."

"And if you'd found it, you'd have taken it?"

Sunil nodded vehemently.

"And when you didn't find anything, you took the tape recorder?"

"Yes, Nicholas, yes. I thought you wouldn't mind. Tape recorders are so cheap in Tangier and—"

"Forget it," I said. "Forget it," and gave him his hand back. Goods smuggled in by a gullible foreigner and left lying around in a hotel room. Sunil must have dreamed about that for years. It was the perfect deal, all the rewards of smuggling and none of the risks, and no way the smuggler could tell the police he'd been robbed. If I'd been in Sunil's situation, I'd probably have done the same thing. "Sit down," I said. "Have another beer."

Sunil sat, rubbing his stiffly splayed fingers, looking anxiously at the dark weals across the phalanges.

"No hard feelings," I said. "Just wanted you to know I don't like having my things nicked."

"No hard feelings," Sunil said, subdued.

I looked around the verandah. Three beginning-of-season tourists sat at the far end, sipping beer. Our scene had apparently gone unnoticed by even the waiters. I waved to one and ordered beer.

Sunil said, "Look, I give you tape recorder back. Okay?"

"Okay," I said.

"Then we go on tour, right?"

I didn't say anything.

The waiter brought two bottles of Lion Lager, large, brown and dripping with condensation. The beer was a trifle heavier than I liked, a trifle sweeter. I hated to think what it would do when it met the sweet drinks I'd had.

A loudspeaker came to life playing soft Muzak. The Platters. Bringing back memories of a single speed record player, a boy alone in an attic room in the Cotswolds. Did anyone remember them now?

Sunil asked, "Did you bring anything in yesterday?"

I looked at him. He'd recovered most of his composure. He was still rubbing his hand. I sipped my beer and thought, it made sense. If there was anyone in Colombo likely to be on intimate terms with a fence, a pimp, or a bent jeweller, it was Sunil. "Yes," I said, "Watches."

"And you have problem?"

I nodded. I reached into the briefcase and gave him a watch.

Sunil examined the watch carefully, turning it over in his hand, holding it up to the light, dangling it from its strap, finally laying it beside his own vulgar timepiece which had enough dials on it to initiate a moon landing.

"Is nice," Sunil said. "Is very nice."

"I want to sell them," I said.

Sunil, confidence returning reached out and took one of my cigarettes. "No problem," he said.

"I want to sell forty of them," I said.

Sunil wreathed the table in smoke. "How much?"

"Two thousand rupees each."

He stared unseeingly at me. "Maybe too much," he said. "Maybe a little less, huh."

"If it's only a little," I said.

He circled an open palm in front of my face. "A little this way, that way, but don't worry. I get good price for you. Don't worry. I fix."

And with that he slipped the watch into his own pocket and led me out of the hotel.

14

WE DROVE THROUGH THE FORT, lurched over a railway line and crawled into the Pettah. The Pettah was as old as the first Portuguese fort. It had been burnt down innumerable times through carelessness more than conflict, and now survived on a mixture of cheap goods, low rentals, and a Levantine love of bargaining. It was a miserable huddle of fly-blown shops, pressed together on high pavements, overlaid with a fine layer of dust, and smelling of over-ripe fruit. Crowds milled along the pavements, women in saris, men in sarongs, itinerant vendors selling balloons and dolls and chunky wooden toys, bearing glass cases with bangles and combs and cuff-links and greasy looking sweets. In the narrow street between the pavements, lorries shunted, cars glinted with impatiently idling engines. Cyclists twisted past, bells pinging.

Sunil edged down the street, horn-blasted his way to a parking slot. "Wait here," he said. "I come soon." I waited, and sweated. The area around me was more open and slightly wider than the average casbah. Which meant it was rather cooler, rather cleaner and I was only rather less likely to be beaten over the head, knifed or robbed.

The air in the car became dank, dried out. I sweated freely. My mouth and throat became parched, and my neck started to ache from the constant twisting effort of vigilance.

I ran a parched tongue over dry lips, feeling completely isolated. I didn't speak the language. I didn't even know the phrase for "Help me, I am lost." Everything around me was extra-foreign, mysterious, oppressive, and the raised car windows didn't help one bit.

It seemed like hours later when I spied Sunil jogging along the pavement, leaping lightly off it to pass an obstructing hawker. He was breathing quickly when he reached the car and wrenched open my door. Hot, steamy air rushed in, a damn sight cooler than the air inside.

"Come," Sunil said. "All fixed."

I climbed onto the pavement, pressing into the crowd, feeling ludicrously distinctive in my lightweight suit. I pulled past a gang of youths, past a shop selling cloth by the bale, twisted round a tout offering picture postcards. Twice I lost Sunil and jumped off the pavement, dodging between the cars till I glimpsed his eye aching batik shirt. We stopped outside a jewellery shop.

The shop was small, dark and cool and smelt of dried fish and coconut oil from the provision store, next door. Small glass cases held the usual sample of pendants and ear-rings, brooches, necklaces and carved elephants. Opposite the show cases an old man squatted on a counter, washing gold into a rusted basin, full of soapy water. He did not look up as we went in.

Sunil waved to the single salesman and led me to the back of the shop. A black and white plastic sign attached to a shiny brown door announced, Emir Latif, Managing Director.

"Go in," Sunil said. "He's expecting you."

Latif was a large man, heavy and slow. A grave-like mound of stomach rose from behind the green metal-topped desk, subsiding into a wide udder like chest and rounded plump shoulders. Latif's head was small, perched on two rolls of fat. His hair was thick and close cropped. He was about as agile as a beached whale, and he didn't bother about standing up when I entered.

He pointed a chubby hand and said, "Sit down Mr. Maasten."

I sat.

He studied me carefully, with large dark eyes that had that permanent semitic sadness which tells you business isn't good.

"You have watches to sell?" His voice was soft, precise, slightly tired, the lips that mouthed the words thick and fleshy. I reckoned that Latif was about forty, and that he had eaten well in every one of those years.

I dived into the briefcase and brought out half a dozen watches and put them on the desk.

Latif let them lie there, still studying me carefully. "You came to Ceylon, when?"

"Yesterday," I said.

"On the UTA flight?"

"BOAC."

He rocked his tiny pea-like head in comprehension. "How did you bring the watches in?"

"In a waistcoat, underneath my shirt."

"And you didn't declare them?"

"Of course not."

Latif sighed, as if he had reached the point of maximum exertion. "Are you sure you were not detected, Mr. Maasten?"

I shrugged. "If I was, would I be here now?"

He said, "I can't afford any risks. You realise that."

"Sure," I said.

"Or any careless talk." He rocked his head again. "I dislike amateurs," he said.

I wasn't exactly an amateur, but I didn't tell him that. "No-one knows about the watches," I said, "except us." Us was a wide word. It had a wide sense of togetherness.

Latif rested a hand on the desk. "Could I see your papers please?"

I hesitated. The podgy hand on the desk remained implacably outstretched. No passport, no deal, that's what the podgy hand said. I reached into my jacket pocket and handed Latif my passport.

"This your first time in Ceylon?" Turing over the pages casually, stopping to look at my photograph and personal details.

"Yes."

Latif sighed. "What would you like to drink? Lanka lime or beer?"

"Beer," I said. One more sweet, iced drink and I'd throw up.

He pressed an intercom switch and ordered a bottle of Three Coins lager. The assistant from the shop brought it in, with one glass.

"Aren't you?"

"No," Latif said. "It is forbidden by my religion." Latif was a Moor, a descendant of those fierce seamen who had lived in

Ceylon for over eight hundred years and had once controlled the cinnamon trade. His office was unimpressive, though functional. Walls a bare green except for a couple of calendars, a row of grey metal filing cabinets, a desk, bare of everything except a wooden correspondence tray. There was nothing to show how rich Latif was, or how important, except the safe behind his desk and the telex machine at the far end of the room.

Latif sighed and dragged a watch across to him. He split open the back and stuffed a watch-maker's glass into the rolls of fat around his right eye. He took his time examining the watch, and when he had finished, he clipped the back on and put it away. Then he drew another watch towards him.

That was when I began to worry. Neither Elmer nor I had checked the watches in Dubai, certainly not with the care and precision that Latif was showing now. It would have been easy, and tempting for Hassan to have slipped in half a dozen samples, with the right watch face and the wrong movement. Probable, but unlikely. I had always found the Arabs particularly correct in matters of business, especially that of smuggling. But there had to be an exception to the rule. There always was a first time.

Latif looked up from his examination. "How many watches have you got?"

"Forty," I said, and remembering Sunil, "thirty-nine."

"Let me see." Again the hand lying outstretched on the desk. I took the watches out of the briefcase and heaped them on my side of the desk. Latif picked one for further examination.

I drank beer and worried, feeling strangely like a fish in an aquarium, insulated from the outside world by the fast shut door and the bare green walls, yet aware that at any time, anyone could walk in and ruin everything. After all, I had no way of knowing that Sunil hadn't rushed off to his favourite police constable, to claim ten per cent of the fine that the customs would levy on me.

"Do you mind if I smoke?"

Latif nodded over the watch.

I lit up. The cigarette tasted cool with the artificial air, slightly sweet with the beer. Time passed slowly.

Twenty minutes later Latif had all the watches on his side of the desk. He worked the eye glass out of the folds of fat and looked at me, right eye tearing slightly. "They're good," he said and waited.

I waited, too.

Latif asked, "Sunil? Is he a friend of yours?"

"He's been driving me around."

Latif acknowledged the truth with a curt nod. "Is there anything you wish to buy, Mr. Maasten. Blue sapphires? Cats eyes? Rubies? Ceylon stores are very good, and very cheap. I could get you a blue sapphire at three hundred rupees a carat."

"There are problems in taking them out," I said.

"A smaller problem than bringing watches in, surely."

I shook my head and smiled. "I'd rather not," I said.

Latif shifted his gaze to the blank wall behind me. "How much?" he asked, floating a flabby hand over the watches.

"Two thousand rupees each," I said. Seventy-eight thousand rupees the lot."

Latif shook his head. The sadness in his eyes deepened. "Mr. Maasten, that is what I can sell them for. If it is so destined and I have the luck."

I said, "Those that preserve themselves from their own greed will surely prosper." The quotation was from the sixty-fourth chapter of the Koran. The one entitled "Cheating."

Latif smiled thinly and picked up one of the watches. "Where do you come from, Mr. Maasten? Not England, surely."

"I live in Tangier," I said.

"And do business with Dubai?"

"Occasionally," I said.

Latif put the watch down. "Thirty-nine thousand rupees," he said. "One thousand rupees each."

It was my turn for head shaking. "That's what they cost in Dubai," I said. "On top of that there's freight, there's duty and there's risk."

"There's also the customers, Mr. Maasten. Times are very bad. These are very nice watches, but who can afford to buy them? Ceylon is not a rich country."

"There are still people who pay a hundred and fifty thousand rupees for a six year old Mercedes," I said. "They need watches. Besides your clock tower's stopped."

Latif sighed, as if I didn't understand.

"There's India," I said, "and a lot of hot money."

"There's also a lot to organise, and there's transport and dealers. There's no profit in that."

"One thousand seven hundred and fifty," I said.

Latif sighed again and asked me to be reasonable. Because I was a friend of Sunil's he would consider eleven hundred. Seventeen fifty would bankrupt him.

I said eleven hundred would bankrupt me. I'd been looking forward to Ceylon, and if I didn't get a good price for the watches I'd have to go back straight away. I was sure that Latif was a decent man, and being a decent man wouldn't want that.

No, Latif said, he wouldn't want that. But business was difficult.

For someone who was so good a businessman as he was, I told Latif, things would surely get better.

Latif shook his head dejectedly. He offered one thousand two hundred and fifty.

It was tempting. I was already moving into profit and pushing the price higher could blow the whole deal. I reached across the table for the watches.

Latif let me put six into the briefcase before he said, "You won't get a better offer anywhere else. Twelve fifty. Take it or leave it."

"I know someone who'll pay sixteen hundred for them," I said with a confidence I didn't feel. "I thought since Sunil knew you, we could do business together." I put three watches into the case. Latif scratched the flat of his nose methodically.

"No-one will give you sixteen hundred," he said.

"That's always the problem," I said, slipping two more watches into the case. "Doing business with friends. They only expect favours."

Latif asked, "How do you want to be paid? Sterling, dollars, Swiss francs?"

"Ceylon rupees," I said. Swiss francs, dollars or sterling weren't any good for buying local bronzes. Besides Latif would discount them heavily anyway.

"Fifteen hundred," Latif said, turning to his safe, "Cash."

15

ELMER LAY ON THE FLOOR of the room, eyes tightly closed, naked except for a small white towel draped around his middle. The purpose of the towel was largely negated by his upraised right leg, which pointed directly at the ceiling.

As I came into the room, the right leg came down and the left leg went up. It was a skinny leg with a large round knee and muscles looking like strips of leather. Downy, brown hair grew sparsely along the outstretched limb, except on the outside of the calf, where the constant rubbing of trousers had produced a surface as smooth and shiny as a billiard ball.

I moved five stubby pink toes from the region of my stomach and stepped over Elmer. "I got the money," I said.

Elmer grunted. The leg thumped down. "How much?" he asked in a strangled voice.

I told him.

His face had turned as red as the carpet. I felt sure he would do himself an injury.

"It's enough money," he said, raising the other leg.

I poured out a glass of water, sat on the bed and watched him. The muscles of his tiny, lute-like stomach rippled like snakes. Elmer's body was compact and firm, his chest surprisingly deep. He never would be very big or very strong, but what he had Elmer exercised and developed and intended preserving.

"It wasn't as much as you'd said we'd get," I said, raising my voice over the sound of his breathing.

The legs flashed up and down alternately. Elmer grunted. It

wasn't helping the conversation at all.

"I don't know that it will be enough to buy bronzes," I said.

Elmer began to raise both legs at the same time. Very difficult, and very hard on the stomach muscles.

"I'm glad you're feeling better," I said.

The legs arced down. And up again. I watched Elmer. The little bugger was incredible. Heaven knew how long he had been exercising before I came in. His face and the long cavity between his pectorals were covered with a shiny patina of sweat. He breathed in tight, explosive gasps, like a wrestler gripped in a half-nelson. I wondered if in the days he had been a seven stone weakling, Charles Atlas had been as unsociable.

Elmer stopped exercising his stomach muscles, turned over and started to do press-ups. I counted twenty-five and because there wasn't any sand I could kick in his face, I hit him with a chunky wad of ten rupee notes.

Elmer stopped on flexed arms and looked at me with round, surprised, blue eyes. "You spoilt my rhythm," he said, reproachfully. Then getting to his feet he began to jog.

"Don't," I said. "It's obscene. And you'll go through the floor."

"Pick the money up, sir," Elmer panted, still jogging. "Someone may come in."

"Somebody bloody well will! Especially if you carry on like that."

Elmer kept on jogging, rising onto the balls of his feet, moving lightly round the room. I picked up the money. He jogged up to me. "Put the money in the hotel safe deposit," he said.

He jogged over to the dressing table and opened a drawer. Still jogging he pointed to a collection of envelopes. It was like being in a room with the all American football team. "Pack the money in there, sir," he said.

I put the money into the envelopes, twenty wads in each, twenty-nine envelopes in all. By the time I had finished, Elmer was standing in front of the closed window, taking deep gulps of sterilised air.

I put the envelopes back in the briefcase and asked, "Where's the safe deposit?"

Elmer came across to me, breathing hard, and picked up a

key from the dressing table. "Ask the receptionist downstairs where the safe deposit is," he said and held out the key. "Ours is number three."

I could hardly wait. I lugged the briefcase downstairs and the receptionist took me past the Accountant's office to a small, windowless room with a large safe, marked "Excelsior," built into the wall. A row of five deposit boxes coloured in gun-metal grey stood by the safe. Four of the boxes were open.

I slotted the key into the lock of number three and eased out the drawer. It was packed with fourteen by ten envelopes, the same size as mine. The only difference was that the money inside was packed in wads of twenty-five, and the notes were in hundred rupee denominations.

I put my envelopes in, locked the deposit box and went back upstairs. Elmer was standing in the centre of the room, doing sideways bends.

"You miserable little runt," I cried. "What have you been up to?"

From eighteen inches above the floor, Elmer's lopsided head mouthed, "I did Hassan a favour."

"Some favour! What did you do? Promise to buy him an elephant?"

"No sir," Elmer said. He straightened up and came and stood six inches in front of me. Dropping his voice six octaves, he whispered, "I brought in some gold."

"You sneaky, little swine," I cried remembering that it had taken Hassan a remarkably long time to fit Elmer into his waistcoat. At the time I had thought it had been because of Elmer's size. "How much gold did you bring in?" I asked.

"Seven kilos."

That was about fifteen pounds, worth at current prices, around fifteen thousand dollars, over one hundred thousand rupees. "No wonder you could hardly walk off the bloody plane," I said.

Sitting for six hours with a strait jacket of gold bars is deadly uncomfortable and deadly tiring. In fact, some professional outfits actually buy used air line seats so that they can train their couriers to long distance discomfort. Trying to walk normally afterwards is like trying to go fifteen rounds with Muhammad Ali. It isn't only the weight, which if carried long enough, drains your strength, but the nervous tension. I've known of gold smugglers who have collapsed on customs floors, with the most embarrassing clanking sounds.

"It's no bloody wonder you were ill," I said. "It's no bloody wonder at all."

"There was the heat as well," Elmer said mildly.

"You might have told me," I said. "I might have carried half." Or more likely taken another flight.

Elmer looked down, shyly. "We thought of it, but decided, no."

"Because you didn't sodding well trust me, I suppose?"

"Oh no, sir." Elmer shook his head violently. "It was nothing like that." Again the shy smile. "Nothing personal, but it's your hair. We thought customs might search you for drugs."

"Thank you very much," I snorted. "And what about the customs searching me for watches?"

Elmer moved back a couple of paces. "It was a justifiable risk. Nothing ventured, nothing gained."

"Try doing it to a duck with a feather," I suggested.

Elmer smiled. "I got a hundred and twelve thousand rupees for the gold, sir, and fifteen per cent of it is ours."

That made me feel a little better. Fifteen per cent meant a further sixteen thousand eight hundred rupees in the kitty. Half of it, mine. I thought of something. "Elmer," I said, "You're so smart, it hurts. Have you wondered what Hassan is going to do with rupees in Dubai?"

Elmer kept smiling. "No-one's going to use the rupees in Dubai. We're going to use them here. We are going to use them to buy bronzes and manuscripts and find Dirkian's temple."

"And does Hassan know of this?"

"He does. He doesn't mind, as long as we get the money to him in the end."

I let out a long, slow whistle. I had a vivid idea of what Hassan would do to us if he didn't get the money in the end. No smuggler of Hassan's stature could afford to be diddled. It set an example and gave too many people ideas.

"You realise that if we can't pay Hassan back, he won't even send round a dead fish as a warning," I said.

"You've been seeing too many movies," Elmer replied. "As

soon as we inform the Reede Museum of what we've acquired, they will credit our bank accounts with the full cost price of the goods. That will be enough to take care of Hassan, and more besides."

"What about the rest?" I asked.

"They'll pay a further fifty per cent on delivery," Elmer said. "You see, it really is all quite simple. There's nothing to worry about."

There wasn't. Not unless I chose to worry about finding a hundred and fifty thousand rupees worth of bronzes.

16

As it transpired I didn't have to find the bronzes. The bronzes found me.

I was seated alone on the wide, shady verandah of the hotel, having tea. Outside the sun was still hot. The sea still beat at the wall below the esplanade. Elmer had gone out to look at some Kandyan daggers and old Sinhalese swords.

I sipped tea and thought about Dirkian and Cindy and Sunil and blackmail. There was no doubt that Dirkian had been blackmailed. But not, I thought, by Sunil and Cindy. Blackmail called for a special quality of sneakiness which neither Cindy nor Sunil possessed. In any case Cindy and Sunil were hardly more than petty confidence tricksters, and their own engaging naïveté would prevent them from organising blackmail on an international basis. But if not Cindy and Sunil, who? And more important, why?

It was time, I thought, for another conversation with Cindy. Twenty-four hours was long enough for her to worry about what I knew. Three weeks without Penelope was long enough, too.

I went to a pay phone and called her. Yes, she said, after static filled hesitation, we could meet later that evening and finalise arrangements for the tour.

I came back to the verandah and drank more tea. I thought some more about Cindy, and a little less about Dirkian and Sunil. I wondered if she had principles and how strong they were. I wondered about the hotel management and if they had principles. Idle concupiscent thoughts on a somnolent, humid afternoon.

I was thinking about concupiscence so hard that I didn't hear my visitor come. There was a discreet cough over my right shoulder, hardly a foot from my right ear. I jerked upright. A soft, lilting voice said, "Mr. Maasten," raising the last syllable in semi-doubt.

He was a small, distinguished-looking man, with thin, sharply defined features, and a deeply professorial air. He was hardly more than five feet six, with a large head, showing a circular patch of brown scalp in front, and a shaggy silver thatch at the back. His face with its firm, well-shaped mouth and sharp patrician nose belonged to a Roman senator. The eyes, under bushy white eyebrows, were soft and brown and full of intelligence. He was wearing a creased white suit and a dark tie, shiny brown shoes with pointed toe-caps. His collar was threadbare with too much washing.

As I turned, he spoke again. "Forgive my impertinence, sir, in intruding upon your solitude. You are Mr. Nicholas Maasten?"

Behind my visitor, I could see the waiter who had pointed me out. "I'm Maasten," I said.

"Pray allow me to introduce myself." He held out a rectangular visiting card, printed in Roman type, the kind of print *The Times* used thirty years ago at the head of their court circulars. The card said:

ARTHUR RUBEIRO DIAZ
Historian and Dealer
in
Fine, Rare Antiques
*
Bronzes A Speciality

At the bottom of the card was an address and telephone number. It was an odd combination, especially the antiques that were both fine and rare.

Arthur Rubeiro Diaz stood hesitatingly in front of a chair.

"Sit down," I said and offered him tea. I had nothing important to do till dinner. Correction. I had nothing to do till dinner.

He perched lightly on the edge of the chair and said, "It is very gratifying to meet you, Mr. Maasten. It is very gratifying to meet anyone from Europe with an interest in Oriental art."

"How do you know that?" I asked. "How do you know I am interested in Oriental art?"

"Ah, Mr. Maasten, you obviously are unaware of the nature of the country in which you are presently residing. Ceylon is a small country. Colombo is a small town. There are those amongst us who believe that it is the centre of the globe. But I have travelled, Mr. Maasten, I have seen London, Frankfurt, Zurich, Paris, Amsterdam, Rome, the capitals of Europe, and believe me, Mr. Maasten, there are a few of us who know and do not agree."

"I see," I said, even though I didn't, and wondered why Diaz had never been to Bonn.

"So in a small place like Colombo, people are loquacious. In Colombo, Mr. Maasten, you are famous. Ah! Allow me."

He leaned forward and poured tea from the fresh pot. "There is an art, Mr. Maasten, in pouring and drinking tea. Tea can be as fragrant and delicate as the most exquisite claret. But it has to be poured properly."

Arthur Diaz poured properly. I couldn't tell the difference.

Arthur Diaz raised his tea-cup, little finger outstretched. "Are you enjoying your stay in this fair island?" he asked. "This God-given paradise, where every prospect pleases and only man is vile. I quote from Bishop Heber, an ecclesiastic poet, who never had the privilege of observing the country he wrote about."

"It's fine," I said. "The island, not the poet."

"You are already remarkably brown."

I didn't say anything. We sipped at our tea.

Arthur Diaz said, "If this is your first visit to Ceylon, you must visit the ruined cities, the game sanctuaries, the Temple of the Tooth in Kandy. For someone with your deep interest in art and culture it will be profoundly rewarding."

He set his cup down with a tiny clink and eased further back in his chair, reassured by the sound of his own voice. "Wherever you go in this delightful island, Mr. Maasten—a word of warning." He paused like an actor waiting for silence and full attention. "Do not buy anything from touts. Whilst looking at the splendours of Ceylon's past, while watching a pre-Christian civilisation come alive before your very eyes, you will be offered ola leaf papyri, stone carvings, old jewellery and pocket-sized Buddhas. Do not buy them, Mr. Maasten. They are either fraudulent, tasteless or overpriced." He reached into the inner pocket of his jacket. "Here let me show you."

He brought out two pieces of flat, slim wood, fastened together with string, separated by what looked like the folds of a fan. Diaz unfastened the string and drew out the upper strip of wood. Underneath were what looked like dried leaves, covered with writing.

"The process is the same," Diaz said, handing the wood and leaves to me. "Dried leaf, with characters dug out with a sharp implement. The point of a pin will do. A mixture of soot and oil is then rubbed over the leaf and this adheres to the indentations." He looked at me triumphantly. "The process is the same," he repeated, "but the language is different. That ola leaf you are holding is written in modern Sinhalese. The ancients used Pali. Few visitors know the difference."

"Very interesting," I said, handing the leaf back.

Diaz fastened them together and put them away, saying, "So you must exercise great caution, Mr. Maasten, especially with strangers."

Diaz obviously considered himself a friend.

"Now," Diaz continued, "I have some works of art to show you." "Originals, not fakes. Works of the highest artistic standard and consequently expensive." He smiled. "A thing of beauty is a joy forever, Mr. Maasten. Its loveliness increases; it will never pass into nothingness. Keats. The price is unfortunately commensurate."

"I'm not sure," I said. "I don't know, if . . ."

"But you are interested, Mr. Maasten. You are an aesthete. You are attracted by beautiful things. You will please allow me to show you some exquisite examples of tenth century bronze sculpture. You do not have to buy and your delight and appreciation of these rare sculptures will be sufficient satisfaction for me."

I'd heard the same theme countless times before, but not in so many words. Before I could protest, Arthur Diaz had walked to the edge of the verandah, where a battered black Chevrolet crouched. In a totally unexpected stentorian voice he commanded the chauffeur to bring the statues up to me, whilst he himself, climbed into the car and brought out a bundle of thick envelopes.

The statues were wrapped in sacking, tied loosely with coir rope. The chauffeur heaved them onto the verandah, and stood them around my chair. I began to feel like Snow White surrounded by five shrouded dwarfs.

Arthur Diaz laid his bundle of envelopes on the table between us. "All these bronzes, Mr. Maasten," he said, "were found in Polonnaruva, the mediaeval capital of the Sinhalese renaissance. They were discovered during the course of an archaeological dig conducted by Dr. W. C. Muir in 1962."

"How did you get them?" I asked.

Diaz was not embarrassed. "At the time when Dr. Muir was conducting his excavations, I was working as an adviser to the Archaeological Commissioners Department." He pulled out a silver cigarette case and handed it to me. It was empty, apart from an inscription which read: *"To Arthur, from all who worked with him. Archaeological Dept. 1964"* "These bronzes were not recognised for what they were. They had been buried in the earth for countless years, they were mouldy, corroded, unsightly, and of no obvious artistic or historical interest. I acquired them."

The story was possibly true. The cigarette case was a tangible fact. Quite often archaeologists obsessed with their search for a lost culture, missed that which was beautiful or expensive, especially if it had been covered with earth for nearly three hundred years.

"You have receipts, of course, bills, proof of ownership?"

Arthur Diaz leaned forward and looked me directly in the eye. "Mr. Maasten," he said in a low voice, "I am a gentleman. You too are a gentleman. I would not offer to sell you something I did not own. I do not have any receipts, or any other documents which you might call evidence of title. As you well know, these documents are not always possible to obtain. But I am, I repeat, Mr. Maasten, a gentleman. I will give you a certificate of authenticity." He looked around the verandah, now filling up with guests, having tea. "If I had anything to hide, Mr. Maasten, I would not be displaying it here."

With that he stood up and tugged at the rope holding one of the sacks. The sack peeled off revealing a darkly gleaming statue of Siva.

The statue was about two feet high, mounted on a decorated pedestal. It depicted the dance of Siva, right knee bent, left foot curved in front of the body, the whole caught in a moment of perfect balance, frozen in time and space, yet so free, I could feel the statue move. The casting was so delicate that you could distinguish between clothing and what appeared to be bare flesh. I felt I could see muscles flex in metal.

Streaming hair, wide-spread arms and tassels stretched out to a circular frame ringed with tongues of leaping bronze fire. A figure huddled, crouched under the foot of the dancing God. It was all so light and mobile that one thought not of bronze but of fire and rain and the wind that came from the sea.

The statue of Siva's consort, Parvati was equally fine. No flaming circular frame this time, only a high pedestal, the figure of a woman wearing a high conical head-dress. She stood on a shaped pedestal, an arm outstretched before her, right hip thrust sideways, again in a posture of perfect balance. The bronze was as smooth as flesh, the calf length trousers seemingly transparent. Parvati herself was ideally proportioned. Perfect rounded breasts and narrow waist. Gently rolling hips and rounded navel, Parvati, sensuous woman-child, mother, eternal Goddess.

Slowly Diaz took away the sacking from the other statues. Krishna and two Saivite saints, dating probably a century later. They weren't as good or as beautiful, but that was only because the Parvati and the Siva were superb. Beside them, the others looked somehow unbalanced, unrefined, lacking grace and delicacy.

My lips had gone suddenly dry. "They aren't new?" I asked.

"I have restored them, where necessary," Diaz admitted. "And polished them. And preserved them. There are two attitudes towards restoration, Mr. Maasten. Repairing the damage caused by age and wear, or re-creating the artist's vision. I have done a little of both."

"Why do you want to sell these?" I asked. While Diaz was

an antique dealer, these were undoubtedly his prize possessions. There are some pieces a dealer never sells.

Diaz's face drooped with sadness. "You are a visitor, Mr. Maasten. All you see are beautiful beaches and laughing eyed children, an unspoilt, undeveloped land of picturesque squalor. For those of us who live here, it is not as pleasant. Food is expensive, rents are high and there is not enough work. In my case I have lived my full span. I seek nothing more than to be buried under a palm tree on yonder shore. But my children, Mr. Maasten, I have six, their future is important. For their sake I must leave this land and build with them another future."

"Why can't you take the bronzes with you?"

Diaz shook his head. "It will not be allowed. In your case it is different. You are a foreigner. You would have legally acquired these bronzes. No-one will prevent you taking them away."

"I have read that works of art over a hundred years old cannot be exported."

"And who is to say, Mr. Maasten, that these bronzes are more than a hundred years old? Our customs people are neither historians nor art lovers. And look at the way the statues gleam. They could almost be new."

"But no-one casts bronzes nowadays."

"But they did, fifty, sixty years ago. Besides I would give you a receipt stating that they are bronzes of no historical or artistic importance. I am an authority on bronzes, Mr. Maasten. If there were any doubt the customs would consult me."

I looked at the bronzes. "How much?" I asked.

"At this juncture let me inform you of one fact. I know how valuable these bronzes are. I know their true worth. I will not bargain about the price. To haggle about these would be desecration."

"How much?" I asked.

"What do you want to buy?" Diaz asked.

"The Siva and the Parvati. How much?"

Diaz smiled. "You have excellent taste, Mr. Maasten, you are a man of great discernment and sensitivity. Had I been a salesman I would not have shown you those two statues till after I had sold you the other three. You must agree that beside the

Siva and Parvati these others look insignificant."

My palms were sweating. "How much?" I repeated.

"For the Siva and the Parvati, nine hundred pounds each. It is expensive but—"

"A thing of beauty is a joy forever."

"Precisely, Mr. Maasten."

17

DIAZ SAT DOWN AND ASKED if I wanted more tea. What I really wanted was a large, straight Chivas, topped with ice. But it was only five o'clock. I lit a cigarette and settled for tea.

Diaz said, "Now let me show you something else." He tapped the envelopes on the table. "Manuscripts. Old European manuscripts, not ola leaf papyri. Are you interested, Mr. Maasten?"

To be frank, I wasn't. Somehow Diaz did not look the sort of person who would have both valuable bronzes and manuscripts. Besides the statues had excited me to the point of satiety. After them, I felt there could be no sensation. There could be no emotion. After the statues everything had to be an anticlimax.

I was wrong.

"These manuscripts," Diaz was saying, "Are mainly Dutch. They are not collated in any way and they certainly do not have any artistic merit. But it is these pedestrian pieces of paper that form the corner-stones of history."

For politeness sake I took an envelope and extracted its contents, four thick, dusty sheets of paper, held together by a clip. The paper was very old and dry to touch. The ink was brown. It began with a great flourish of handwriting, settling down to neat script with the continuations written in below the level of the first page and at the top of the succeeding one. It seemed to be a report of some kind with an accounting. Half way down the second page were figures, showing the result of trading in elephants.

"Interesting," I said, handing it back, "But not for me."

Diaz took the envelope. "As you wish, Mr. Maasten, but please look at the others. You might find something you like."

The other documents were much the same, letters, reports, a diary of a journey along the western coast of Ceylon. I couldn't evaluate them and I didn't find them interesting. Not until I opened the last envelope.

It was a sheaf of even older paper, held together with a metal clip. The paper was stained, browning, its edges torn as if it had been ripped from a binding. This manuscript was in Portuguese, not Dutch, and an English translation of one section was attached. It was headed, "The Pagode (trans. Doctor Francesco Cabraal)."

My palms were sweating so much I thought the papers would drop from my hands. Diaz was watching me coolly, with the patient eye of a psychoanalyst.

"This looks interesting," I said.

"It is, Mr. Maasten."

"Could I ask how much?"

"It is expensive, Mr. Maasten, more expensive than the statues."

"But it is of little value. It has no artistic merit, you said so yourself."

"That document is in Portuguese, Mr. Maasten. There are very few original documents left relating to the Portuguese period in Ceylon. The Portuguese were a carefree people and their attitude to records was well—*etourderie*. The Dutch, who were great conservers of space burnt what few records the Portuguese left."

"It is still only of local interest."

"True, Mr. Maasten. But to me it is of great sentimental interest," he said, "Pray observe the signature at the end."

I observed. The signature was neat, precise and clearly legible. In those days writing was an art form. One learnt not only how to write but to write beautiful characters. The beautiful characters at the end of the sheaf of documents, said, Rubeiro Diaz.

"An ancestor," Diaz said solemnly. "The founder of the Diaz dynasty in Ceylon. For over four hundred years, that diary has been in our family. It is of great value to us, and I would not be selling it, if not for," he shrugged, "circumstances."

Diaz leaned forward. "For this manuscript, the price is three thousand pounds. Take it or leave it."

I really didn't have any choice. I took it.

* * *

The hotel didn't have Chivas Regal so I settled for Johnny Walker. Diaz had more tea and gave me a rapid summary of recent Ceylonese history. "For twenty years, Mr. Maasten, we have been preoccupied with symbols, with problems of language that have created three nations instead of one. After twenty years all we are capable of is symbolic action."

Diaz said, "It is ironic. Here am I striving to emigrate to the West. And every Western businessman is giving himself ulcers so that he can retire to a sandy beach, sit under a palm tree in the sun and do nothing. I can sit under a palm tree any time, Mr. Maasten."

I began to wish Diaz would go away and leave me alone with the manuscript and the bronzes.

Diaz said, "Mr. Maasten, you are a gentleman and I will not ask you to sign anything to confirm the arrangements we have made today. But you will be the first to admit that what you have bought from me is unique. Irreplaceable. Therefore after we have met tomorrow and arranged the financial side of this transaction to our mutual satisfaction, I will deliver to you what you have bought." He waved to the chauffeur.

"Wait," I said. If he took the bronzes and the manuscript back, anything could happen. He could switch them, damage them, or make them simply disappear. "I've got cash," I said.

Diaz's hand froze in mid-air. He sat down again. "That is a most charming way to do business," he said.

I went over to the safe deposit and collected the right quantity of envelopes. Returning to Diaz I said, "Let's see, the statues came to one thousand eight hundred pounds, the manuscript to three thousand. I make that four thousand eight hundred."

"Agreed, Mr. Maasten."

"Four thousand eight hundred pounds is one hundred and twenty thousand rupees, at the official rate of exchange." I laid the envelopes on the table. "You will find exactly that in there,

7—TPF * *

Mr. Diaz. Please feel free to count it."

Diaz did not make any move to count the money. In fact, Diaz didn't make any move at all.

"I am sorry, Mr. Maasten, I cannot accept payment in Ceylon rupees." He took a deep breath. "I expected you to have sterling, or dollars. I explained to you that the only reason I was selling these unique objects was because I needed money to ease my passage in a foreign land. Rupees are of no use to me, Mr. Maasten."

"I have no foreign currency," I said.

Diaz repeated, "Rupees are of no use to me, unless I can convert them." He gave me a worried look. "I have friends who will convert these rupees for me. But these are friendships tinged with gold. My friends will expect to be paid for their services." He paused, while he calculated. "I will accept one hundred and sixty thousand rupees from you, Mr. Maasten."

"But that's more than thirty per cent—"

"That is what it costs, Mr. Maasten. The labourer is worthy of his hire. St. Luke chapter ten."

And Latif had chosen that good part which shall not be taken away from him. That wasn't quite St. Luke but it explained the alacrity with which Latif had bought the watches for rupees. He had got rid of a chunk of depreciating currency for something that was more readily negotiable and whose value in terms of the external world would not, at least diminish—if he didn't drop them. I hoped Latif dropped and rolled over them.

"A hundred and sixty thousand is still too much," I said. It was nearly all the capital we had, and I didn't know how Elmer would react.

"I am sad," Diaz said. "I am sad for me and sad for you."

To add to our mutual sadness, a dusty jeep pulled up under the porch, with a harsh grating of brake drums. Barney Goldman got out. He was wearing an open necked, check, cotton shirt and khaki shorts. His legs were bare, his dirty feet were thrust into dusty sandals. There was a pale powdering of dust over his beard and hair.

"Arthur," he cried, "Nicholas! Hey man, I could really do with—" He saw the bronzes and went silent. Then he said, "Shit! They're fucking beauti—"

"They're mine," I said. "I've just bought them." My voice was tight, possessive.

Barney turned to face me. His teeth cut a white slash against the sunburned skin. There were tiny sun wrinkles around the corners of his eyes, and the edges seemed wildly flecked with orange. "You haven't, Nicholas man!" he cried.

I nodded.

"You lucky son of a bitch," Barney Goldman said.

For the moment I decided to leave it at that.

* * *

"Ge-ro-ni-mo!" Elmer breathed. And again, "Ge-ro-ni-mo! Heavens sir, they're beautiful!"

We were in my room. The statues stood by the floor of the bed, glistening darkly. Elmer reached out for my bottle of scotch and poured it directly to the back of his throat. Afterwards he wiped his mouth with the back of his hand, tears sprouting from the round blue eyes. "They're fantastic, sir! They're incredible! Those statues are going to make us a fortune!"

He hadn't seen the manuscript yet. I showed it to him. Before he could react there was a knock at the door.

"Come in," I cried, and George Ponsonby walked in.

18

PONSONBY WAS DRESSED FOR AN EVENING STROLL along the Via Veneto. He wore a silvery grey lightweight suit with silvery black charcoal stripes, a Cardin tie, hand made yellow moccasins with plaited tops, the whole snazzy outfit crowned with a pale grey fedora. He must have attracted all the touts in Colombo, the way an aniseed ball attracts dogs.

"Have a drink, George," I said. "You must be thirsty, wherever you've come from."

Ponsonby had a drink. "Nice," he said, looking at the bronzes.

"And all perfectly legitimate," Elmer said.

I asked, "You don't think the British Museum—"

"No," Ponsonby said. "They've got enough." He sipped my Chivas. "What you did wasn't very nice, Maasten. I've come for the manuscript you took from Dirkian's safe."

"What manuscript?" I asked.

"You know what I'm talking about, old boy. Now stop being silly and give it to me. It belongs to the British Museum."

"Really," I said. "Then perhaps the British Museum can ask for it nicely, with a large cheque."

"They've already paid McGregor," Ponsonby said. "Perhaps you don't know it, but the Moroccan police want to talk to you about Dirkian's death."

"And you," I said. "You were there too, weren't you, George?"

"Yes. But I'm not going to admit to that, am I?"

"I will," I said and smiled.

Ponsonby looked confused. His face flushed behind a moustache that had begun to wilt with the heat and look like twists of old rope. Despite the air conditioning, Ponsonby began to sweat. "You wouldn't," he said, in a small voice. "You wouldn't, old boy."

I said, "Why don't you be a decent chap and tell us about the manuscript. Then maybe we can get somewhere."

Ponsonby cleared his throat and looked about the room. "I think I'd better sit down," he said and went over to the bed. I filled his glass with more Chivas.

"Dirkian's Swiss bankers wanted to know about the manuscript," Ponsonby said.

"That's unusual."

"Not really, old boy. Dirkian's bank had been making payments in exchange for a manuscript. They'd made four payments and there were three more to be made. They wanted the manuscript so that it could be valued and then they could decide whether to obtain the rest of it for Dirkian's estate."

Cool, I thought, cool and discreet, arranging blackmail through Swiss banks. It was like payment of bills of lading. One bank paid the money against delivery of documents, and both intermediaries were honest, discreet and above all, anonymous.

Ponsonby said, "The manuscript wasn't there, old boy."

"So you thought I'd taken it?"

"No, old boy." He smiled apologetically. "I saw you take it. At least I saw you putting something into your case that could have been the manuscript."

Then Dirkian had arrived and nearly driven Ponsonby out of his tiny mind. "Perhaps you were mistaken."

"No," Ponsonby said. "I wasn't. You know I have the authority to order you to deliver up the manuscript. You're still working for me."

"Try that out on McGregor," I said. "Try and get your five thousand pounds back." I shook my head. "The deal was one job, George. That's how it stays. Unless . . ." I left the word dangling in the air.

"Unless what?"

"Unless you can guarantee clearing me in Tangier, and Elmer in Spain. You will also have to pay for the manuscript."

Ponsonby said, "Dirkian was murdered. That's difficult to clear. But I'll try. However I don't intend to pay for the manuscript, unless of course you're talking about expenses for the time you have been here."

"Twenty pounds a day?"

"Something like that."

"Stuff it," I said. "The deal is immunity in Tangier, immunity in Spain and a large sum of money."

"Couldn't do it old boy," Ponsonby said. "With the best will in the world, couldn't do it."

He paused and gave me one of those belligerent, beady looks. "I could tell the Moroccans about the manuscript," he said.

"Then we would both lose it. Have you thought about that?"

"I have, old boy. But what difference does it make. I don't have the manuscript anyway."

I sighed. Ponsonby wasn't a complete fool after all. "Alright," I said, "We'll cut you in." I told him very briefly about Dirkian being blackmailed and showed him the page of the manuscript that had been translated by Dr. Cabraal. It might not be such a bad thing to have George on our side, I thought. He did have contacts, he might be able to find out more than we could.

"What do I have to do?" Ponsonby asked, finishing reading the manuscript and handing it back to me.

"Ask questions," I said. "Use your contacts and try to find out exactly what Dirkian was doing here, whom he met, where he went, what he did."

"And the manuscript?"

"I'll find the missing fragments," I said.

"And then?"

"We'll play it by ear," I said. It was about all I could say.

* * *

That night, I had dinner with Cindy. She took me to a place that wasn't in any tourist guide, a converted residence with plastic covered tables spread out on the verandah and in the main rooms, with waiters in grubby white coats and sarongs, a crowd of hungry Ceylonese and a kitchen that smelt delicious, never mind what it looked like. The food tasted just like it smelt.

There were stringy cakes of steamed flour, half a dozen curries, prawns fried in batter, pickles, a *sambal* of ground coconut and chilli to take the roof off your mouth and green coconut milk to put it back again. Delicious. I ate hugely.

Conversation teetered round local politics, the travel business and pop music. Then Cindy asked, "What about the tour? I'll make the price more reasonable."

"I didn't really want to talk about that," I said. I wanted to talk to you about Stavros Dirkian." I pushed my plate away, picked two Sobranies, lit them and passed one across to her.

Cindy inhaled deeply. "You asked me about him last night. I told you I didn't know him."

I passed her the photograph and watched her face go four shades paler. "That's Stavros Dirkian," I said.

She looked up at me. She was not only pale, she was also frightened. "He was here about a year, fifteen months ago. At the time of the insurgency."

"And you met him?"

She looked down at the table. "Yes. They hired a car from us."

"What were they doing in Ceylon?"

"I suppose they were on holiday. They were diving."

"What for?"

Cindy said, "Just diving. For fun."

"There was something more than that, Cindy. Stavros Dirkian is dead. I'm trying to find out who killed him."

"Are you a policeman?" she asked in a strained voice.

"No, not a policeman. The police think I killed Dirkian. I'm looking for his killer. What was Dirkian diving for?"

She shook her head and covered her face with her hands. She took a deep breath and said in a muffled voice, "Claude told me they were trying to salvage the *Malabar*." She took her hands away and looked at me. "It's a steamship that was wrecked just outside the breakwater in Galle. Claude said it had a hundred and fifty thousand dollars of gold bullion on board."

"Were there only the two of them?"

Cindy nodded.

Salvaging anything from the sea is difficult. It is also dangerous and expensive. If Dirkian and Claude were going to salvage a ship, they were going to need loads of equipment, pumps, compressors, under water cutting and welding machinery, a whole team of divers and boats. They would also have had to get permission from the government.

Cindy said, "They hired a boat from Latif. I took them down to the south to test their equipment. That's when that photograph was taken. Afterwards I took them to Galle and brought them back." She began to sob.

"What happened in Galle?" I asked.

She shook her head, reached for her purse, took out a handkerchief and dabbed at her eyes. "It was nothing to do with what you want," she said. "Please, let's go."

I went with her to the car. She got in and began to drive towards the hotel.

"I'd like you to show me," I said, "where Claude and Dirkian went diving."

"I don't know where they went in the boat," she said.

"But we can still go diving tomorrow?"

"You'll have to go with Sunil," she said. "I've got a hire. An elderly German couple. I'm taking them to the hill country and the East Coast. I'll be away for a couple of days."

"Sure," I said. Two days. Two days bright with sunshine and scorching heat. However I looked at it, two days could be a long time. In two days anything could happen.

19

THE NEXT DAY IT RAINED.

It started in early morning darkness, a harsh spattering of thick drops against the windows and a great rushing of wind. Then a steady cascade of water, washing against the walls of the hotel in an unceasing stream. Gutters burbled and ran. Thunder rumbled hollowly over the sea.

Sunil came, a dark, solitary figure standing by the reception desk in the dismal grey light. Rain slanted across the esplanade. Large patches of brown water bubbled on the driveway and on the water-logged grass. Slung underneath his arm was my cassette recorder.

"No diving today," he said. "But I brought you this."

There was a wariness about Sunil this morning. Perhaps because it was early and he hadn't got it together yet. Or perhaps he too was worried about Dirkian.

"Thanks," I said and took the tape recorder. I looked out at the rain. Even if it did clear up later, the sea would be swollen and rough and probably quite cold. "We'll have to make it another time," I said.

Sunil nodded. "Oh sure. Is no good for diving now."

* * *

Rain fell all morning. Yellow bulbs battled forlornly against the gloom. I pottered and read, played all my cassettes and had a drink with Elmer. Afterwards I went into the Fort and bought a few tins of artlessly vivid paint.

One way of smuggling the statues out would be to make them look garish and cheap, so that any customs officer looking at them would think they had been made in Hong Kong. After that I took yet another of those ancient perpetually cruising Morris Minor taxis and went to see Latif.

Latif's shop was darker than ever, the smell from the dry goods store must-damp from the rain. The old man still squatted on the counter opposite the showcases, washing jewellery, impervious to the occasional wind blown scatter of rain. The assistant switched on the lights in the showcases. They didn't do much for the gloom and the whole shop felt clammy with damp. I told the assistant it wasn't the weather for buying jewellery and asked to see Latif. He disappeared to the back of the shop, returned and waved to the door with the plastic sign that said Emir Latif was the Managing Director.

Latif hid his surprise at seeing me. It was easy for a man his size, to look solidly impassive. "What can I do for you, Mr. Maasten?"

"A favour," I said. "I want to hire a boat."

"A boat?" He looked suitably mystified. "What kind of boat?"

"Something large enough for about six divers to work off. Something with a bit of power."

Latif rolled his head from side to side. "Why come to me? I deal in jewellery."

"Stavros Dirkian said you hire boats."

For the first time expression floated across the round, plump face with the bloated jowls. An expression of concern, perhaps even fear. "I don't have boats for hire."

"Funny, Dirkian told me you did. He said you hired him a boat about a year ago. I want to do some diving, too."

"One of you must be mistaken," Latif said. "I've never hired a boat to anyone in my life."

* * *

I came back to the hotel, had lunch with Elmer and watched the rain clear, bringing with it the burnt bracken smell of soaked earth and a brightening of the sky. The chunky buildings of the Fort shone with glistening water.

After lunch I read some more and played my cassettes over again. I thought of the money we would make on the statues, but that wasn't much help with the weather. Or Dirkian. Elmer went out to look at more daggers and swords. I stared at the ceiling and wished I'd had the sense to supplant Cindy's tour with one of my own. Then Ponsonby rang.

"I know what Dirkian was doing in Ceylon," he said, his voice throbbing with excitement.

"Let me guess. He was trying to salvage a hundred and fifty thousand dollars of gold bullion from a steamship wrecked near Galle Harbour."

"Wrong, old boy," Ponsonby breathed. "Absolutely wrong. He was smuggling arms."

Smuggling arms for Barney, I thought. Perhaps that was the money Dirkian owed Barney and his friends. I thought about it quickly. Money owed was the only fact that made sense.

"He was here just before the uprising," Ponsonby went on, "He chartered a boat and kept cruising off the south coast with someone called Claude Cesari. Our people think he was making contact with a ship carrying arms for the rebels."

"Do you know what kind of boat he had?"

"A largish one, perhaps a converted MTB."

Converted MTB's were the commonest craft on the smuggling run between India and Ceylon. Latif undoubtedly used them, and if he didn't hire them out, he certainly could make them available.

"Diving for treasure was just a cover," Ponsonby said.

That made sense too. Because it was only a cover, there were different stories about buried temples and buried bullion. But what was the significance of the manuscript?

"What else have you found out?"

"They were in Ceylon for four weeks," Ponsonby said. "They stayed in a hotel for only five days of that time. They spent the rest of the time cruising. Dirkian left a week after the uprising, as soon as flights out of Colombo were operational."

"And Claude?"

"I haven't found any trace of him, old boy. But things were

in a confused state. I mean, our chaps had to pitch in with arms and planes."

"Thanks George," I said.

"I'll keep on keeping on for a bit," Ponsonby said. "I'll call you later tonight if I find anything more."

* * *

I was playing *Tapestry* for the third time when Elmer came in, looking excited. His collar was standing up and his check sports jacket was unbuttoned. Beads of sweat stood on his high freckled forehead. "I've had a cable from the Reede Museum," Elmer said.

I stretched and lit a cigarette. "Oh good. When are they sending the money?"

"They aren't, sir." Elmer shifted uncomfortably. "At least they aren't sending the money yet."

"We can wait," I said. In two days Cindy would be back. In two days I would have found out more about Dirkian.

Elmer moved silently into the room, stopping in front of the statues, reaching out and fondling them as if they were alive.

"What's gone wrong?" I asked.

"Nothing really. Nothing really." He stared, broodingly at the statues. In a small voice, he said, "They're sending an expert to examine what we've bought."

Carole King sang, "You sat down on a river rock and turned into a toad."

I shrugged. "That's not unusual. Museums normally send experts."

"That's precisely what I thought," Elmer said. "The expert is coming in tonight. He's on a flight from Bangkok." He looked at his watch. "It's due in two hours time, and I think we should go out to the airport and meet him."

"Great," I said. It sounded like a very sensible idea.

* * *

I had a shower, a sandwich, changed and half an hour later, with Elmer calling out the roadsigns, was driving to Colombo's

International Airport. Elmer had rented a Peugeot 403, a squarish, solid looking car, with eighty-five thousand on the clock and a hundred and eighty-five thousand mile clatter from the suspension. Despite this, it felt dependable, with that sempiternal feeling Peugeots seem to build into all their cars.

We reached the airport with time enough for a drink in the bar and a walk onto the cool and deserted waving bay. We waved to the Air Ceylon Trident as it flashed along the runway in a blur of streaking light accompanied by a thunderous roaring of engines. We waited till the jet taxied back to the apron in front of the terminal, with a great subdued whistling. Then we went downstairs and stood by the Tea Propoganda Board counter where we could look through glass doors into the customs area.

There hadn't been many passengers on the plane. I counted five. None of them looked like Dr. Lindsay Hamilton. Four of the passengers were Thai, the fifth European, dressed in a brown knitted cotton, short sleeved sweater, a wide, brown leather belt, brown hot pants and brown boots.

I watched the passengers file past the customs desk in a patient queue, at the same time watching the back of the building for late arrivals. There weren't any.

The five passengers moved in an orderly line, clutching passports and forms, were cleared, moved together in a tight knot towards the glass doors. Still no Dr. Lindsay Hamilton.

"Just our luck," I said to Elmer. "He's gone and missed the plane."

I started walking towards the incoming passengers, thinking to ask if there had been anyone else on board. Then two things happened. I was giving the incoming passengers the broad, welcoming grin of a Port Said tout. As we drew closer, I decided to address my question to the European girl. She looked as if she spoke English and my smile was beamed directly at her.

She saw me approach, altered direction slightly, and smiled too. I began to have serious second thoughts about Cindy, but I wasn't the only one with second thoughts.

From behind me, Elmer choked, "I'll see you back at the hotel, sir."

I half turned, but Elmer was already travelling quickly towards the exit, check coat collar pulled up against the stubble on the back of his neck. Undecided, I turned back. The girl was standing two feet in front of me, her smile just below my own eye level. "Hi," I said and took two steps back to get a better view.

She was well built, with great big cocoons of breasts amply filling the thin, cotton sweater. She had broad shoulders, with a smooth wide look of a swimmer and her waist tapered to a hand-span behind the broad leather belt. She had an alert, intelligent face, framed by shoulder length brown hair that had a marvellous tint of deep red in it. A sharp, no-nonsense nose, a firm cupid's bow of a mouth and a chin that was pointed, dimpled and gave more than a hint of aggression. Her skin was evenly tanned to a reddish copper colour and her eyes were startlingly green. She stood about my height on magnificent legs, firm booted calves and full, flaring thighs. There was only one word to describe her. Statuesque.

"Hello," I said. "I've lost a passenger."

"Or two?" A thin eyebrow curled.

"I'm looking for a Dr. Lindsay Hamilton. Tell me were there any—"

She stretched out a hand, squarish, with short, unpainted fingernails. "I'm Dr. Lindsay Hamilton," she said. "How do you do?" Her grip was firm as a man's, the palms slightly rough.

"There must be a mistake," I said. Dr. Lindsay Hamilton should have been a thin, stoop-shouldered archaeologist, wearing half-lensed, square-topped spectacles and an absent minded expression. Dr. Lindsay Hamilton couldn't be a woman, especially not a woman who would have looked so much better in a bikini.

"It's not fair," I said.

The real Dr. Lindsay Hamilton laughed. "Don't worry. It's happened before. I don't know why everyone expects me to be a man."

"I'm glad you're you." I said, with feeling. "My name is Nicholas Maasten. I've got a car outside."

"Whacko," she said.

I picked up her bag, which was sensibly light and walked with her to the door.

"Lindsay is a girl's name as well, you know," she said striding beside me. "Even though I was called after Lindsay Hassett."

"Lindsay what?"

"You know, the Australian cricket captain. A fine batsman."

If he looked anything like Lindsay Hamilton, I thought, the bowlers must have dropped him lobs.

"I'm Australian," Lindsay Hamilton said, just to make everything crystal clear. It also enabled me to place the nasal twang, the dipthongal rise and fall in her voice, like so many question marks.

"Wasn't there someone else with you?" she asked.

We walked through the door. There was no sign of Elmer outside the airport building. "Yes," I said. "I mean, no."

She gave me a hard look. "Which is it? Yes or no?"

"No," I said. "I always say yes when I mean no, if you know what I mean."

"I don't know what you mean," she said. "You sound like a very confused person."

"I am," I said thinking of Cindy. "Very."

We walked along the drive to the car park. I opened the passenger door for her and slung her bag onto the rear seat. Then I got in and began to drive quietly back to Colombo, hoping I wouldn't get lost.

Lindsay, as she insisted on being called, had been working in Bangkok for a Paris based organisation that had a rather specialised interest in Oriental art and archaeology. Her contract had expired six days ago and while she was hesitating whether to go back to Europe, or return to Australia, she'd had this beaut offer from the Reede Museum.

"Lucky for them," I said.

"What do you mean?"

"Oh—that you were free. That sort of thing." Again I had that feeling of not being exactly original, of being rather second-hand.

She said, "You are a very confused person, aren't you?" And leaned against the door.

For a while she stared in silence at the darkened countryside. Then she said, "Ceylon hasn't changed much, has it?"

"You've been here before?"

"Yes, two years ago. I was with Dr. George Varsaly." She

paused for applause.

"Oh, yes," I said, thinking that if George Varsaly was so famous, why hadn't I heard of him.

"We were investigating a dagoba. You know dagobas?"

"I've seen them," I said. "Great big domed things, with a pinnacle on top. Religious, aren't they?"

"They're more than that, Nicholas," she said. "A hell of a lot more than that." During the rest of the journey, she told me.

We reached the wide, rutted bridge with its unlit concrete bollards and wandering cattle. It was one of the two northern entrances to Colombo. "What happened at the excavation?" I asked. "Did you find anything?"

She laughed. "Not a zack," she said. "We ran out of funds and into a lot of interference. People thought we were there to desecrate the dagoba and to smuggle its treasures out of the country. It's a very serious offence, smuggling treasures out of Ceylon. Did you know that?"

I wished I didn't and twisted the car round a bullock cart. After that, for my own peace of mind, I concentrated on driving.

20

WHILE DR. LINDSAY HAMILTON CHECKED IN, I asked for my room key. The receptionist looked at the vacant slot behind her, shouted a question along the counter, checked the empty slot again and told me that my friend had taken my key.

I caught Lindsay looking at me, interrogatively. I shrugged and gave her a helpless smile that I hoped, indicated that the receptionist was not entirely sane. Lindsay's room was four doors along the corridor from mine. I walked up the stairs with her and suggested that she looked at the bronzes as soon as she'd finished unpacking.

My room door was open. Elmer was hunched at the foot of the bed, between the statues. His knees were clasped to his chest and he was staring broodingly at the carpet. As I came in he stopped staring broodingly at the carpet and began staring broodingly at me.

I closed the door softly behind me. "You look great sitting there," I said. "Dressed in doublet breeches and stocking cap, I could sell the lot of you—Siva, Parvati and plastic gnome."

"We're in deep trouble," Elmer said, gloomily.

I went round the bed, pulled out the chair in front of the dressing table, swivelled it round and sat on it. I shot my feet out onto a corner of the bed. If we were in deep trouble, I thought staring at my shoes, then I might as well hear about it comfortably. My Pinet suedes were scuffed around the toes and the instep. When we left, I decided to fly back through Rome. They made lovely shoes in Italy and perhaps on this trip, I could afford them. I brought my mind back to Elmer and the probability we could be in deep trouble.

Elmer said, "That girl."

"You mean, Dr. Lindsay Hamilton?"

"The very same, sir. The very same. I didn't recognise her name on the cable. I was expecting an esquire."

"She's used to being mistaken for a man."

"I recognised her at the airport."

"And you ran." I shook out a cigarette and fumbled for a lighter.

"She works for ICOM," he pronounced it eye-com, as if it were a left-wing conspiracy. "The International Council of Museums."

"I thought she was with the Reede people in New York."

Elmer shook his head, "Seconded, sir, on loan. You know about ICOM?"

I shook my head, spilling ash over the carpet.

"ICOM's based in Paris."

"Yes. She told me that."

"Dr. Lindsay Hamilton works for their Ethics of Acquisition Department."

I blew out smoke, watching it cloud over my pale blue, brushed cotton pants, making my suedes look even more battle weary. Ethics of Acquisition sounded like something the Pope had to deal with cataloguing the Vatican treasures. "I suppose," I said, "she must be a Catholic." Disappointing. If she was a Catholic and if she worked for the Pope, she would have principles. It wasn't fair. Especially with the body she had on her.

"For heaven's sake! Why should she be a Catholic?"

I told Elmer.

He shook his head, reprovingly. "Ethics of Acquisition is nothing like that."

I brightened. "In any case she's left ICOM. Her contract expired a few days ago."

Elmer brooded. "I doubt the relevance of that. In fact, I doubt it very much. Once a policeman, always a policeman."

Smoke caught at my throat. I coughed, violently.

"The Ethics of Acquisition Department investigates the ownership and the authenticity of works of art. But their main concern is maintaining records and circulating descriptions of works that have been stolen. They also persuade private collectors and museums to return illegally acquired material, and most important, they work closely with Interpol."

I began coughing again. I had heard of Interpol. Worse. Interpol had heard of me. When I had ceased working for the Department, some bastard had passed Interpol selected extracts from my personal file. Nothing serious. Nothing penal. Just enough to ensure Interpol's continued interest in where I was and what I did. Just enough to warn me to stay on the Department's side of the fence. With the Moroccan police wanting to talk to me, all I needed was someone asking Interpol for a reference.

"I suppose we'd better get the hell out of here," I said and stopped. I remembered Hassan and decided it wasn't going to be as easy as that. There were also the problems of Dirkian's death and where to go.

Elmer had a different idea. "I'll go," he said. "You stay."

Nice, I thought, friendly. Greater love hath no man than this that he hands his friends over to Interpol and the Moroccan police. "I've got a surveillance and report file with Interpol," I said.

"That doesn't affect the situation. You are now engaged in a perfectly legal business venture."

Until the Moroccans found me or until I smuggled the statues out. "Almost perfectly legal," I corrected.

Elmer ignored me. "My situation is rather different. I've met Miss Hamilton before." A warm flush was creeping up from his open shirt, moving slowly all the way up to the high, domed forehead. "Miss Hamilton and I had a difference of opinion over an American Indian necklace."

I sighed. "What went wrong? Couldn't you stay with Velazquez?"

"Velazquez was too dangerous, sir. He's too well known."

"So you ended up with an American Indian necklace and Miss Hamilton. What happened?"

"In the end, nothing. I returned the money to the purchaser and we all agreed it was a mistake."

"Sure," I said. "Could happen to anyone."

"But I don't think Miss Hamilton entirely believed me. I think she will examine anything I sell with extreme suspicion."

"Let her," I said. I looked fondly at the statues. Eternally dancing Siva and divine girl-goddess, Parvati. Lindsay Hamilton could examine the statues as closely as she liked. "We've nothing to worry about," I said. "You stay."

"But—"

"It's going to be very difficult," I said firmly, "if you keep disappearing like a frightened rabbit each time Miss Hamilton appears."

Elmer pursed his mouth into a tight line, making his face look like a collapsed orange. "I think it would be better if you dealt with Miss Hamilton."

"What happens if the Reede Museum has told her there are two of us?"

"You'll think of something. You always do."

At that moment the door opened and my mind went blank. Lindsay Hamilton stood in the doorway, mouth rounded in surprise. Elmer gave a small, strangled cry and made for the bathroom.

I grabbed Elmer by the trouser band and turned him round to face Lindsay Hamilton.

Lindsay Hamilton said, "I'm sorry. I just touched the door and it opened." She had changed into a sleeveless white blouse, cotton jeans and sandals. A leather satchel drooped from her right shoulder. She still looked as big and as beautiful as ever. I couldn't believe she was a policewoman.

Still gripping Elmer firmly, I said, "Come in. Meet my associate, Elmer Robey."

While they stared at each other, I released Elmer, took out the bottle of Chivas and filled glasses.

"I thought I saw you at the airport," Lindsay said transfixing Elmer with a gimlet stare. "I'm sure it was you."

"Soda or water?" I asked, handing out the glasses and standing pacifically by with the syphon. "I'll have to ask room service for ice."

They both took soda.

"Elmer wasn't at the airport," I said. "He was in Colombo,

looking at daggers."

"Oh," she said.

I was relieved to see that she was a trifle unsure, that there was the smallest hint of self-doubt in her expression. I offered her a cigarette. "What do you think of the statues?" I said. "Aren't they fantastic!"

She held her own cigarette, chest high and ignored my outstretched Ronson. Still staring at Elmer, she said, "I thought you specialised in American Indian decorative art."

Elmer reddened. Then his face took on the innocently happy expression of a child at its first birthday party. "Until I met you, ma'am. Until I met you, I thought I knew all about American Indian art." He laughed, ruefully. "You sure proved me different."

Lindsay Hamilton reached into her satchel, took out one of those cylindrical French lighters and lit her cigarette. "And you are now specialising in Oriental art?"

Elmer flinched under the sarcasm in her voice. More than that. He even managed to sound hurt. "Look at those bronzes, ma'am," he said, "and decide for yourself."

Dr. Lindsay Hamilton gave us all a look which said that that was precisely what she intended to do.

21

STRONG-FINGERED HANDS HOLDING HER GLASS before her like a votive offering, she walked slowly round the statues. Soft, russet brown hair flowed over one shoulder as she tilted her head to one side, and looked. The thin cotton blouse did little to hide the firmly muscled body underneath, and there was an entrancing streak of brown as she leaned forward to observe the Siva, more closely.

Elmer came round and sat on the edge of the bed, hands clenched between his thighs. I smoked and slopped more Chivas into my glass. I had the same feeling of incomprehension and helplessness, of not knowing quite what to do next, that you get waiting in an airport lounge just after a saccharined voice announces that your flight will be delayed.

Lindsay squatted beside the statues in a magnificent, rippling movement. The jeans stretched sensuously against her thighs, taut against her round bottom. She reached out and ran a finger along the Siva, brow slightly furrowed, mouth compressed into a narrow line, totally absorbed. The expression in her eyes was hard, cold, impersonal.

As I watched her, I seemed to see the statues through her eyes. The bronzes somehow ceased to be delightful, fluid sculptures. They ceased to be masterpieces created by a marvellous, forgotten artist. As I looked, they became mere masses of worked metal, capable of analysis, of interpretation, of evaluation.

Lindsay stood up and walked round the statues. Disdaining

my help, she moved them around, to get a better view. I began to see little bubbles I hadn't noticed before on the smooth surface of the bronze, almost as if holes had been filled in. I noticed rust-like marks, where the patina hadn't taken properly.

Bending over the Parvati, Lindsay said, "The patina is unusual."

"It's a lovely green," I said.

She straightened and looked, frowning. "I don't know . . . It's . . . There are traces of corrosion."

"They're old statues," I said. "Over a thousand years old. What do you expect?"

She looked directly at me, brushing hair from her face with impatient fingers. "Perhaps you're right. Perhaps. Do you know how patinas are formed?"

I nodded quickly. I knew that bronze is an alloy of copper and tin, that exposure to the atmosphere corrodes the copper, forming a thin green skin over the bronze. I didn't think I needed a lecture on that.

She said, "You know green isn't the only colour. Sometimes you get patinas that are blue or grey, even black or red."

"Really," I said, interested.

Lindsay explained. Patinas were usually constituted of basic copper carbonates, the vivid green mineral malachite found in nearly all copper mining districts, and the blue carbonate, azurite. It was these that gave bronzes their usual green or greeny blue skins.

But patinas were affected by the chemical composition of the bronze, by location and by time. Thus a bronze exposed to volcanic winds could turn black due to the presence of sulphur in the air. A bronze buried in an alkaline soil free of carbonic acid would turn red, due to oxidization of the copper. The presence of zinc in bronze would darken the patina appreciably; the presence of tin oxide or lead carbonate would produce a patina that was greyish green.

"Remarkable," I said. I was impressed and I looked at the statues with new interest. "Still they do have a lovely patina."

"Such a vivid, dark green," Elmer contributed.

"I noticed that," Lindsay said and squatted down, absorbed once more in her examination.

I lit another cigarette and relaxed. The lecture on patinas had had a useful effect. We had communicated. Elmer and I had shown that we were interested, we had I thought, made Lindsay aware that we appreciated the difference between sculpture and scrap metal.

Then she said, "Have you got the invoice for these statues?"

I was glad we had anticipated that. I gave her the invoice Elmer and I had prepared. It was headed Maasten-Robey Associates and was for seven thousand six hundred and eighty dollars. Using dollars on the invoice had been Elmer's idea. That way, we made a small additional profit on the rate of exchange.

Lindsay glanced cursorily at the invoice and placed it on the carpet beside her. "I'm not interested in this," she said taking another look at the bronzes. "I want to see the invoice from the person who sold you the statues."

I said, "I'm not sure that's ethical. There's such a thing as trade secrets, you know."

She got to her feet. The cold hard light in those startlingly green eyes had changed to something much hotter. "I'm interested in three things," she said, softly, "That these statues are what you say they are," a quick glance at the invoice by her feet, "tenth century bronzes, that you have acquired them legally, and that the Reede Museum pays a fair price for them. I am not interested in your profit."

Elmer said, "The young lady is right, Nicholas. We have to prove authenticity."

After that there wasn't much I could say. I picked up the invoice from the dressing table drawer and handed it to Lindsay.

"Thanks," head lowering over the piece of paper in her hand, hair flowing in a glistening river. Then, "This invoice says that the bronzes are warranted to be less than one hundred years old?"

I sighed. Life would be so much simpler if people took each other's word for everything. "That invoice is for customs," I said. "We've got to get the statues out."

"You mean you've got to smuggle them out?"

"What do you think? They aren't going to swim to New

York and the Ceylon Government isn't going to give me any Duke of Edinburgh awards for taking them out."

"But it's wrong, Nicholas!"

"It's in a good cause," I said. Smuggling the statues out would benefit the art lovers of New York, the Reede Museum, Elmer and me.

"You obviously believe that the end justifies the means."

"I also believe in just wars, the survival of the fittest and Nicholas Maasten." We stood facing each other with the belligerent air of swordfish in the mating season. "Look," I said, "half the museums in Europe are filled with stuff that has been smuggled or stolen from other countries. Only because the thieves or smugglers had political and military power behind them it wasn't called theft. It was called patriotism. Theft is still theft, however many Acts of Parliament might have been passed to prove otherwise."

Lindsay said, "All that is no justification for what you're doing."

"We both work for the Reede Museum. This is what our employer wants. You do your job and I'll do mine."

"Perhaps afterwards, you will return the Elgin marbles to Greece," Lindsay said.

"Perhaps," I said. "If you'll help me carry them."

She smiled tightly. "Who is this Arthur Rubeiro Diaz?"

"He's a dealer. He used to work in the Archaeological Department."

"And he acquired the bronzes legally?"

"He says so. He will give me a certificate if I want it."

"He sounds very obliging."

"He's a gentleman," I said. Arthur Rubeiro Diaz would certainly have agreed with that description.

Lindsay knelt down again by the statues, taking out a small slab of metal from her satchel. Carefully she applied it to one of the tiny marks on the Siva that I had thought was a bubble. The slab of metal stuck fast to it.

"How old are the statues, Nicholas?"

"About nine hundred, a thousand years."

"And this is what Arthur Diaz told you?"

"Yes. He'll certify that too."

She removed the slab of metal and pressed it twice more against the Siva. Then she did the same with the Parvati. "These markings," she said, "are magnetic."

"Bronze is an alloy," I pointed out.

"An alloy of copper and tin. These markings have iron in them." She slid the magnet over Parvati's bosom. "They're a different mixture from the rest of the statue."

I said, "These statues are very old. They must have been repaired from time to time, touched up. Arthur Diaz told me that he'd done some restoration work on them."

"Really," she said, "Let me show you something else."

I went and knelt beside her. She traced a finger down the Parvati. "See that line?"

"I see it," I said.

"Now look at the Siva."

There was the same faint line, bisecting the statue. "I wouldn't worry about that," I said. "They're mould marks that have been filed off."

"I'm glad you agree," she said and stood up. "I'm certain that these statues have been cast in the sand mould process. I'm certain that those markings are plugs filling the holes made by the iron wires which held the sand core in place."

I gave the Parvati a friendly wink and a tap on the rump. I stood up too. The trouble with experts was that they always wanted to impress you with how much they knew. "That's very interesting," I said.

"It is, Nicholas. You'd be surprised how interesting."

I hoped she wasn't going to give me a lecture on the sand mould process. I hoped she wasn't even going to start a lecture on that or any other process. Once she started, she was going to be impossible to stop.

Lindsay didn't give me any lectures. What she did was much worse. She said, "What I find difficult to understand is if the statues were made in the tenth century, how they could have been cast in the sand mould process that wasn't invented until the fourteenth."

Thoughts jammed my head. Panic. The Sinhalese were four hundred years ahead of their time. Probable, but not necessarily possible. I knew the Sinhalese had performed great feats of irrigation, that they had built vast tanks in the North Central Province. There must have been great architects amongst them, engineers, sculptors. It was possible —

"Prior to the fourteenth century," Lindsay was saying, "Bronze was cast in the lost wax or *cire perdue* process. A model was made in beeswax and covered with malleable clay . . ."

I wasn't listening. It couldn't be true. The Siva and the Parvati were genuine. I was sure of that. I had to be. Otherwise, whatever happened over Dirkian, Hassan would be using me for a lampstand.

"Molten bronze is then —"

"Are you saying that these bronzes aren't a thousand years old?" I demanded, harshly.

Lindsay looked levelly at me. "In any investigation of this type, Nicholas," she said, "It is difficult to reach conclusions which are definitive. All one has are certain lines of probability, certain elements that individually might be irrelevant, but taken together form the basis of a conclusion. Take these statues for instance."

I took the statues.

"To be definite about them, I would like to have samples of the bronze and the patina chemically analysed. I would want the statues subjected to a gamma ray shadowgraph. I would want to make many other tests, none of them possible here and now. But it is here and now that I have to make a decision. I have to make a decision on such facts as are available."

She wasn't sure, I thought. She couldn't be certain. Her own words were, no definite conclusion. And if she couldn't be sure, the statues *could* be one thousand years old.

Lindsay said, "Let's look at the evidence. It is claimed that the statues were made in the tenth century. Yet they were cast in a process that was not invented until the fourteenth. That must throw some doubt as to their being one thousand years old."

"But they could be six hundred years old?"

"The statues have, as you have repeatedly pointed out, a deep green patina. I would imagine that this is caused by the presence of zinc in the bronze. Zinc is a product of a much later age. It forms three per cent of United States Standard Bronze, the material commonly specified today, in contracts for art bronzes.

"And while we are talking about the composition of bronze, it was quite common in the East, to mix bronze with lead. This served to make the bronze easier to work with, and also gave the finished work a deep black patina, the colour of polished ebony. Like this."

She reached into her satchel and brought out two postcards. "My fourth and most conclusive reason," she said.

The cards were photographs of my Siva and my Parvati. Except they were clearer, smoother, darker and somehow more perfect than the originals. The cards were copyright, a product of the West German firm of Defot Werkstätten, and the cards were available at thirty-five cents each from the Colombo National Museum, Edinburgh Crescent, Colombo 7, where no doubt the originals could be inspected.

"Nothing is really conclusive," Lindsay was saying. "But you must admit, it all adds up." She pointed casually to the bronzes. "I doubt if either of those is over fifty years old."

She couldn't have done better if she had clobbered me with both statues, from a height of fifty feet.

22

LINDSAY SAID, "I'M SORRY, I'D LIKE to help you, but I can't recommend that the Reede Museum buy these bronzes."

"Not even at four thousand dollars?" I asked, hopefully.

She shook her head. Hope died. "They aren't worth a brass razoo."

I lit a cigarette, went over to the dressing-table and picked up the manuscript. "I suppose you'd better take a butchers at this," I said. "Then I can go out and strangle Diaz and get our money back." I would also find out what the manuscript meant and that would be some consolation.

She toook the manuscript from me and looked at it.

"Well?" I asked. My throat seemed to be stuck to the back of my neck, and all I could think about was that if the manuscript was genuine, then we'd only owe Hassan one thousand pounds.

"It looks old enough."

My heart leapt.

"So would any respectable forgery," Elmer said.

"Aren't there any tests you can make?"

"No," she said thoughtfully. "Not here. They wouldn't tell me anything, anyway, except how old the paper is, and the ink. Age can be faked too, you know."

"Will the Reede Museum take it?"

"Let me translate it first. Then we'll see."

She went to the door and turned. "I'm sorry it hasn't worked out for you two," she said, and smiled encouragingly.

I even believed she meant it.

* * *

As soon as the door shut behind her, I turned to Elmer. "Holy, flaming snakes! Just wait till I get my hands round that bastard's stringy throat!"

Elmer said, "We'll still have Dirkian and Hassan to worry about." He reached out and passed me the Chivas. "Have a drink, sir. It will relax you."

I didn't want to be relaxed. I wanted to smash Diaz' fragile skull against a wall until his brains popped out like egg yolk. "Sod Diaz!" I said and I put the Chivas back, untouched.

Elmer said, "I hope the manuscript is the same one Dirkian had."

"And that it's genuine."

"Don't worry," Elmer said. "We'll think of something." "We'll rob a bank, or sell an Utrillo, or something."

"I could sell the bar," I said, sombrely.

"When they let me back, I could raise some money on the plane."

I pulled Elmer to his feet and crouched till my face was on a level with his. "We could," I suggested, "sell the statues to Barney Goldman."

Elmer blinked quickly at me. Then his tiny mouth split into a tiny grin. "In many ways," he said, softly, "that would be simpler. Much simpler."

Later that evening Ponsonby telephoned again. When Dirkian had left Ceylon he had gone to Thailand. Subsequently he had visited Thailand twice accompanied on both occasions by an ex-OAS man called Dupré, who was a known arms-smuggler. Dirkian's last visit had been four months ago. And that only made everything more confused.

* * *

However confused the Dirkian situation might be, I was clear about one thing. I was going to sell those bronzes to Barney Goldman. Barney had once had an interest in antiques, and now despite what Ponsonby had discovered about Dirkian, Barney was into art smuggling.

I decided that my meeting with Barney would have to be casual. There could be no hint of strain about it, not the slightest amount of pressure. Barney should never know that I had to sell the bronzes.

So I spun out most of the next morning seated under a fan in the lobby of the hotel, reading. The other, low, comfortable chairs were empty and from where I sat, I could see the large counter of the reception area, the verandah and the porch. No-one could go in or out without my noticing. In any case, business was slow that morning. Everyone was either sleeping late, or the tourist season had not yet begun.

It was a few minutes after eleven o'clock when Barney came out onto the verandah, with the stretching, well-fed-cat look of a man who had slept long and peacefully and was just beginning to feel the first pangs of thirst on a hot day. He stretched out comfortably along a chair on the verandah and ordered beer, staring vacantly along the esplanade, with the air of someone settling in for a long stay.

I picked up my book and wandered off towards the swimming pool. Barney would be all the more mellow for two more beers, and business would be easier.

Half an hour later I was back. Barney was still slumped in his chair, arm trailing to the cement floor, a tall, frothy glass of beer resting casually on his stomach. He had also been joined by two other men.

They were dark, bearded, deeply tanned, dressed like Barney in loose batik patterned shirts, khaki shorts and sandals. They were leaning forward in their chairs, elbows resting on bare knees, talking in low voices. There was a fierce intensity in their eyes.

All conversation stopped as I approached. I smelt caporal, saw a crumpled blue pack of Gauloise amongst the cool green of the bottles, and the rings of damp on the table. "Hello Barney," I said.

Barney opened his eyes. There was a moment's hesitation, before the smile crossed his face, travelling slowly without impression, like the shadow of an aeroplane across a field.

"Nicholas man," he said. "Good to see you."

The other two men were watching me with a hard, blank look that I'd seen before. Barney introduced them as Maurice and Pierre. Pierre was the shorter one, the one with the tough looking shoulders and a fading inverted V of a scar across the bridge of his nose. Maurice was leaner, wirier, older with flecks of grey in his hair and beard. He looked just as tough.

Neither of them smiled or offered to shake hands. Only the tersest of nods acknowledged my presence. That and the chilling, empty watchfulness.

"Take a pew," Barney said lazily. "Slake your thirst." Pierre and Maurice began speaking quickly to each other in French.

I sat down. "Nice day," I said. It was a stupid thing to say in a country where every day save one is nice, but I had to begin somewhere.

They let me pour out my own beer. Maurice shook out a Gauloise and lit it, You saw men like them in bars in Jo'burg or Salisbury. You met them in steamy, tin roofed buildings alongside desolate runways; you even saw them in pubs around Earls Court, wearing expensive, drip-dry nylon shirts and knife edged trousers, always talking softly amongst themselves, always creating a tight, tough enclave and looking vaguely military.

Pierre and Maurice were, or had been mercenaries. I'd been long enough in Commando 15 to know that.

Barney asked, "What's new?"

I shrugged. "Nothing's ever new." I waited. No-one said anything. "The only thing new," I said, "is that I have some bronzes for sale."

Barney stretched hugely. "Always hustling, Nicky baby. Always trying to make a deal." He smiled. "You haven't changed, Nicholas, man."

"I've grown older," I said. "And more beautiful. And I've got some exquisite bronzes for sale."

"What's wrong with them?" Barney gave me a big grin. "There must be something wrong or you wouldn't be selling them."

"There is," I said. "I can't get them out of the country. The export of works of art over a hundred years old is banned."

"Bloody unjust," Barney said. "That's what I think. Bloody

unjust. So unjust it's even taught you honesty."

"I'm letting you have them at a special price," I said. "I'm letting you have them at less than I paid for them, taking account of the risk."

Barney placed his beer on the table and sat up. "What makes you think I could get them out, Nicholas baby?" The smile was only an empty crease on his face. His eyes were saying something very different.

"Because you've got imagination," I said. "And you're intrepid.

Maurice and Pierre had ceased their low, rumbled conversation. They were staring past me, over my left shoulder. Barney turned and looked, too, getting the full benefit of Lindsay who was bearing down on us, breasts in full flower, thighs rippling under the shortest and hottest pants of the year. "Oh Nicholas," she said, "I've been looking for you. Would you lend me the car?"

I let out the breath that had somehow stuck in my throat. "Sure," I said, diving into my pocket and tossing her the keys.

She caught them with a swift, snatching movement that would have delighted her cricket loving father. "I won't be long," she said. "See you."

But it was four of us who did the looking, as she walked straight and erect, with only the slightest wiggle, along the verandah, down the steps and into the car park.

"Boy," Barney said, "Boy oh boy. You sure pick 'em, Nicholas baby."

"Sure," I said. "I'm beautiful."

"Bet you smell nice too." He kept looking at the car park. "Boy oh boy, right out of the pages of Playboy. And those legs! Jesus! All the way up to her fucking arse."

"Barney," I said sharply. "You're drooling, and it isn't nice. Sit up like a man and drink your beer and stop looking at that car park. She isn't going to walk past again."

He turned to me and winked. Maurice leaned across and said something to him very rapidly in French. Then the amusement faded from Barney's eyes, burying itself deep, replaced by something much colder, and very much harder. "You're right, Nicky baby," he announced firmly. "Let's go and take a look at those bronzes."

*　　*　　*

Upstairs, in my room, I whipped the sacking off the bronzes, as if I was a bullfighter practising a veronica. The bronzes still had that rich dark gleam, they still looked just as beautiful and expensive as they had done that sunny afternoon, Diaz had brought them to me. Barney must like them, I thought. Barney had wanted them. I only hoped that my own diminished excitement about them, wasn't contagious.

Barney knelt down before them, running his fingers gently over the smooth surfaces, as if they were flesh.

"They're beautiful," I said, softly. "They're worth a fortune."

Barney kept touching the statues and I wondered if he imagined he was feeling up Lindsay. "I know half a dozen people who would buy them for three grand each," I said.

Barney turned. "Do you Nicholas?" He asked softly and looked back at the statues. His fingers had never left them.

"Yeah," I said. "There aren't many pieces like this outside museums. And with private collectors the way they are—well—"

"How old are they?"

"Oh," I said. "Tenth, twelfth century, something like that."

"You bought them from Diaz?"

"Yes and I'll sell them to you at the same price. Twelve hundred pounds each."

"Reasonable," he said, but he took his time considering that. He stood up and walked around the statues looking at them from every possible angle. He crouched down and touched them. He tilted them and looked underneath their bases. He moved the curtain so that the light washed over them at a specific angle. I smoked two cigarettes and tried to look unconcerned. I even hummed a tune about raindrops and happiness.

Barney said, "Odd things, statues. They've got such a sense of history." He pointed. "What are those markings, do you know?"

"Yes," I said. "They're quite usual. In the old days they

had difficulty keeping the furnace at the critical temperature. Consequently there always were slight imperfections, which the sculptor had to rectify by hand. It is these imperfections which give the statue its value and enable it to be so precisely dated." I hoped Barney knew as little about bronzes as I did.

"They look like holes that have been filled up," Barney said.

"Oh yes," I pretended to look. "That one does. But what do you expect? These statues weren't made yesterday, and a thousand years is a hell of a long time. Just think of it, a thousand years."

I paused to give Barney time to think about a thousand years.

Then I said, "These statues have been repaired from time to time. But that doesn't make them less valuable. All that shows is that they have been well looked after. The value of these statues lies in their whole concept, their age, their rarity. They don't make statues like this any more, Barney."

Barney looked blankly at me. "Diaz does." he said.

"He does!" My surprise and disappointment were genuine. I didn't think Barney knew about Diaz.

"These two statues," Barney said, "Are known as Diaz's Divine Deceptions. He's been trying to flog them for years." With that he burst out laughing, throwing his head back, screwing his face up, his whole body shaking as if he was being jolted by electric currents, the sound of his cackling filling the room. He was still laughing when the door opened.

Lindsay stood there, arms piled high with books, the car keys twined round her little finger.

Barney subsided with four long cockerel like crows. "Hello again," he said, squeezing a tear out of the corner of his eyes.

Lindsay gave him a curt nod. "Your keys," she said to me, waggling her finger so that they dropped on the carpet.

"You interested in Ceylon history then?" Barney asked, looking at the books. "You going to spend a lot of time reading then?"

"I don't think so," Lindsay replied. Again she spoke to me. "Nicholas, can we go to Galle this afternoon. I want to look at a fort."

Which reminded me that I had to go to Galle too. To look

at a harbour.

I said, "If you want to."

"Beaut, we'll go after lunch. And Nicholas, the manuscript is incomplete. There must be more of it somewhere."

I looked at my watch. I still had time to see Diaz.

23

DIAZ LIVED IN A LARGE, GLOOMY HOUSE, made to look even gloomier by the heavy shade trees that grew alongside it. The house was at the end of a short, rutted, driveway of red earth, a haunted, brooding presence of stained and faded cream, with a long verandah slashed by a diamond-patterned trellis of grey wood that began at waist level and ended about six feet from the cement floor. A battered, black Chevrolet dripped oil under the peeling porch, and a dented tricycle stood with one wheel resting on a grubby, plastic doll.

The slam of my car door brought a small servant boy onto the verandah, rapidly unhitching a blue striped sarong. Behind him, Diaz appeared, a bird-like white clad figure in a shady doorway. I raced on to the dusty verandah, past the row of cane backed, wood framed chairs and the mirrored umbrella stand with its crown of antlers. "Diaz!" I shouted, "I want you!"

He took two tiny steps onto the verandah. "Mr. Maasten," he said quietly, "What a surprise."

I stopped with a slight feeling of shame, as if I'd just been discovered stealing money from a child's piggy bank. I said firmly, "I want to talk to you." I wasn't shouting at him anymore. "I want to talk to you about your bloody statues."

"With pleasure, Mr. Maasten. With pleasure." He waved a fragile hand at a set of dangling plastic strips, which separated a small room from the verandah. He followed me in, pulling the wooden doors shut after him.

We were in a small room, crowded with glass fronted cupboards containing old medical and biological text books, whose yellowing pages spilled out of the broken bindings. There were also, I noticed, a 1936 edition of the *Encyclopaedia Britannica* with two volumes missing, and a complete set of *The Book of Knowledge*. Dusty photographs paraded up one wall, topped by a sepia toned portrait of a heavily moustached man in a topee, who must have been Diaz's father. A copy of the Dali "Crucifixion" slanted over one of the two barred windows. A small desk filled the centre of the room, crowded with what looked like dreary government circulars and stained copies of *Hansard*. There was also a large framed photograph, facing the single straight backed chair on the further side of the desk. All I could see of it was its dark wood and spatulate stand.

"Those statues are fakes," I said. "They aren't a thousand years old."

Diaz sighed, patiently. "The precise dating of works of art has always been one that has confused experts."

"There's no confusion about these. These statues are less than fifty years old and you know it. I want my money back."

Diaz said, "Those statues may well be a thousand years old, Mr. Maasten. Who can tell?"

"I've brought them back," I said. "They're in the car. Now I want my money back."

Diaz sighed again. "It isn't as simple as that," he said. "You see Mr. Maasten, even if I wanted to give you your money back, I couldn't. The money is gone. If you had spoken to me yesterday, last night even, I might have been able to do something. But today it is too late. The money is gone."

"What the hell do you mean, gone?"

He made an open palmed gesture of wonder and incomprehension. "Who can tell, Mr. Maasten, who can tell? The money is perambulating, circumlocuting, diversifying, converting, all on a circuitous route, that with luck and good fortune, will end in some part of the world where currency values are stable and exchange control does not exist. It is a process that takes many weeks, Mr. Maasten, and would take twice as long if it were to be reversed."

"Give it back to me in rupees, then."

"Mr. Maasten, believe me, if I could, I would. I am a poor man. I do not have a hundred and sixty thousand rupees to give you."

It was then that I tried to grab him, but the desk got in the way. Diaz twisted away and as I reached across the desk, the narrow frame of the photograph pressing into my stomach, he was standing against the window, under the picture of the Dali "Crucifixion." From his closed fist there protruded the ugly blue black barrel of a Webley .32.

"I deplore violence," Diaz said softly. "I really do."

I picked myself slowly off the deck. At that range even a .32 was lethal. At that range even someone as feeble as Diaz, couldn't miss.

"You'll never get away with this," I said, pulling the photograph away from my middle, realising how futile my words sounded.

"I would suggest, Mr. Maasten, that if you are dissatisfied with the statues, you sell them to someone else. There is nothing else you can do. If you were to go to the police, they would be more concerned with why you want to buy statues that are more than a hundred years old, knowing they cannot be exported. They would be more concerned with how you obtained a hundred and sixty thousand rupees to pay for them. I think, Mr. Maasten, that the most sensible thing for you to do is to find another buyer for the statues. Or return them to me, and I will try and sell them on a commission basis."

"Go bite your own backside," I snarled and dropped the photograph on the desk. I didn't know what else to say, or what to do. I took my eyes away from Diaz and looked down at the desk, at the photograph. And nearly died of shock.

It was a conventional family group, Diaz seated proudly in the middle, his six children lined up behind him in a roughly triangular shape, so that the older and taller children stood together in the centre. It was the older and taller children that I was looking at. I was looking at Cindy and Sunil.

"My children." Diaz said. "My family."

I looked slowly up at him.

"They do not all look like me," Diaz said. "They have had different mothers. I have been married three times, Mr. Maasten. I find this in the lives of others too, that great intellectual power is linked to great sexual passion."

I was not interested in Diaz's sexual proclivities. I pointed to the photograph. "Cindy is your daughter?" I began to feel angry again. The whole thing was one great big rip off. They had all conspired to trick me into buying the statues.

"Her name is Miranda," Diaz said. "I don't know why everybody calls her Cindy. Miranda is such a lovely name, don't you think?"

And then everything came together. The manuscript, the bank account, the other photograph, everything.

"I prefer Stavros Dirkian," I said.

Diaz made hard work of looking incredulous.

"I can take the statues out now," I said, making it sound like tea-party small-talk. "All I have to do is tell the customs that the money was paid to the Union Banque Suisse in Zurich. I could even tell them the number of the account."

Diaz went as white as the shirt he wore. "How do you know that?"

"I know more than that," I said. "I know that you could spend a long time in jail for having an undeclared foreign bank account."

The gun wobbled dangerously in Diaz's hand.

"Put the gun away," I snapped, "before we have an accident. I'm not the only one who knows about your account."

"The American gentleman who came with you?"

I nodded. "What about the money for the bronzes, Diaz?"

"It will take time," Diaz cried. "I swear to God that is true. But leave the bronzes. I will see that you are paid."

If that was fine with him, it was fine with me. After all I was the one who knew about the account and he was the one who shouldn't have had it. "One more thing," I said. "The Rubeiro Diaz diaries I bought from you are incomplete. I want the rest."

"Mr. Maasten, what are you trying to do to me? I showed you two sections of the diaries and you bought them. What more do you expect?"

"The rest," I said tightly.

"There are two more sections. I can let you have them at the same price, two thousand pounds."

"Done," I said. It was the same price Dirkian had paid for them. "As long as it is the complete diary and as long as you take the money out of what you owe me."

Diaz opened a drawer of the desk, took out a small bunch of keys and used it to open one of the glass fronted cupboards. He took out a slim leather bound volume.

"This is all there is," Diaz said.

I looked at it. It was dusty, with brown acidulous holes, where the yellow paper had been eaten by termites. The ink was brown with age. It certainly looked authentic and presumably Lindsay could soon tell if it wasn't.

I said, "One more thing, Diaz. What was Stavros Dirkian doing here? Why did he buy part of the diary?"

"When you read the diary you will find that somewhere under the sea is a temple. Precisely where, no-one knows. That is what Dirkian was looking for. That is what he was doing here."

"I was told he was trying to salvage a ship."

"No. He was looking for the temple."

"How come, if you sold the diary to Dirkian, you still have it?"

"I only sold Dirkian a copy. You have the original, Mr. Maasten. It is worth much more. If I were not being forced — "

"But Dirkian paid you seven thousand pounds. Why the difference?"

"Ah, that was an agreed price. As you well know quite often the value of an object lies in the eye of the beholder."

"I think Dirkian was being blackmailed."

"Blackmailed Mr. Maasten! Whatever gave you that idea!"

24

When I returned, Lindsay and Elmer were seated on the hotel verandah, reading and looking like illustrations to the cover of a travel brochure. Sunshine slanted over coffee cups, thin wisps of cigarette smoke hung in the bright air and the sound of the gentle, Victor Sylvesterish muzak was punctuated by the regular, rolling, rumble of the sea. Lindsay had changed into a square necked white dress, which was less sensational than the hot pants but only by about four inches and the thickness of a reel of cotton thread.

Elmer's stumpy, bare legs were stretched out onto a low stool and he wore a bright red and white check shirt that would have received whoops of admiration at any mid-western rodeo. I seemed to be the only one around with covered knees. For some reason, loose cotton pantaloons felt cooler than shorts and they prevented third degree burns from the hot vinyl of car seats.

"Hi!" I said, throwing myself into a vacant chair.

They looked up from their books. Lindsay was reading *The Temporal And Spiritual Conquest of Ceylon* by Father Queroz, S.J., and Elmer, E. F. C. Ludowyk's *Story of Ceylon.*

"Am I in time for the tutorial?" I enquired.

"This is jolly interesting, sir," Elmer said. "We're checking out the manuscript."

"Is that why we are going to Galle? To verify the manuscript?"

"In a way, yes," Lindsay said. "I've made a rough translation of the manuscript. It deals with a siege of Colombo Fort. I want to see what one of those Portuguese forts looked like."

"I didn't know there were any Portuguese forts left."

She looked slightly surprised. She was supposed to be the one with the answers. "Dutch forts were usually built on Portuguese sites," she said. "They were bigger, stronger and better constructed, but the basic principles remain the same. I want to get the feel of the place."

I beckoned a waiter and ordered a sandwich and a beer.

Elmer moved Ludowyk's *Story of Ceylon* from his lap onto the table. The sun caught his lenses, turning them into square silver flashes. "How did it go with Diaz, sir?" he asked.

"It depends," I said, "how you look at it."

"You haven't bought anything else have you, Nicholas?" There was a warning undertone of incredulity in Lindsay's voice.

I looked from Lindsay to Elmer. That crafty little sod seemed to have got her on our side. "Let's look at it this way," I said. "We've lost the statues but we've gained the rest of Rubeiro Diaz's diary." I pushed the stiff covered book across the table.

In the strained silence that followed, the waiter brought my sandwich and beer. I drank thirstily.

Lindsay said, "You're bloody mad. Can't you see the man's a babbling brook."

"Babbling what?" I said, my mouth full of soft bread and even softer chicken.

"Brook, crook. It's Aussie for people like Diaz."

I swallowed. "There were problems of exchange control," I said, "and circumlocution of money. This was the only way I could get Dirkian's manuscript."

"You really believe in that temple under the sea, don't you?" Lindsay said.

I looked from her to Elmer. The little sod had been whispering things in her ear. I said, "Yes. I think when we find the temple we'll find out who killed Dirkian."

She gave me a sarcastic smile. "And," she pointed out, "you'll be rich."

"That too."

Lindsay said, "If you want to be rich, you'd be better off selling the manuscript to the Reede."

"Oh well," Elmer said quickly, "In for a dime, in for a dollar."

"One for all, all for one," I said looking directly at Lindsay.

"Oh yes, sir," Elmer said. "I forgot to tell you. Dr. Hamilton is now associated with us."

"As well as George Ponsonby?"

"I'd forgotten about him. Dr. Hamilton is now in charge of the Manuscript Authentication Division of Robey-Maasten Associates. We haven't any money to pay her, so she gets twenty per cent of the profits."

"It makes sense," Lindsay said. "I've got to verify the manuscript and the Reede Museum won't pay for an expensive research job. So if we can't use conventional methods, I will have to help you find the temple."

"So you believe in the temple too," I said slowly. "Howdy, pardner."

With an angry toss of her head and a harsh scraping of wood over cement, our new partner thrust her chair back and said she was going up to her room to collect her dillybag.

I watched her go. The absence of Cindy, and the presence of Lindsay, were doing awful things to my libido. It was as confused as a Chinaman with a stutter and had gone a long way past brisk walks and cold showers.

* * *

Elmer stayed behind to complete his reading. Lindsay and I drove south, along the crowded four laned carriageway leading out of Colombo. The atmosphere inside the Peugeot was as friendly as a Ku-Klux-Klan lynching.

I let her smoulder for a bit and concentrated on driving, nearly deafened by the tuneless symphony of horns. We left Colombo and got onto a dangerously pitted dual carriageway, full of sarong clad pedestrians ambling aimlessly across the road, the inevitably wheeling cyclists, and cars darting haphazardly around the pot holes. Light industrial factories bordered the road, set behind high walls and equally high guarded gates. Occasionally cattle pausing in the centre of the road to stop and stare brought us to a nose dipping halt.

Moving away from one of these interludes, I said, "Stop worrying about Diaz. It's over and done with and we'll have to do the best we can."

She emitted one of those long-suffering sighs, as if she was listening to an off-colour joke for the seventeenth time.

"You're right. I'm sorry. I just think you were so stupid, that's all."

"We all make mistakes," I said. "You make me sound like a professional victim."

"You're not doing so badly. What's annoying me is that I could have got you hordes of legal, authenticated manuscripts in Thailand. And they would have been cheaper too."

"And how many sunken temples?" I asked.

"None," Lindsay laughed.

The road narrowed abruptly to a smooth, pre-mix surface, just wide enough for two vehicles. We drove through the crowded main streets of towns, pressed between fluttering sarongs and vivid saris. We followed buses around small Dutch clocktowers, drove across narrow iron bridges, past gigantic sloe-eyed Buddhas, with close cropped hair and robes of gilt saffron. I drove steadily, settling well into the local rhythm of a horn blast every fifteen seconds and forcing my way past slower traffic with two wheels on the parched grass. From time to time a red blur glinted in my mirror. Another car driven equally fast.

"Tell me about the manuscript," I said.

Lindsay inserted a lit Marlboro between my fingers. "The translation so far tells of a siege and a temple. We don't know how they are related to each other, or if they are related at all. What I am trying to do is to place the siege in time, by studying the history of the Portuguese period. After that I will investigate the temple by checking records at the Government Archives, checking any religious records relating to temple construction, generally studying Ceylonese history from the beginning."

"It sounds a long and complicated process."

"Not necessarily. We are concerned with about fifteen hundred years, from the beginning of recorded history about the fifth century B.C. to the time the Portuguese left the island, in 1658. Our biggest problem is not the length of time, but the fact that the temple appears to be Hindu. Most of Ceylon's early history was recorded by Buddhist monks and was intended to glorify the Sinhalese kingdom and the Buddhist religion."

"Perhaps the rest of the diaries would help."

She laughed. "If they're genuine."

"If they aren't," I said, "And Diaz has conned Dirkian and us, we're right up the creek."

"Without a paddle," Lindsay said and laughed again.

25

OUTSIDE THE TOWNS, THE SUN BEAT PITILESSLY down on mud walls and thatched roofs, on the dark narrow outrigger canoes looking like beached logs on the diathermant sand.

The road outside the towns was fringed with palm trees, bordered by a railway line, the beach and the sea.

Lindsay told me that Galle was one of the oldest known natural harbours in the world. It was the Tarshish of biblical times, a whirling entrepot where the Arab and Chinese worlds met and traded, where Solomon's galleys had called, loading gold and silver, ivory and peacocks and apes. Marco Polo stopped there on his way to China, and Fa-Hien, and Ibn Battuta, a Moor, who also came from Tangier. With the building of larger ships for whom the coral reefs at the mouth of the harbour became an even more dangerous hazard, and the development of the harbour in Colombo, Galle had lost its traditional importance.

I told Lindsay about the *Malabar*.

"Do you dive, Nicholas?"

"Sure," I said.

"You might try salvaging the *Malabar*."

"Only if the diaries aren't genuine." I came hurtling around a corner and crashed to a stop, to avoid running into someone celebrating his funeral in the middle of the road.

For some distance past the road had been lined with palm fronds, suspended from ropes strung between hurriedly planted stakes. Now a line of white clad mourners stretched in front of the car, following an ancient Ford V8 travelling at walking pace.

In front of it a group of men shouldered a coffin, and in front of them, eight agile youngsters unrolled a continuous stream of white cloth.

With much shouting and hand waving, the procession was moved to one side of the road, the Peugeot to the other. I had just drawn alongside the hearse when there was a sudden, violent shrieking of brakes. My mirror filled with the glinting, twisting shape of a red Volkswagen, tilting horribly to the right and flinging its arched tail sideways as it skittered to a halt. I accelerated as quickly as I dared. I liked funerals even less than the thought of a runaway Volkswagen smashing into my boot.

Galle had all the excitement of a seaport without ships. The Fort was built around a small hill, overlooking an esplanade and the sea. Heavy, solid, black battlements separated by six foot high orifices ringed an area of about a mile, menacing, even in the bright sunshine, a permanent tribute to man's fear of man.

We entered through a narrow archway, plastered with advertisements announcing the visit of a local pop group and the current exhibition of a five year old spaghetti western. There was a narrow perimeter road running round the inside of the ramparts and this was joined at various points, by the three or four tiny streets that still comprised, the Fort. We drove round the perimeter road, climbing up the hill and down again, flanked on one side by shabby single storey houses and on the other by grassy green mounds leading up and sometimes over the massive granite walls.

We had tea in a small hotel, overlooking the harbour. The harbour was a web of idle rusted cranes, an idling tramp steamer, a lot of sea and multi coloured buoys. Not much chance of two men salvaging a steamship there.

Orange jacketed waiters moved with discreet efficiency and we sat on green cushions on low cane backed settees, under whirling fans, amongst copies of *Time* and *Newsweek* and *German International*. Afterwards Lindsay said we should walk around the Fort.

We walked outside, it was still hot, the sun beating back from the solid buildings onto the narrow street. The houses opened right onto the street and there was an air of stillness everywhere as if heat and time had sapped the will to live. A buggy cart jangled by, the head of its emaciated bullock, drooping listlessly.

"It's still a Muslim town," Lindsay said, pointing to the garish blues and pinks and greens inside the houses and the men walking splay legged, handkerchiefs pulled tight over close cropped heads, only rarely wearing the traditional red fez.

We walked and sweated. There was a large Dutch church in the centre of the town and dull looking administrative buildings. Up on the ramparts we looked down into the harbour, at a sailing boat whipping along the waves. Up on the ramparts, at least it was cool. We walked up to the eye-achingly glaring lighthouse, threw our legs over the edge of the ramparts and sat down.

The wind whipped at our clothes, everything seemed nicely peaceful and still. Galle may have lacked the excitement of Tarshish but with that loss, perhaps it gained something more valuable. Contentment.

I turned and looked around, down the narrow street that led to the hotel. A red Volkswagen was parked behind the Peugeot and a tall young man with a thick head of curly brown hair, wearing a camouflage jacket was peering into the Peugeot.

It was the memory of the glinting red blur on the drive to Galle that moved me to action. That and the camouflage jacket and the fact that the man was European.

"Wait here," I said to Lindsay.

"Where are you going?"

"I left my cigarettes in the car."

I dropped into the crevice between the ramparts, climbed out onto the grass mound and walked away from Lindsay, along the perimeter road. At the first intersection I turned right, doubling back so that I would come up on the hotel from behind. As soon as I turned the corner, I began to run.

Running wasn't easy in that heat, and in my condition. Eight months of owning a bar in Tangier had put on six pounds and had done nothing to increase lung capacity or firmness of muscle. Sweat poured down my face as I ran, pasting my shirt to my body in a hot embrace. People turned lazily to stare at a lunatic Englishman running in what was still noonday sun. An emaciated dog, startled, gave chase and decided it was more sensible to walk.

I made another turning and came up the hill towards the hotel,

10—TPF • •

lungs bursting, legs feeling as if they had been twisted through a mangle and strung out with lead. There was no sign of the stranger in the camouflage jacket.

The Volkswagen had the deep shiny look and uncreased upholstery of a car that was relatively new. It had seven thousand miles on its Vdo tripmeter. About a hundred yards ahead of me where the perimeter road curved, I could see Lindsay, all white and golden, seated on the black topped rampart. I sucked warm air into dry lungs, felt the sweat prickling out like boiled water. From the balustrade of the hotel, an orange jacketed waiter, stared at me without curiosity. It was then I saw the man again. He had been walking on the narrow ledge of grass and rock, on the outside of the rampart, over the harbour. The ledge was broken in places and occasionally came to an abrupt end, leaving a gap over which it was impossible to jump. The man had obviously come to one of these gaps and crossed through one of the crevices between the huge mounds of stone, to by-pass it on the inside. As I watched he ran quickly across the top of the grass mound, swerving hurriedly into the next crevice. He ran with a loose athletic movement, with the flowing rhythm of a trained runner. Only his right arm was out of balance. It was trapped firmly above his trouser pocket, knuckles pointing outward, thumb folded over, as if resting on the butt of a hand gun.

I pushed myself away from the cars and ran. I sprinted across the road and half leapt, half dragged myself onto the mound of grass.

Rocks wedged into the top of the embankment tore at my shins, my sweaty hands slipped over close cropped grass. I dragged myself up and ran, air wheezing into my tortured lungs with all the sound effects of a dying asthmatic. If I followed the path he had taken, along the outside of the ramparts I would never reach the man. Running on the inside meant a long uphill diagonal, absolutely without cover.

I ran straight up the hill and scrambled up to the top of the ramparts. It was about six foot wide, filled with patches of grass, scrub and broken stones. Below me the wall fell away in a sheer, unbroken drop to the boulder strewn beach and the diminutive fishing ships below. Keeping to the inside, I began to run.

Lindsay was leaning forward to the sea, chin cradled on cupped palms. Sweat trickled into my eyes and stung as I reached the first gap between the ramparts. Hands tearing at my face I jumped, landed, staggered, sprawled face downwards on the rough earth. Still moving forward, scrabbling with hands and knees, I climbed erect and kept running.

The gaps were about three to four foot wide and each time I landed it felt as if my legs would be driven through my body. Each time I landed I felt my legs would snap off like dried twigs.

Fortunately, the further I ran, the hill became lower, drawing nearer to the yellow beach and the glistening sea. Unfortunately, the slope made me run faster. I hurtled over the gaps, hoping I wouldn't catch my foot when I landed, hoping I wouldn't pass over the gunman in mid flight.

A stone stairway with a rusted handrail skimmed by, the triangular roofs of warehouses disappeared. Ghastly, panting sounds filled my ears and my tongue felt dry, swollen as if it had been rubbed with a pad of wire wool. I saw the man as I braced myself for the next crevice.

He had the side of his face pressed to the far edge of the wall, only the tip of his nose and his arm extended beyond the line of the ramparts. At the end of the extended arm a snub nosed pistol was pointing straight at Lindsay's unprotected back.

I stopped, twisted, hurled myself to the ground. My elbow jarred on the edge of the rock wall and then I was slipping into the crevice, feeling rock tear the shirt and flesh away from my back, pound against my body with bone shattering force.

The man stopped and turned, startled. I landed all crumpled up, half lurched towards him. My arms grabbed him round the waist, struggled for balance and I brought a weak knee up into his groin.

It had little effect. He swung a left hand into my stomach, but because he had little room to swing, that too had little effect. I concentrated on the gun. I locked his wrist with mine and let him hit me twice more. That hurt. He took a swing at my face and I rolled with the punch. Even so my head swam and I tasted the hot, salty tang of blood. I swivelled my hips, swinging the man round, the effort draining all the strength out of me. His outstretched wrist connected with the sharp edge of the rock wall and he screamed. I felt his hand go limp, heard the gun bounce once against the rock and explode with a sharp crack. Then he shouldered me away and bracing himself against the wall aimed a kick at my middle. It was one of those high, wheeling, pushing kicks. It connected somewhere on my chest. As the man kicked me he moved round adding force and direction to his attack. I felt my feet lift off the ground with a surprising lightness. Then I was plunging backwards through the crevice onto the rock strewn beach below.

There was a brief silent moment while the regular shaped granite stones passed before my eyes, while I resolved I should train with Elmer, while my stomach contracted in panic.

Then I slammed into the water with a stinging breath shattering force and the whole world became a roaring red charisma of pain.

26

WAVES WASHED LISTLESSLY OVER ME. I turned on my face and floated. Tattered strips of shirt exposed my lacerated back to the water and the sun. The combined effect of salt and heat made me feel as if I was being branded. I rested my cheek on the water and breathed, long and deep. I was too exhausted to even sob with the pain. A wave brushed me lightly against the rock I had missed by the width of a guppy's fin. I realised I was an easy target for the gunman in the camouflage jacket, on the ramparts fifteen feet above me. But I couldn't care.

There wasn't enough air in the world to fill my aching lungs, there wasn't enough ether to end the searing pain. The whole world tasted of salt. My tongue was swollen and heavy, my spine felt as if the flesh was being inched off with red hot tweezers. I let the waves bear me to the shore. My hands and knees grated on sand. Soft, hot crystalline mud trickled into my mouth and ears. Painfully I dragged myself further up the beach and flopped, the water still lapping round my feet and ankles.

That was how Lindsay found me, stretched out, wet and half-dead. Awareness came and went in a miasma of golden sand and blazing sunlight, came and went with sounds of harsh breathing and racing footsteps, with visions of crumbling black walls of rock pressing down upon me. I lay on the beach and retched, forcing mucous over dried lips onto damp sand. Voices, the sight of dark spatulate feet spread out around my head, feet as rough as grained leather, with stunted toenails, brown and tough as horn, the tight snapping sound of sarongs flicked by the wind. And Lindsay's voice, crying, "Nicholas, Nicky, are you alright!"

I looked up her sun bronzed legs, all the way up her skirt, without feeling. Then arms gently pulled my shoulder round, arms cradled my neck, soft, woman's arms. Lindsay's arms. I stared wordlessly into her anguished face.

"Nicky, honey, are you alright?"

I moved my head gently in a semblance of a nod. Nothing untoward happened.

The pairs of feet and the tightly flapping sarongs around me grew in number. I concentrated on breathing, slow in, slow out, slow in, slow out, trying to think of nothing but air moving slowly in and out, gritting my teeth against the stinging pain.

"You?" I croaked.

"Of course, I'm alright. What happened?"

"I fell." Two more breaths. "I was running . . . Top of the ramparts . . ." Pause. Breathe. In, out. Slow and easy. "I fell."

A new, lilting voice, said, "Is very dangerous, Missy. Master running like the devil on top of ramparts. I get doctor here, now."

I succumbed to a puritanical British dislike of fuss, and a more primeval of fear of involvement. I squeezed Lindsay's hand and said, "No, later."

"Alright," she said. "Alright."

We waited.

After a while I forced myself to sit up. Slowly, easily, supported by Lindsay's willing hands, I raised my head up from the ground, arched my body away from the sand. A hazy red curtain swam before my eyes, my breathing became more difficult and my body filled with sharp, stifling jabs of pain that had nothing to do with the gashes on my back. I sat and waited for the haze to disappear, for the pain to go away. So far, so good. I was able to sit up without the ugly grating sound of bone ends rubbing together, without the thick twisted prick of a nerve trapped between torn ligaments.

I sat and waited. There were about twenty people around me now, men and boys, discussing my fall in a rapid babble of excitement. The man who had offered to get a doctor squatted in front of me, dark, wavy haired, moustached, a big brass badge pinned to his shirt, proclaiming "Tourist Guide No. 1478."

"Why you run?" he asked. "Is very dangerous."

"I'm trying to keep fit," I said.

He stared uncomprehendingly at me. "How you feel now? Better?"

In fact, I was feeling a lot better, except the crowd pressing round me had cut off my supply of fresh air. I pointed to my chest and made fish-like gasping faces. With a great show of ferocity, Tourist Guide No. 1478 jumped to his feet, cuffed the two smallest and nearest boys and moved the crowd eighteen inches back. I kept breathing slowly, allowing the air to fill my chest cavity, letting out the air in long, slow whistles through my mouth. My head was clearing rapidly and a few minutes later, with the help of Lindsay and the guide, I got to my feet.

A fit of dizziness nearly overcame me. An overwhelming feeling of nausea, did. I dry retched a few times, then still leaning on Lindsay and the guide, shuffled slowly along the beach to a stone stairway guarded by a single rusted rail. The crowd followed expectantly and at the foot of the stairway were shooed away again by the guide.

I took the steps slowly, one at a time, pausing each time I felt dizzy or short of breath. By the time we got to the top, the nausea had gone and I was breathing almost normally. My legs had the strength of wet sponge and I had an almost irresistible desire to lie down and sleep. Gradually the raw, aching sore of my back, eliminated all other sensations. I walked down the grass mound barely supported by Lindsay and the guide, and stepped down onto the narrow street. The Peugeot was still there. Behind it was an empty space where the Volkswagen had been.

* * *

The guide led me to the hotel, past a crowd of anxious eyed day trippers, past a line of peering waiters. The manager himself ushered us into a room and waited, till the doctor he had sent for, came.

The doctor was a chubby, well spread man of about forty,

wearing a floppy white suit and an expression of deep harrassment. He had large, slow eyes and a large, thoughtful mouth. His hands were like scalpels.

"How did this happen?" he asked, probing the wounds.

I lay on my face wrapped only in a towel, wincing at his touch. "I was running along the top of the ramparts, and I fell."

"You were lucky," he said. "You might have been dead."

There was nothing I could do to stop the shudder that ran through my whole body. Only I knew how close I had been to dying and it wasn't a very pleasant sensation. I'd always believed that because I wasn't rich, I was lucky. That afternoon I'd used up a lifetime's quota of luck.

"The sea water should have disinfected the wounds," the doctor said. "But being so near the harbour, I don't know."

He took his time cleaning and dressing the wounds. Then he gave me an anti-tetanus jab and advised me to rest for a few days. "You're still suffering from shock," he said. "You might even have slight concussion."

He checked my pupils and my reflexes and told me it was alright for me to be driven back to Colombo, and again advising me to rest once I got there, left.

* * *

Lindsay drove. I lay on my side with the passenger seat fully reclined, clad in a clean shirt and sarong that I'd had the hotel buy for me. I took the doctor's advice and slept.

When I woke, there was a continuous passage of lights flowing over the car. I reckoned we were nearing Colombo. I sat up and put the world into focus again. We were travelling along the stretch of dual carriageway, by the factories. Lindsay was driving slowly in the centre of the road, to avoid the larger potholes.

"How are you?" she asked.

"OK, so far. Who was the man?"

Lindsay said, "Man. What man?"

"The man in the camouflage jacket. About six feet tall, lean, thick curly hair, round faced, clean shaven, blue eyed."

"That description would fit anyone," she said.

I said, "Anyone's tried to kill you."

She braked smoothly for a corner, pulled round and took her time passing a Renault Dauphine, all narrow cycle tyres and smooth, slip streamed back. Ceylon, I thought, was like a car museum of the fifties.

Lindsay asked, "Are you sure it was me he was trying to kill?"

I said, "When I caught up with him, his pistol was pointing at you."

She said, "And you stopped him?"

"I stopped him shooting you. Didn't you hear the gun go off?"

"No," she said. "You'd hardly hear it would you, if it was a pistol. All I had eyes for was you, hurtling out of that crevice like a throw-away doll."

"Your friends kick hard," I said.

She braked the Peugeot to a gentle stop, then twisted it round a wandering bull. "I'm sorry," she said. "What on earth do you say when someone has saved your life?"

"As someone with a great deal of experience in being saved, you start off by saying, thank you. Then you kiss the person tenderly and passionately, and then, you tell him all your guilty secrets."

She laughed. "In your state, bazza, a tender kiss could be fatal."

"You're half right," I said, regretting that for all practical purposes, I was half dead. "Let's save the kissing till afterwards and start with the guilty secrets, now."

She thought that over for a while, taking care to drive smoothly so as not to aggravate my wounds. "It isn't a guilty secret," she said at least. "It's a hypothesis."

"Must you always use such big words?" I asked.

"I'm a big girl and I was educated properly. No, Nicholas, I can't think why anyone should try to kill me."

"Except," I prompted.

"Unless," she corrected, "it has something to do with my last assignment, the job I did in Thailand."

"What were you doing in Thailand?"

"I suppose, you could say, I was investigating a murder."

"Who are you, really? Lady Ironside of the Yard?"

"Don't be silly. I was working for ICOM and it ended up

as a murder hunt. A gang of armed bandits broke into a Thai temple and looted it. They got about two hundred thousand pounds worth of stuff, Buddhist statues, jewels, silver ornaments, even the gold leaf from the offerings pillar. They shot and killed the temple guards."

"Did you find the men?"

"No," she said, "but I spent a lot of time looking and helping the Thai police. From the way the robbery had been carried out, we deduced that they were a gang of well trained people, experts in the use of arms and explosives. They were disciplined as well as ruthless and they knew exactly what they were looking for. They took only the most portable and the most valuable pieces."

"You make them sound like that group of ex-army men in, what was it—*The League of Gentlemen.*"

"Not ex-army," she replied. "Ex-mercenary. With the decline in the number of irregular wars, there are a lot of them about, and it isn't a big step from irregular warfare to irregular crime. The same thing happened in France, after the Algerian troubles ended."

I thought of Barney and Pierre and Maurice and wondered.

"Thefts of art and antiquities are the second biggest racket in the world, after narcotics," Lindsay said. "Every year millions of pounds worth of valuable pieces are stolen or destroyed. Quite often what is lost, are the last traces of forgotten civilisations, and while the art world is always poorer, the sum of potential knowledge is always diminished."

"ICOM are trying to stop this?"

"Yes," Lindsay said, "but like all voluntary organisations it is short of money. That's a problem the criminals don't have."

I asked, "Are you still with ICOM?"

"No," she laughed. "For the present I'm on the side of the professional victims."

We swept into Colombo over a wide, white bridge. Lindsay asked, "Who were the men you were talking to last morning?"

"Barney Goldman used to be a gun runner," I said. "I don't know what he does now."

"It might be useful," Lindsay remarked, "to find out."

"That might be pushing the business of a professional victim, too far."

She said, "We all have a duty, Nicholas, to prevent robbery and murder."

"Hold on a sec. No one said Barney and his friends had anything to do with the robbery in Thailand."

"No," Lindsay said. "No-one said that. All the same it would be useful to check."

"I'm not sure—"

"If it's them, you're already a little too late to avoid the issue. You see, Nicholas, now they might want to kill you too."

My mouth went suspiciously dry. "Not Barney," I said, and thought, why the hell not. Barney owed me nothing.

"I'm sure you could search his room or something," Lindsay said. "You must have some way of finding out what they are doing."

"I have," I said. Searching their rooms wouldn't place me in any greater danger than I was in now. After all, I did know someone who was an expert at that kind of thing.

27

LINDSAY FOLLOWED ME TO MY ROOM, bringing with her a translation of the second instalment of the manuscript. I called Barney on the internal telephone. Yes, Barney said, he'd love to have a drink with us and yes, he'd ask Maurice and Pierre. An hour would be fine and did I still have the bronzes?

I turned to Lindsay. "You've been invited too," I said.

"Why?"

"He fancies you," I said. "We all do."

I reached over the telephone and kissed her lightly. She kissed back, also lightly. No tenderness, no passion, not even for the half-dead. Nevertheless for me it raised other problems.

* * *

I went to the bathroom and sponged away the white salt that had formed into a thin powdery crust all over my body. There was a sharp, dry crack of pain along my back, as if the lips of the wound were opening and closing. When I finished bathing I called Sunil, poured out a glass of Chivas and settled down to wait with the manuscript. This section of the manuscript was entitled, "The Siege."

THE SIEGE

It was the fourth month of the siege and our situation worsened every day. Two ships which had been sent from Goa to relieve us of our adversity, bearing a force of three hundred Indian Christians and one company of soldiers, bringing dried meat and flour and rice and butter and other provisions necessary for the survival of the people of Colombo had been wracked by the inclement weather which prevails in these parts at this season.

For seventeen days past our rations have been reduced still further so that each fighting man whatsoever be his rank or title receives one medida[1] of rice each four days, and all other persons whether man, woman or child, received but half that quantity, the sum of which is barely sufficient to sustain life.

There is also a proclamation punishing by death any person who knowingly eats human flesh, for there are some who are so crazed with hunger that they would pickle and eat the flesh of the fallen.

Father Joao has also condemned those who are thus not able to contain their appetite, all the more because the transgressors do not observe fast days.

Outside the Fort to the south and the south-east are the armies of the Chingala King in great mass.

The Chingala King who rules over the army surrounding us, they call Raju[2] and also apostate and heathen, for in his anger he had bestowed that mountain with the imprint of the Boudhou, whom the Chingala hold sacred, upon some Indian personages of doubtful holiness. He is also a parricide, having murdered his father, who was called Maya Dunnai, who also gave us much harassment. Yet the people follow Raju[2] because he is a strong warrior and is feared of no man.

By treachery and violence he succeeded in taking the Kingdom of Candea and there raised an army of fifty thousand men, with elephants and cannons and batteries, good guns and other diverse war-like implements, wherewith he had surrounded us for four months and more.

On the thirteenth day of the fourth month of the siege that the Captain-General sent for me, that is to say, three

1 A Portuguese measure of grain, about 5/6ths of a pound.
2 The Sinhalese king Raja Singha (1581-92).

days after my master, the factor, had been killed at the gate of Saint Sebastian. Since my master's death I had taken it upon myself to perform his tasks, keeping a good accounting and a faithful record, maintaining the roll of those persons killed in defence of the fortress so that the correct sum of the quarterages[1] and moxaras[2] due was known, and also the amount of conduto[3] due to the Captains and soldiers, which last had not been paid since two months. The consequence thereof was that I had not left my billet, overlooking the harbour, for two whole days, for there was much other work to be done also.

On receipt of the summons, I laid aside my manifold tasks and hurried past the house of Saint Francisco to Straight Street, that I might comply with the directive more quickly. The air was heavy with the smell of sulphur and burnt powder and dust from broken masonry hung in the air. Further along the street, near the bastion of Saint Philip, houses which had been hit by cannon, lay gaping and open, their contents exposed to every passer-by. A ball had scored a direct hit on the roof of the Church of Madre de Dios and the streets were littered with rubbish and filth of all kinds.

The Captain-General admitted me without formality. During the days of the siege he had grown old. His countenance was ashen, and there were black smudges, as of tar, underneath his eyes, for he had not slept regularly for four months and more. He bade me be seated, for he had known my family, and in a low voice asked me about my work and in particular what provisions we had and for how long we could withstand the siege.

I told him that I had not fully completed my master's books but that in ten days our supplies would without doubt, be exhausted. He showed no surprise at this news, being a man driven beyond all feeling, except fatigue. Still keeping his voice low, he told me that there was no hope

1 Bi-annual payments.

2 According to Pissurlencar, this means a salary. It is not defined elsewhere.

3 Curry allowance.

for Colombo, unless we could divert some of Raju's forces and at the same time obtain food. Accordingly he had decided that he would send a small band of men by sea, to land at points on the coast and attack villages loyal to Raju, and at the same time obtain sufficient provisions to enable the siege to be withstood, until assistance came from Goa.

He was sending, he said, two small craft and a band of thirty soldiers under the command of Gaspar Saldhana, the very same who had but recently engaged in a night foray against the Chingala, and lost an entire company of men, he being fortunate to escape with his life.

The Captain-General was sending eight casados[1] amongst the thirty soldiers as more fighting men than that could not be spared from the defence of the fortress. He said they were still short of persons and though I was an escrivao[2] he would oblige me to serve under Gaspar Saldhana.

I thanked the Captain-General for his consideration, and though it grieved me much to serve under someone such as Saldhana, who was no fidalgo but pressed for service from the Limoeiro[3], and obtained to his present position by showing great cruelty, and it must be said, great bravery to the enemy, I agreed. There was no help for it and therein lies the cause of my misfortune.

Sunil came a few minutes later, hesitating in the doorway before summoning up the courage to come in. I had him sit on the chair by the dressing table and gave him a large glass of Chivas while I changed into mauve pantaloons and a red and gold embroidered shirt with a high pointed collar. With the neck of the shirt open, anyone could see the bandage around my ribs. That was how I wanted it. I felt Barney's reaction to my accident was going to be the high-spot of the evening.

Sunil raised his glass and asked, "How are you, man. What you want?"

"A little job," I said. "A nice easy simple job."

1 Young married men normally exempted from military service.
2 Scribe or clerk. Usually attached to the factor who was responsible for overseeing the trade of the Fort.
3 A prison in Lisbon.

Sunil sipped at the Chivas, put it down and fingered my comb and wristlet watch. "How much you pay for nice little job?"

"Two hundred rupees," I said.

Sunil turned my wristlet watch over in his hand and then placed it beside his own. I'd seen that happen before. Gently, I took the watch away from him.

"What happened to your chest, man?"

"I fell off a step."

He sipped at the Chivas. "What you want me to do?" His fingers carressed the top of the cassette player.

I told him. All he had to do was sneak into three rooms and take a look around. He had only to find out what the occupants of the rooms were doing in Ceylon. It was dead simple, and wouldn't take long. A quick look at some letters, papers, that kind of thing, and he was two hundred rupees richer. And nothing was to be nicked.

"While I'm doing the rooms, where will these people be?"

"Downstairs," I said. "They'll be in the bar, drinking with me."

Sunil did a little twisting with his mouth. Then he said, "Five hundred rupees."

"That's a lot of bread."

"Nick," Sunil asked, "If it's as easy as you say, why aren't you doing it?"

He had me there. I couldn't tell him I wasn't doing it, because I wasn't as good as him, and that I really didn't want to get involved with Barney. "OK," I said. "Five hundred," hoping ICOM would pick up the bill for this job.

Lindsay came in, all fresh and smelling of Patou's "Joy," wearing a white open necked shirt and hip hugging, flared, midnight blue pants. The view through the open neck of her shirt was far more exciting than my bandages. "Hello everybody."

I introduced her to Sunil. "He's going to do it," I said.

She gave him a dazzling smile. Under that wattage, Sunil simply had to melt. "You're very brave," Lindsay said.

Sunil positively dissolved. He expanded his chest half an inch and tried to look as if this kind of thing happened every day.

"He's doing it for five hundred rupees," I said.

"You should never undersell anything," Lindsay said sweetly.

"Or anybody. Do you know what you're supposed to do?"

"I've told him," I said.

Just to make sure, she told him again. She was that kind of person. And being a perfectionist she had to include a few details like the robbery in Thailand and the shooting incident that afternoon. I could sense Sunil's price rocketing by the second. "Remember, we are depending on *your* assessment of the situation," she told him. "Everything depends on that. We must find out what terrible thing these people intend to do. Remember it's your country they're plotting against. Remember everything depends on *you*."

Behind Sunil's head I played an invisible trumpet. Next time she could stand in for the Duchess of Kent and give the ball boys at Wimbledon a pep talk.

Meanwhile Sunil looked dazed, and it wasn't because he'd just joined the Boy Scouts. If there was any profitable crime around, I felt sure Sunil would rather be doing it, than preventing it. Except the poor bastard had fallen in love.

She laid a hand on his shoulder and led him to the door. He was to wait in the bar for us, and when we were all gathered together, make his search and return to my room. I remembered to take my travellers cheques with me. Sunil marched bravely out into the corridor, walking on cloud nine, a con-man knight without even a dilapidated charger.

"That was great," I said. "If Rommel had you on his side, the Suez Canal would still be German."

"It was necessary," Lindsay said. "Sunil has to be involved. He's got to know what he's doing, and why. He's got to be able to evaluate the significance of what he finds. After all, Nicholas, everything depends on that."

"That's one way of looking at it," I said, and suggested we went down. We were already ten minutes late for Barney.

11—TPF • •

28

BARNEY WAS WAITING FOR US in the bar, without Pierre and Maurice. Sunil sat in a corner, sullenly nursing a beer. His face lit up when he saw Lindsay and for one frightening moment, I thought he was going to come over and join us. But discretion or the thought of five hundred rupees won and he relapsed into hostile glaring.

Barney made cordial drink buying noises. I ordered a large scotch, not only because that was what I'd been drinking.

Barney's reaction to my bandages was negative. Like one of the proverbial three monkeys he was seeing no evil, and even if he did, he was certainly not speaking about it. He handed round the drinks, Lindsay's gin and it, my scotch. Barney was staying with beer. "Here's to you," he said. "Whatever you're doing."

"And you."

"Tell me," he asked, "whatever happened to that shop of yours in Camden Town?"

"I've still got it."

The antique shop in Camden Town was one of the little businesses into which I'd invested my gratuity from Commando 15. The last time I'd seen it, it was full of imitation Hepplewhite tables and curlicued wrought-iron cemetery gates. Keith, who managed it for me, spent half his time flirting with Bumtit Cameos up the road and the rest investing shrewdly in stuff that would be fashionable the year after next. The year after next we would be rich. Meanwhile, we broke even. "It's doing alright," I said.

Out of the corner of my eye I saw Sunil move. Too soon, I thought, keeping my face firmly turned towards Barney. "Whatever happened to your shop?" I asked.

"Antiques were just a phase," Barney grinned. "I guess I moved into the big time. About those bronzes . . ."

"About those bronzes," I said.

"I think I might have a buyer for them."

"Even though you think they're fake?"

"Christ! That doesn't matter, man. My customer doesn't care how old they are."

"Really," I said. "Aren't you lucky."

"Where you been living, Nicky baby? Don't you read the papers or anything? My customer doesn't want the statues because they're works of art. He wants them for their copper content."

"How much?" I asked.

Pierre and Maurice came in. Barney performed the introductions, made more drink buying noises and got them a couple of beers.

They were on a job, I thought. If they were on beer, they had to be. There are many things that make a man become a mercenary, love of adventure, a reaction against boredom and the dullness of modern life, a desire to use his military training to the full, a need for army type, male-hearty living, even, as in my case, accident. But whatever the mixture of reasons compelling a man to become a mercenary, one ingredient is always present. Money.

But the mercenary's desire for money is different from the avaricious hoarding of say, the merchant banker or the slum landlord. He does not risk death in battle, or the greater risk of being shot in the back by his own ill-trained soldiers, only for money. He does not risk dying of malaria or typhoid or the tsetse fly because he needs a mansion in the country, a Rolls Royce and an increasing investment in property bonds. To the mercenary, money is something else.

To the mercenary, money is happiness between wars, it is comfortable flats and fast two seater sports cars, it is agile dolly birds and fancy gear, it is first class air travel and sun soaked afternoons on private beaches. Which is why, there are few mercenaries I know, who left a war rich.

If Pierre and Maurice were on holiday, they wouldn't be sitting up in a hotel bar and sipping beer. Not even in a place like Colombo where the night life ended just before the radio station closed down.

"Six hundred pounds and a penny for your thoughts."

"A thousand," I said, "And you can have the thoughts for free."

"Six hundred it is, Nicky baby. It's a fair price." He turned to Lindsay. "Go on, tell your old man it's a fair price. Six hundred pounds for the content."

It wasn't as teasing as it sounded. Barney was throwing bait. He wanted to see what role Lindsay would adopt, naïve little woman or tough archaeological expert.

She took the middle course. "I only know about art," she said. "Things like world prices, baffle me. I'll have to talk to my economist."

Shrewd, I thought, laughing. Barney wasn't laughing, but I could see he thought she was shrewd, too.

"I'd like to think about your offer," I said. What I wanted to think about was why he was offering me more than a fair price. I estimated that the statues were worth about two hundred pounds each as scrap. I didn't know how, or even whether it was possible, to extract copper from bronze. In any case it couldn't be a cheap process and on top of that there was freight and duty.

"What do you want to think about, Nicky baby?" He leaned across the bar and ordered more drinks.

I wished Barney wouldn't call me Nicky baby, especially in front of Lindsay. It made me sound either infantile, or queer, or both.

"I'm thinking about it," I said, "because I haven't got the statues." I held out my hand for the next large scotch. Shock or no shock, the scotch was doing me a power of good, and the surprise on Barney's face was worth a dozen Nicky baby's.

"Who's got them, man?"

"Diaz," I said. "I exchanged them for an old Portuguese manuscript, the manuscript Dirkian had a copy of."

"I'll be goddamned," Barney said.

"The manuscript is about an ancient temple. Dirkian was looking for it, the last time he was in Ceylon."

"So it was you at Dirkian's."

I asked, "What was your connection with Dirkian?"

Barney laughed. "I told you. He owed us money."

Pierre asked, "Why you sit like that?"

"Because I gashed my back," I said. "Falling off the Galle ramparts."

They accepted the accident, stolidly. That also, was give-away, I thought, unless by now, they were immune to violence.

Barney said, "That was a damned stupid thing to do."

I decided to push him further. "No," I said. "Someone was shooting at me."

"Don't be absurd, Nicholas. The troubles in Ceylon ended months ago, and all the shooting stopped. Your problem is you read too many thrillers."

"Dostoevsky's more my line," I said. "Heavy, Russian, and morbid. He was wearing a camouflage jacket, you know the kind of thing that kids wear these days, because they haven't been in a war. He was also using a Browning P.35."

"I still think you're mooning, man."

"He was driving a red Volkswagen," I said. "I've got the number."

Barney said, "I still can't believe it. You must be going mad."

But I knew that he believed it. I knew that he knew I wasn't mad.

"He isn't mad," Lindsay said. "The man was shooting at me."

Barney looked from me to her. His expression said that we were both mad. But there was relief in his voice when he said, "Let's drink to your survival, then." And he launched into a story of how a busload of tourists had been held up on a desolate stretch of road in the eastern part of Ceylon.

Pierre enquired how long the manuscript was and what it was about. Lindsay told him it was quite long and all in Portuguese and even she hadn't understood it yet.

"What'll you do with the manuscript?" Barney asked. "Sell it?"

"Once we've found the temple," I laughed. "What are you

lot doing then?" I mean it seemed only fair, after he'd spent so much time and money pumping us.

"An archaeological survey," Barney said promptly. "Matter of fact, we are waiting for some equipment to be flown in. Then we're going right back to the Central Province."

"What exactly are you surveying?" Lindsay asked.

That was exactly what Barney declined to tell us. Instead he rambled on about the splendour and the beauty of the ruined cities, of a lost, ancient civilisation and how there was so much work to be done, how the government was hampered by the lack of funds and volunteers. I gathered that some institute in Washington had financed their survey. Whoever they were, if they had engaged Barney, Maurice and Pierre, they must have been as idiosyncratic as the Reede Museum.

After a few moments of polite conversation, I left, pretending I wanted to go to the loo. I went to an internal phone and checked all the rooms. There was no answer from any of them. It was logical to conclude that Sunil had done his job, perfectly.

When I went back, Pierre was already inviting Lindsay out to dinner, and Lindsay was already refusing.

I said we had to work on the manuscript and they said they had to go out anyway.

On the surface it seemed a very civilized evening. But only on the surface.

* * *

Sunil was waiting for us in my room, eyeing my tape recorder thoughtfully, and listening to the funky guitar of Wes Montgomery.

"Well," I asked. Barney's scotches had started me off. I pulled out the Chivas.

"I looked through all the rooms," Sunil said.

"Great! What did you find out?"

"I don't know."

Hell, I thought, another five hundred down the plug hole.

"You went into all the rooms?"

"Sure, sure, yes. I went into all three rooms."

"And you found nothing?" It was possible, that all Sunil

had done, was walk around the hotel a few times and come back to my room.

"I found plenty, but I don't know what they're doing." He walked over to the side of the bed and picked up a large number of folders. "Here, I brought everything."

"Jesus!" I cried, "Who's going to put them back?"

* * *

Lindsay had no such inhibitions. She went through the files like a kiwi after birdseed. From time to time I gave the papers a cursory glance, and wished she'd hurry up. With the most uninhibited intentions in the world, there was nothing in Colombo that would keep Barney and his friends away from the hotel for very long.

The documents Sunil had brought seemed to confirm Barney's story. There were maps and sketch plans and an elaborately drawn sectional plan of a stupa. There were photographs and letters, permissions to photograph ancient monuments and receipted bills for self-drive cars. There was also a series of illustrated notes, elaborately explaining the construction of dagobas. They were all signed by Stavros Dirkian.

The dagoba is a development of the tumulus, a kind of ancient sepulchre found in southern India and the Deccan. These tumuli are low circular mounds of earth, surrounded by a ring of boulders, firmly planted in the ground to keep the tumuli in position and to mark the sacred spot. Dagobas are much bigger. They are huge dome like structures reaching a height of as much as three hundred feet and a diameter of up to three hundred and fifty. They are shaped like bubbles or bells and are topped by a square superstructure and a spire which in the old days was ringed with crystal and formed the setting for a great precious stone.

The dagobas are built of earth and brick and enclose relics of the Buddha. More important, they also enclose more commercial relics, gold and silver images, precious stones, jewellery, coins, all extremely old, all extremely valuable.

Sunil said, "There was also this." He held out a bundle of what looked like candles, wrapped in blue oiled paper.

Lindsay asked, "Nicholas, have you got a camera?"

"Was there more of this?" I asked Sunil.

He nodded.

"I hope whoever is storing it, has given up smoking."

Lindsay asked again, "Have you got a camera?"

"There's no time for photographs," I said. "Sunil had better get this stuff back, before Barney and the others return." I turned back to Sunil. "You remember where you took these from?"

"Sure," he said. "Sure, sure."

Lindsay said, "It'll only be a few minutes."

I said, "Perhaps you're getting excited about nothing. It isn't unusual, you know for archaeologists to use dynamite."

"Not in great quantity," she said. "Anyway, look at this."

I looked. Lindsay pointed to the sectional plan of the dagoba. "It's their work," I said. "It isn't ethical to copy it."

Finger jabbing at the paper, she asked, "What about this? And this?"

Lindsay was pointing to what looked like two tunnels, superimposed on the plan of the dagoba. Then she showed me a way bill for a consignment of drilling equipment, that was arriving on a BOAC flight, the next day.

"Can't you see, Nicholas. They aren't trying to reconstruct a dagoba. What they're trying to do is blast their way in."

I gave her the Pentax. She worked rapidly, using two spools of film, long time exposure and Sunil's body as a tripod. Sunil loved it.

Then I collected the stuff together and gave it to him together with the five hundred rupees. "You'd better get all this back, fast."

Sunil looked hopefully at Lindsay. "You want to visit ruined cities, tomorrow?"

"No," Lindsay said. "Not just yet." She led him by the hand to the door. "It was great meeting you," she said, "We can all go to the ruined cities afterwards."

Sunil smiled, hopefully and went.

I replaced Wes Montgomery with Bacharach, smooth, easy to listen to, swinging.

"Sit and talk," I suggested, with just a hint of lechery.

She smiled. "I've got things to do," she said.

"Like what?"

"I've got to find some way I can get the film developed and translate the rest of the Diaz diary."

I moved closer up to her. "That can wait," I said.

She smiled. "Besides, I prefer Mozart."

I once knew a girl who who could turn on to the Horn Concerto. It was just my luck. The only cassettes available in Colombo featured the top of the Chinese hit parade, and were imported from Hong Kong.

"In any case," Lindsay said, "the doctor said you should rest." She touched two fingers to her lips and pressed them to my forehead. "Good night, Nicholas. Sleep well."

Afterwards I lay down on my bed, but sleep proved impossible, till much later.

29

THE SLEEP THAT CAME FITFULLY WAS DISTURBED by the jangle of the telephone and Ponsonby saying, "I hope it isn't frightfully inconvenient, old boy, but do you happen to have a gun?"

I came bolt upright hurting my back. My watch glowed five past one. "I haven't got a gun," I said. "What do you need a gun for?"

"Actually, I've got to the bottom of the Dirkian mystery," Ponsonby said. "I know who his killers are. And they're right here, in Colombo."

"Who are they?"

Ponsonby said, "It isn't wise to mention their names. I think we can do some kind of deal."

"You don't deal with killers," I said.

"I thought of that, old boy. Which is why I asked you if you had a gun."

"I haven't," I said.

There was a brief silence. "I suppose you wouldn't like to come," Ponsonby asked, "We're having breakfast in my hotel at seven."

I thought about it quickly. Then I said, "I'll be there," and put the phone down.

* * *

I drove through cool streets, silvered by the early dawn, along Galle Road looking vast in its emptiness. From behind the swaying bunches of bananas at the dark entrances to the boutiques came the clatter of tea being stirred in brass utensils. People melted in and out of narrow turnings and waited hopefully for buses.

Ponsonby's hotel was a few miles out of Colombo, overlooking the sea. The entrance was across a thin bridge spanning a railway line. I entered and parked under the large shady tree that stood in the centre of the tarred courtyard. Below me gardens damp with saltspray and dew tumbled to a lonely beach. The hotel, lined with wide balconies and potted palms reared whitely upwards.

I went up wide steps to a narrow lobby with a red polished floor, divided by ugly, square white-washed pillars. To my left were the entrances to two curio shops, bigger than Latif's, windows piled hopefully with the same kind of merchandise. There was a stuffed tiger by one of the doors, a scattering of pale cane chairs under brightly coloured notices in German, and along half the length of the room, a deserted, chest high counter.

I went behind the counter and looked up Ponsonby on the card index. Then I went on up the wide stairs covered with springy coir matting, to his room. It was on the fourth floor. Bright light fell on the tall white walls of the stairway, along corridors lined with wood, divided by a central strip of coir matting, on solid, shiny wooden doors.

I went down the corridor and knocked on Ponsonby's solid, shiny wooden door. It opened.

"Morning George," I said and walked in. I was an hour early anyway, and I felt George and I should have a little talk before meeting Dirkian's killers.

The room was high and spacious. The double bed was ruffled but hadn't been slept in, and Ponsonby's hide leather case lay unlocked on a canvas trapezium. Toothpaste and electric shaver were in the bathroom, but no sound of running water or George Ponsonby. No air conditioning either. The high rectangular windows were open, their net curtains ruffled by the sea breeze.

I went to the window and looked out. The dark figures of three boys moved slowly across the sand. In the distance was the straining figure of a lonely runner. From where I stood, I could see the buildings of the Fort coming alive with colour on the other side of the bay. I could also see George Ponsonby.

He was lying four storeys below me, a twisted streak of silver grey on the lawn beside the sea, his body stretched out in the angular stillness of the very dead. A blotch of blood stained the grass where his head had been and his fedora lay crushed beneath him. A yellow, plaited shoe lay sideways on the grass.

Cautiously and suddenly afraid, I backed away from the window and looked around the empty room. Then wiping the door knob with my handkerchief I went back, down the coir matted stairway, through the deserted lobby and into the brightening day.

I drove slowly back to the hotel taking a circuitous route, all the while trying not to think about what was left of Ponsonby's head.

* * *

When I got back to the hotel, Lindsay had gone out. I told Elmer about Ponsonby and stayed in my room till lunchtime, thinking. My thoughts were like the parts of a jigsaw, only they were larger and fitted together more easily.

I began with Dirkian. Stavros Dirkian who'd started life smuggling sponges and ended up smuggling art. Now the business of art smuggling, is a very confined one. It isn't every day that someone has a hot Van Gogh or a disguised Carravagio to be smuggled. Artists like Van Gogh or Carravagio are too well known, and if they are stolen, no collector dares show them. No, the bread and butter of art smuggling comes from the lesser known pieces of art, those which are beautiful in their own right and created by little known artists, or those that are valuable for the sake of their content, gold statues, jewel encrusted tiaras, that sort of thing. In order to be rich and successful, Dirkian must have made a speciality of a very special kind of smuggling.

But here again, supply was limited. The last time he'd been in Ceylon, Dirkian had obviously taken steps to end that state of affairs. Whatever he might have been diving for, he had brought an architect with him and made plans for the sacking of a dagoba. He had also since then made visits to Thailand.

A temple *had* been robbed in Thailand. As a result of that robbery, someone had yesterday, tried to kill Lindsay. Moreover Ponsonby had quite definitely referred to killers, and he had equally obviously been reasonably sure of doing a deal with them. The gun and me were required only if anything went drastically wrong.

The only people I knew who had been in Thailand, who'd been in Tangier at the time of Dirkian's death, and were now in Colombo were Barney and his friends. Whatever doubts I had about Barney's potential as a killer, I had no doubt about the other two.

It appeared that Barney and his friends had robbed the temple in Thailand. They had taken the proceeds to Dirkian, or alternatively Dirkian had organised the robbery. In any case he had kept too much and they had killed him. They had then come to Ceylon bringing his plans for the sack of a dagoba. Recognising Lindsay, they had tried to kill her. When Ponsonby had got too close to them, they had killed him.

The only problem now, was proof. The Thai police hadn't found the temple robbers. The Moroccan police had no means of showing that Barney and his friends were at Dirkian's the night he was killed. Which left me.

I went down to lunch with the problem of proof still unsolved.

* * *

The verandah was lined with rows of widely spaced tables. Small groups of tourists wearing shirts and shorts, print dresses without sleeves, ate fresh lobster salad. Elmer sat at a table alone, nursing a beer and looking out over the parched grass of the esplanade. I joined him and looked at the shimmering buildings of the Fort.

I lit a cigarette, drank some of Elmer's beer and listened to the steady beat of the waves and the faint rumble of the lunchtime rush hour. Lindsay joined us, very business-like in a green spotted shirt blouse, grey skirt and black low heeled slippers. A green scarf was knotted loosely about her throat and there was a sense of smugness about her, like a cat that had got both the mouse and the cheese.

"How's your back?" she asked.

"Heaps better," I said. "I recover quickly."

I looked up and down the verandah. There was no sign of Barney or his friends.

Elmer asked Lindsay, "What sort of a morning have you had?"

She lit a Marlboro. "I've spent all morning with the police," she said.

"For heaven's sake! Have you gone mad or something? What do you want to spend a whole morning with the police for?"

"Simple, Nicholas. It is the duty of any responsible citizen who has information relating to a crime that has been, or is about to be committed, to lay such information before the appropriate authorities."

"That's bloody stupidity," I said. In all my years of living within the hairline of legality, I had learned that there was one thing you must never do. That was never, never get involved with the police, any time, any place, any situation. Very rarely, the police just might help you. Most times all they did was create more problems. I had a depressing feeling that this was going to be one of those times.

Lindsay said, defensively, "I had reasonable suspicion."

"That's hardly enough. And it isn't as if we're pure as lilies and smelling of air freshener." Besides the combination of Lindsay's reasonable suspicion and that of the police would have frightened off Barney and his friends for good.

"I showed them the photographs and told them about the shipment of drilling equipment. They picked up Barney and Pierre at the airport this morning and they found some way of impounding the equipment."

"Are they in jail, then?"

"No. When the police came to the hotel and searched their rooms, there was nothing there. No maps, no plans, no bills, nothing."

"And no dynamite?"

"No," Lindsay said.

"I suppose no one thought of looking for a radio set?"

"I saw them leave," Elmer said, "All loaded up in their jeep and travelling very fast."

And with them, I thought grimly, went my last chance of showing that I hadn't killed Stavros Dirkian.

30

THE POLICE CALLED ON ME that afternoon. Just one man, in white shirtsleeves and slacks, wearing a broad, gaudy tie that was standard apparel for all Hollywood gangsters in the forties. His brown shoes were polished to a military shine and he wore an expression of patient good humour, for the same purpose that an exhibitionist effected a raincoat. His name, he said was Inspector Harvid and he was sorry to trouble me.

I said go right ahead. I was doing nothing that afternoon except wondering how to keep out of the way of the Moroccan police for the next twenty years, but I wasn't going to tell Inspector Harvid anything about that.

Inspector Harvid suggested we went up to my room where everything would be more discreet. He made it sound as if discretion was important. It would also, I knew, give Harvid a chance to inspect my room. There was no point in my telling Harvid that I knew about that either.

Harvid was a stocky, heavy shouldered man with close cropped prematurely grey hair, and a thin, sensual mouth. His face under the grey hair was unlined, with skin the colour of capucino coffee. His eyes were black and held the stolid, unemotional expression of a cow chewing cud. But that was only the impression, Harvid chose to give.

In my room he sat on the chair by the dresser and looked at my passport and currency form, jotting down a few details in a brown, leather covered note book. "Thank you," he said, leaving the documents on the bed, beside me. "You know a young man called Sunil Diaz? I understand he has driven you about from time to time."

It was superbly done. In two sentences Harvid had shown me that he wasn't going to waste time on pointless denials, that he had certain information about me, and left me to wonder how much and what.

"Yes," I said, "I know him."

"You know him well?"

"As well as I know anyone who drives me around in a strange city."

"When did you last see young Diaz?"

This was a little more difficult. I could tell him it was the last time Sunil had driven me. I could tell him it was last night. "Last night," I said. "We had a drink together, here."

"What time?"

"Oh, about seven o'clock or so. We had another drink together, about an hour later."

"Also in this room?"

I nodded.

"Do you usually entertain hire car drivers in this way?"

"Sometimes," I said.

"What did you and Diaz talk about, Mr. Maasten? Anything unusual?"

He was making damn sure that I knew, he knew it was unusual. "It was," I admitted, "pretty unusual. I invited Sunil round here to ask him to search the rooms of some friends of mine who are staying at this hotel. He came back an hour later with the results of that search."

"You're a nice man to have as a friend, Mr. Maasten. What information did Diaz bring back to you?"

There was little point in not telling Harvid what he already knew. I also felt that if I told the truth now, it would help if I was forced to lie later. I told him about Lindsay and Barney and ICOM. I told him about the photographs, the plans and the permissions.

"What are you doing in Ceylon, Mr. Maasten?"

I told him I was buying art for the Reede Museum of New York.

"You have some letter of authority?"

I shook my head. "We have a purely informal arrangement."

"And how do you pay for the goods you buy? You do not seem to have brought enough funds with you."

"The Museum will forward any funds that are necessary."

Harvid absorbed that information in thoughtful silence. Then he said, "You should have come to us in the first place, Mr. Maasten, we might have been able to help you."

I shrugged non-committally. "We might have been wrong," I said, "and caused you unnecessary trouble."

"No trouble is unnecessary, Mr. Maasten, not when a serious crime can be prevented."

I let that ride. We were all entitled to our own views.

"If you had come to us, Mr. Maasten, we might have been able to save young Diaz."

"Sunil. What's happened to Sunil?"

"He was found early this morning on the beach, about three miles from here."

"Drowned?"

"Neither drowned nor dead, Mr. Maasten. At least he's not dead yet. Sunil Diaz had been very brutally and very savagely beaten up. He is still unconscious."

"Hell," I said, "Bloody hell." A hot flame of anger lit through me.

"Was it Sunil Diaz who introduced you to Emir Latif?"

The question had all the power and sneakiness of a well thrown rabbit punch. Mentally, I jolted upright. "What? I'm not—"

"Watches, Mr. Maasten, watches. Let's talk about watches, forty ticking timepieces, let's talk about that and Emir Latif."

"I don't know what you're talking about." Standard reaction of injured innocence, standard phraseology of obstinate denial.

Harvid saw through that, like glass. "I'm afraid you do, Mr. Maasten. I'm talking of the watches you smuggled into Ceylon and sold to Emir Latif."

I felt worried and frightened. Very worried. Very frightened. I was also puzzled. If Harvid knew so much, why hadn't he arrested me. Or did he want a confession giving him an open and shut case. But if so why had he come alone and insisted on privacy.

"I've got nothing to say," I said, "Except that—"

"You have no idea what I'm talking about." Harvid paused and looked at me searchingly. "Would it help if I told you that I'm not really interested in the watches. That is primarily a customs matter, and I do not want to make an issue of it. Would it help if I tell you that I am prepared to forget about it."

He has no proof, I thought, with relief. He's probably picked up the information from Sunil's unconscious babbling. Perhaps it wasn't even true that Sunil had been beaten up. Perhaps it was all a try-on to shock me into—what? Harvid already seemed to know everything the police would want to know about me.

"I'm interested," Harvid said, "in *why* Latif told me about the watches."

Another shock. Another try-on. "I have absolutely nothing to say."

"Let's try it another way, Mr. Maasten," Harvid said equably. "You come into Ceylon six days ago, ostensibly buying works of art for the Reede Museum of New York. But you work as a principal, not as an agent. You bring with you a large quantity of watches to finance your purchases of Oriental art. You sell these watches to Emir Latif. The day after you ask your friend Sunil Diaz to search the room of your other friend, Barney Goldman, Diaz is found thrashed to within an inch of his life, and Latif most uncharacteristically informs the police about your smuggling activities. I think there is a connection between these incidents, Mr. Maasten. In fact, I think you are the connection."

"I don't see it that way at all," I said, truthfully.

"Tell me about Goldman," Harvid said.

I told him what I knew, taking care to leave out the libellous bits. Those, I thought Harvid could find out for himself.

"Miss Hamilton told us you found dynamite. Is that so?"

I nodded.

"Interesting,' Harvid said. "Tell me Mr. Maasten what do you think? Were they surveyors, or robbers or what?"

"It is difficult for me to express an opinion," I said.

"I understand your difficulty. As you may perhaps know, a short time ago we had a small revolution in this country. A band of youths got together and backed by certain countries, seized police stations and took over several towns. They attacked and killed many people. We had considerable difficulty suppressing the uprising and it was only with the armed forces and aid from countries like America, Russia and Great Britain that we were able to bring matters under control. I am wondering, Mr. Maasten, whether there are any political reasons for your friend's presence here."

I had to laugh. "Goldman is totally apolitical," I said. "He wouldn't care who was in power as long as he was making money out of it."

"You seem very sure, Mr. Maasten. What about the other two? How sure are you about them?"

"I don't know about the others," I said.

"But you will find out, won't you? You will stay close to them and find out?"

"They've left," I said. "They checked out a few hours ago."

"But you will find them for me, won't you?"

"That surely is a police matter."

Harvid sighed. "Ordinarily," he said, "yes. But they are Europeans. I have no European personnel. If one of my people were to follow them, they would spot him all too easily. And once they've spotted him they will take steps to lose him and do what they have planned. Alternatively, they might be replaced with others whom we do not know. So you see, Mr. Maasten, I would like to have a friend whom they also call a friend. I want you to lead them to me."

"This is ludicrous," I said. "After what happened this morning, if I got close to them, they'd kill me."

Harvid shrugged and turned out his palms in a gesture of inconsequence. "So? You will have brought them to me."

I tried to be reasonable. "Look," I said, "At worst they're tomb robbers. The police should deal with them."

Harvid shook his head. "I don't think so, Mr. Maasten. I really don't think so. After what happened to them this morning, most criminals would have been grateful for the warning and left the country. But not them. These people are idealists. I think they are revolutionaries filled with passion, with no thought of personal danger, devoted only to their insane cause."

"It's a great script," I said, "but you've got the wrong movie."

Harvid stood up. "That number will find me any time of the

day or night." He shook hands firmly. "Keep in touch, Mr. Maasten, keep in touch."

"I'm not sure," I said, "that there's anything to keep in touch about. I haven't even agreed to do anything for you."

Harvid turned at the door and waved. "Ticky-tock, Mr. Maasten. Remember if at any time your spirit flags, think of watches. Ticky-tock." And he went.

31

I STAYED IN MY ROOM and thought about watches going ticky-tock, and bombs making the same noise, preferably under Inspector Harvid. Harvid hadn't retained my passport, which meant that he was pretty damn sure he could stop me leaving the country. Which left one alternative. Get close to Barney.

Which led to three equally distasteful conclusions. I could let Barney Goldman kill me. Or Hassan. Or surrender to the Moroccan police. Simple. Unless of course I did manage to get involved with Barney without him suspecting anything, unlikely, *and* get a spin-off from whatever Barney was up to, improbable, before Harvid moved in. And perhaps somewhere along the line Barney would confess to killing Dirkian. Impossible. It was nice, easy, wishful thinking. Even if it did work out like that, I had no way of knowing that Harvid wouldn't still stick me with the smuggling charge. All I had was Harvid's word, and even that by implication. I still had to meet a policeman I could trust, especially if there was a chance of a nice, easy conviction.

It was a can of worms, I thought resignedly. It was more than a can of worms. It was worms and slippery, slithering eels.

The house phone gave a strangled squawk. I picked it up. It was Diaz, hoping he wasn't disturbing me. Come right up, I said. After Harvid, Diaz could only be an anti-climax.

Diaz came in hesitantly, clutching a large envelope as if it were a fly swatter. He took the chair by the dresser and leaned forward, steadfastly avoiding my eyes.

"I've ordered tea," I said, "I thought you'd like that."

"I would, Mr. Maasten. Thank you very much," but the voice was unenthusiastic.

"How's Sunil?" I asked.

He darted a quick glance at me and looked away. It reminded me of the way a bird picks a fish off the top of a pond. "He's much improved, thank you."

"Has he recovered consciousness?"

"Yes, about an hour ago. The doctors assure me that with rest and care he will soon be whole again."

"Has he said who attacked him?"

"Attacked him! Oh, no, Mr. Maasten! You must be mistaken. The foolish boy fell off a train. I have warned him many times about the perils of riding on the footboards, but you know what young people are. Heedless, solely concerned with the pursuit of excitement and pleasure."

"Is that what he told the police?"

"The police, Mr. Maasten?"

"There must be a policeman around," I said. "A person gets injured and there's always a policeman around."

"I was there when he spoke to them. Sunil is still a minor, you know, and that's what he told them. He fell off a train. Anything else you have heard is incorrect."

I noticed he didn't call it a lie.

Tea was brought into the room and I let Diaz pour. It still didn't taste like claret, but why on earth should it. Tea was tea, and wine was wine, and why on earth should Sunil, with access to three cars, want to ride on a train? If it was thrills he was after, then he could have got more thrills from a single clapped out Peugeot than a dozen trains.

"Which hospital is Sunil at?"

"Ah, Mr. Maasten, it is so nice of you to enquire. Sunil will be most touched when I tell him. Unfortunately he is not allowed visitors—except close relatives."

"Where is he?" I asked, "I want to send him some flowers." I kept staring at Diaz, forcing him to look me in the face.

Diaz hummed and hawed a bit and told me. The hospital was in Colombo, hardly two miles from the hotel.

We drank more tea and listened to the chugging of the air

conditioner.

Afterwards Diaz said, "I've made a momentous decision. I have decided to confess all."

"I am not really the sort of person you should confess all to," I said. "To do it properly, you need a priest."

"But it is to you I must confess, Mr. Maasten, because you are the one I have wronged."

"You aren't saying—"

"Let me begin at the beginning, Mr. Maasten, so that you will understand all. Let me throw myself upon your mercy and compassion."

"That's expecting a lot," I said and lit a cigarette. It seemed the only sensible thing to do.

"I will begin with the statues, Mr. Maasten. The bronzes of Siva and Parvati, those two delightful deities, whom we both admired so much. Sadly, they are not a thousand years old. They were cast forty-two years ago by a sculptor named Evan Williams, a Welshman who was in Ceylon as a guest of the British Government. In those days, Ceylon was a British colony, and better days they were too. But I divert from my confession. In gratitude for the government's hospitality, perhaps even in payment for it, Williams cast the four statues I brought you, so that they could be used at archaeological exhibitions without exposing the originals to the hazards of travel and pillage. In fact the number of exhibitions was hardly worth the cost of the bronze, let alone the trouble of storing and maintaining them. At the time I was working in the Archaeological Commissioners Department, these statues were an embarrassment, so I bought them. Quite cheaply, I may add. I bought them because I liked them. In some ways they were superior to the originals, which you could see in the Colombo Museum, and I had a feeling that one day they would be . . . I had a feeling that one day something would turn up."

Diaz paused and poured out the last dregs of tea. It tasted tepid and rather bitter.

"It was only recently that I thought of selling the bronzes," Diaz said. "Recently it has become impossible for anyone of taste or refinement, for anyone who was used to the comforts of the West, impossible for anyone far sighted enough to think of the future, of his children and his children's children, after, in other words, this resplendent island became a lot more sordid, seedy and depressed, that I decided to sell the bronzes. I did so out of need, Mr. Maasten, out of dire need. If I came to you and said these were copies, you'd have admired them, you might even have wanted them, but would you have bought them? I think not, Mr. Maasten, and even if you did, you would not have paid eight hundred pounds for each of those statues. You are, I believe, a man of the world. You will appreciate the need that prompted me to pretend that those statues were what they were not."

"In fact, Mr. Maasten, you were not my first customer. I started selling antiques many years ago, genuine antiques, things found during excavations in the ruined cities, things sometimes abandoned or stolen, sometimes even excavated specially for the purpose of sale, but nevertheless, genuine. It was not highly profitable. One couldn't expect to make large profits out of bits of stone and papyri and broken statuary. But at that time, I was not concerned with huge profits. A living satisfied me and I had other business interests as well."

"Like the tourist business?"

"Like the tourist business. It was only when I was in desperate need of foreign currency that I decided to make a killing. I knew I could never do that by selling pottery to tourists. I had to attract the dealers, the men with money, and for that I needed objects that were better finished, clearly dated and obviously priceless. Such objects are hard to come by, Mr. Maasten, so where there was a demand, I created a supply. I started in a small way, with papyri and pottery, then growing more expert, on to statues and artefacts, gradually building up to higher things."

Diaz paused, raised his tea cup to his lips, made a face and put it down, untasted. "In a strange way, Mr. Maasten I have always looked upon the Williams bronzes and the Diaz diary as my masterpieces."

"What the hell do you mean, masterpieces?"

"It was with them that I hoped to make my fortune, and when I met you, I thought I did."

"Are you saying the manuscripts are fakes?"

"It is a foolish man," Diaz said, "who even if he can fool all the people, all the time, thinks he can fool God. The evil that men do not only lives after them, Mr. Maasten, quite often it is visited upon them and their children." He looked up at me sadly. "Yes," he said slowly, "the Diaz diary is a forgery."

"Why are you telling me all this?"

"Because I seek a peace above all earthly dignities, a still and quiet conscience. Shakespeare. Henry VIII, Act 3 Scene II. You understand, don't you?"

"No," I said.

"Don't you see, Mr. Maasten, God has inflicted a visitation upon me. He has sent me a sign, a warning. My eldest son, the delight of my fading years, felled in a meaningless accident. Surely that is what St. John meant in his epistle to the Romans, vengeance is mine; I will repay, said the Lord." He paused and placed the envelope lightly on the bed. "In that envelope, Mr. Maasten, you will find one hundred and sixty thousand rupees, the very sum you gave me for the manuscripts and the statues."

I thought quickly. Diaz was telling me that the diaries were fakes, that there was no temple and that Dirkian had been searching for a dream. He was offering me an opportunity to pay off Hassan, pack up my tent and go. Except Harvid wouldn't let me go, assuming there was somewhere to go.

I drew deeply at a cigarette I didn't know I'd lit. "I think I'll keep the manuscripts," I said. "They must have curiosity value."

Diaz lifted his fingers away from the envelope like a pianist pausing after a pianissimo passage.

"I understand," he said softly. "You wish to turn the knife. You wish to extract your pound of flesh. Very well, Mr. Maasten, make your profit." He sighed, long and deeply. "How much do you want for the return of the manuscript?"

"The last time we met," I said dryly, "You couldn't get the money back."

"I haven't got the money back," Diaz said. "Not yet. Meanwhile I have borrowed from friends and relatives at usurious rates in order to appease my conscience. Please understand, I am prepared to pay anything, anything within reason, to procure the return of that forgery. I do this so that the wrath of God may not be visited upon my family."

I twisted the cigarette between my fingers, and thought. Barney's interest in the bronzes last night, had been genuine. He'd wanted them, but not for scrap. Those bronzes were the most beautiful fakes he or I had ever seen. And there weren't that many people in the world who knew about bronzes.

Provided the acquisition price was right, Barney could always find someone to take the bronzes, especially if their age was evidenced by the manuscript. Why hadn't I thought of it? There wasn't even any need to smuggle the bronzes out of Ceylon to make a huge profit.

"A hundred and ninety thousand rupees," Diaz suggested softly.

I shook my head.

"Two hundred thousand, two hundred and five, I can't go much more than that."

I leaned across and stubbed out the cigarette. "The Diaz diaries are not for sale," I said. "Not at any price."

"But, Mr. Maasten—"

"You've tried hard," I said. "God will understand."

32

I WENT ALONG THE CORRIDOR to Lindsay's room. From behind the solid wooden door came the steady rattle, rattle, ping of a portable typewriter operating at mach one. I knocked, pushed and entered. After all, why the hell not. She was always doing it to me.

Lindsay was in the far corner, by the window, a mischievous tendril of hair dangling over her cheek. She was tapping away at a typewriter that Signor Olivetti must have screwed together himself, by hand. Papers were laid about the table in neat stacks, books stood propped up against the wall in front of her, thin strips of paper markers sticking out limply like fading soldiers. There was a large ashtray full of half smoked cigarette butts.

"Hi!" she said, brushing the hair away with an impatient gesture. "I thought you were room service."

"I'm not," I said, "but I heard you call." All dressed up in hot pants or tight mini skirts, Lindsay undoubtedly looked terrific. In battered jeans and a faded blouse with sweat stains under the arm pits, she looked far less overtly sexual. In fact she looked slightly rumpled and preoccupied and as far as I was concerned, miles more attractive. For a moment I forgot what I'd come about.

"I've sent for some orange juice," she said, reaching for the phone. "Would you like some?"

"No," I said. "I'm just going out."

I walked over to the desk. There was a sort of musty smell about her hair that I liked, must and tobacco smoke. "That the manuscript?" I said.

"Yes. I was just typing up my translation of the last few pages." Very business-like, she added, "I'll drop a copy into you and Elmer as soon as I've finished."

"That's cool," I said. "That's very cool. Tell me are you working from the manuscript?"

"No," she said. "I'm working from my notes."

"In that case, I'll have the manuscript. I'm going to put it in the hotel safe."

Her eyes narrowed. "What do you want to do that for?"

"Because Diaz just offered to buy the manuscript back from me—at a profit."

"And you didn't sell?"

I wasn't sure whether she was surprised at my lack of avarice, or whether she thought I should have sold the manuscript anyway. Her uptilted head was about the level of my chest. When I looked down, her face was hardly ten inches away.

"No," I said.

She twisted a brown arm over the side of her chair. "But you don't know whether the manuscript is genuine or not, whether Diaz conned Dirkian."

"I'm hoping he didn't," I said. My mind insisted on wandering, on having impure thoughts, and there was a tightness at the back of my throat. I was going to have to stand further back or . . .

"But even *I'm* not yet sure if the manuscript is genuine," Lindsay said.

"I am," I said and kissed her.

There was a brief startled moment when her head jerked back and her body went rigid. Momentarily her lips moved moistly around mine and I thrust my body against her chest. Then with an ardour which that Jesuit would have admired, she hit me over the head with Queyroz's *Temporal and Spiritual Conquest of Ceylon.*

* * *

The hospital was a series of long and narrow buildings, painted in a neutral stain absorbing grey, extending from a square two storeyed structure. The verandahs were full of visitors and patients and just within the entrance there was a stretcher on the floor, with a man covered by a blood spotted sheet and everyone waiting with the inscrutable patience of the East.

There was some confusion before I found out where Sunil was. Even more confusion when they found out that I shouldn't know.

"No visitors," the hospital clerk told me forcefully. "Only close relatives."

He was a small curly haired man with a greying moustache and a smooth, shiny forehead. His clothes were well worn and he had the ruffled cockerel air of one used to the exercise of a small measure of authority.

"I'm a relative," I said. "My name is Rubeiro Diaz. I have come all the way from Lisbon to see Sunil."

"You aren't from Ceylon?" the clerk asked.

"No, I am Portuguese. I am a pilot with TAP." There must after all be a few Portuguese pilots who look like sun tanned Englishmen. "I've come a long way," I added. "It is a special case."

The clerk hesitated. If my story didn't convice him, the hundred rupee note folded between my knuckles did. He became quite conciliatory, and said I should have mentioned, that I had come all the way from Lisbon. He led me along verandahs, bordered by half walls inside which were wards full of iron bedsteads and bored looking patients. We went to the central building and up a flight of stairs, along lengthy corridors.

At the end of one corridor he stopped before a closed door. "You mustn't stay long," he said.

"No," I promised. "Just a couple of minutes."

"I'll wait here for you," he said.

"You do that."

Sunil lay on his back in semi-darkness, the saline bottle above his head dripping steadily into the opened vein. His face and head were heavily bandaged and there was a thick plaster across his nose. The flesh around the eyes was blackened, bruised, and his mouth sank inwards with the softness of a baby's.

"Sunil," I said, quietly. "Sunil."

He didn't move. There was no change in the rhythm of his breathing.

I went and stood over him.

"Sunil," I said again.

A swollen eye opened. "It's me, Nicholas. How are you, man?"

The eye fixed on me with a dazed, sedated look.

"I'm sorry, man," I said, "I'm damn sorry."

The eye closed. The deep, rhythmic breathing recommenced. I took the three thousand rupees I had brought and placed it under his pillow. Sunil hardly moved. When he recovered, I hoped he would be able to use it.

I pressed his shoulder and went out. The clerk was waiting for me as he had promised, and at the end of the long corridor, walking briskly towards me, was Cindy.

"Cindy," I cried, running forward.

She saw me, stopped, turned and with a rapid patter of heels ran back along the corridor, the way she had come. By the time I reached the corner she had gone.

* * *

I went back to the car which I had parked with open windows underneath a tree, so that it would be cool when I returned. There were crow droppings on the sides of the seats. I wiped them and drove off, to see Diaz.

Diaz was glad to see me. "Come in Mr. Maasten," he carolled, advancing to the top of the verandah steps. "Please come in. I am so pleased you've changed your mind."

I went up the steps onto the verandah, and took his outstretched hand. "In there," I said, pointing to the room at the end of the verandah, behind the strips of plastic curtain.

Diaz hesitated.

"Let's keep this private-like," I said, crowding him.

I followed him closely into the tiny room, with its glass fronted bookcases and rows of sepia toned photographs. Only this time, I got to the further side of the desk, first. Swiftly I flung open the drawers. Three, two, one. The Webley lay on a wad of tissue paper, in the topmost drawer, an oily green-black. It was a late model .32 with a three inch barrel and the safety at the top of the left hand grip.

"I've started collecting guns," I said, and picked up the Webley.

"But, Mr. Maasten, surely—"

With my free hand I eased out a wad of notes under the desk and counted out ten hundreds.

"You're making yourself a thirty per cent profit," I said. "Got any spare clips?"

"But I need that gun, Mr. Maasten. I need it for my own protection."

I tapped the pile of notes. "You know where you can get them," I said. "I don't."

Still holding the gun, I brushed past Diaz and went out to the car. I drove away quickly, in case he already had another gun and decided to use it.

I stopped along the lovely, shady avenue that ran by the Art Gallery, took out the gun and checked it. Keeping a gun in a drawer for years doesn't help, even if it's wrapped in tissue paper. The magazine was full. The gun hadn't been fired for some time but it was freshly oiled. I breathed a sigh of relief. It seemed that Diaz had looked after the gun, and that was reassuring. If I had to use it, I could be reasonably certain that it wouldn't blow up in my hand. But then, as always, I hoped I wouldn't have to use it.

* * *

I drove past the hotel, filtered into the streaming traffic of the Fort, moved along the one way system past the old jetty towards the Pettah. I bumped over the railways lines, past a rubber tyred cart, and crawled along the narrow main street till I could stop within walking distance of Latif's jewellery store.

His assistant didn't recognise me and switched on a light inside a showcase, talking quickly and pointing to a selection of rings studded with gleaming red pin points of rubies and hard blue sapphires. I walked straight past him to the back of the shop.

He came after me, pawing at my shoulder. I turned round and grabbed him by the loose, flapping shirt. "Go and play with your electric showcase," I said. "I'm going to see Latif."

"Mr. Latif, busy," the man said.

"Not too busy to see an old friend," I pushed him away and kicked open the door to Latif's air conditioned office.

Latif was there, rising black and rubbery above the green topped desk. The man with him was smaller, rounder, wearing a red fez, a white brass buttoned jacket, a white shirt and green and yellow striped sarong. On the desk between them there were three paper handkerchiefs, containing small amounts of moonstones, rubies and quartz.

Latif looked at me and said, "Get out."

I moved to the side of the desk, between Latif and the lapidary. "You heard him," I said. "Out." As I spoke I tugged at the paper containing moonstones, scattering them over the desk with a dry, rustling noise. The lapidary got the message. If I flicked the rubies off the table he could spend a day and a night looking for them and even so, he'd never be sure.

Latif said, "Get out, Maasten."

I picked the rubies up and stood back. "Tell your friend to come back another time. We're going to talk."

The lapidary was already half way up from his seat, looking worriedly at Latif. He had the air of a man who knew trouble when he saw it, and was willing to go to great lengths to avoid it. I balled the rubies up and flung them at him. With a surprising agility, he reached up and caught them, emitting a little squeal. Then he stopped, looking at Latif. Slowly Latif nodded.

As soon as the lapidary had gone, I shut the door and stood with my back to it. Latif got up, moving massively around the desk. "You're playing with the wrong person," he said, thickly. "I can have you cut into little pieces and thrown into the sea." He spoke, I thought, with the authority of truth.

"You haven't got your thugs here," I said. "Here there's only you and me and this." I jerked up the Webley so that he could get a good look at it.

Latif stopped. I didn't think he'd been on the wrong side of a gun before. Or the right side either. He stared at the gun with a horrified fascination.

"Tell me about Harvid," I said. "Tell me why you told the police that I'd smuggled watches."

Thick lids blinked heavily over sloe black eyes. The heavy mouth twisted in concentration. "I never told the police anything about you." He even managed to look mystified.

"Then why are they looking for me?"

"Perhaps . . . perhaps it was someone else."

I stepped forward, swinging the gun butt towards my left shoulder, and lashed out. The barrel of the Webley 1913, .32 is three and a half inches long and has a sighting groove running along the top of the weapon. More important for my purpose, it also has a raised, hemispherical metal sight at the tip of the barrel, half an inch long and quarter of an inch high. The sight gouged into Latif's cheek with a swift, sucking sound. My elbow snapped straight and the sight ripped through the soft flesh, leaving a surprised yellow streak, that rapidly filled with blood.

"Was it Goldman?" I asked.

Latif was crouched, holding his hands up to his face. He tried to twist away as I moved up to him, pulling his hands apart and staring in wonder at his blood stained palms. Blood plopped onto the purple shoulder of his shirt.

"Who was it?" I asked.

Latif's eyes were fixed on the upraised gun barrel. Thin wisps of reddened flesh clung to the sight. "Maurice Brescanon," he said. "We have done business in the past."

"A lot of business?"

Latif nodded.

"Use your handkerchief," I said. "If it's clean."

He found it, formed it into a wad and began dabbing at his cheek.

"Why did Brescanon want you to tell the police about me?"

"I'm not sure why."

"Try guessing."

"They wanted you out of the way."

"When did they ask you to do this?"

"Yesterday night."

"How did they know I sold you the watches?"

Latif hesitated. "I told them," he said and winced.

"Go on."

"I do much business with Brescanon. Gold, diamonds, watches."

"Drugs?" I asked.

"No drugs." He shook his head, spattering blood over the floor. "The local *ganja* is not very good."

"What made Brescanon talk about me?"

"They came to see me last night. They wanted me to arrange an . . . accident. For you and a girl."

"What kind of accident?"

"I didn't agree. With my own people, it is different. But with foreigners, that is dangerous. So when he described you, I told him about the watches. It was safer to tell the police than have an accident."

I took a pace back, raised the gun and clicked off the safety. Latif stared at me in horror, his eyes going wide and round as marbles, the handkerchief dabbing at his face, picking up speed. "Let's get something straight," I said. "This conversation is private. Very private. No one knows about it. Not Harvid, not Brescanon, no one."

Latif nodded vehemently. "And there aren't going to be any accidents," I said. "Definitely no accidents." I showed him the gun in my palm. "Even my ghost knows how to use this. Remember that."

I flung open the door and went out. The assistant slid off his stool and by an automatic reflex action, popped on the light of the showcase.

"It's still the wrong weather for buying jewellery," I said and went out into the sweaty, stench of the Petah.

33

I WENT BACK TO THE HOTEL. There wasn't much for me to do, except think and read the remainder of the manuscript that Lindsay had left for me. I read the manuscript first.

THE VOYAGE

Gaspar Saldhana who had charge of us was a person of belligerent disposition, short and bucolic in appearance with beard and hair of a colour not unlike sand. He brought with him to the Santa Maria twelve men who had served under him many years, in Goa and other places, and bore him loyalty as great as that which they had sworn to our Sovereign Lord. They treated Gasper Saldhana with great respect, rushing to do his slightest bidding, and this they said they did because he was an able commander and had oft risked his own life for such of his own men who were in peril. Moreover he had more frequently than other captains, [given them surfeit.][1] The remaining member of his troop he dispatched to the Santa Cristabel, which was commanded by Miguel de Susa who had with him three other soldiers, the eight casados and an arache.[2]

After having been becalmed for some while amongst the inner roads, we sailed from Columbo, that afternoon. In order that time might not be profitlessly expended, we sailed as close to the shore as our draught would allow,

1 These words missing from the manuscript.
2 Captain of Sinhalese soldiers.

even though the danger of shipwreck was greater thereby, this part of the coast being well populated with rock and protected by reefs. Saldhana kept us to our course even after nightfall, and I was greatly frightened as what we had done by day was many times more dangerous by night. I spoke of my fears to Saldhana whereupon he held me to scorn before his troops, saying the escrivao is frightened of the sea and the dark and wishes to go back to his pen. He urged me to sharpen my quill for I would need to use it and he promised that before the voyage ended, he would make me a man.

In the second watch of the night, with the help of the arache who had sailed with us, he brought us to land. Bidding the Santa Cristabel to await our signal, Saldhana and the arache led us ashore.

We walked, each man behind the other, along a narrow track, and even though the night was as black as a Moor's palm we were led up the smoothest way so that no man stumbled. When we came to a village, Saldhana silently dispersed his men around it, and taking the arache, two soldiers and me, entered the village with great shouts and the discharge of firelock shots.

At this the villagers came out of their houses in great fear and Saldhana demanded the head man be brought to him. When this was done he bade the head man give us food, which they hastened to prepare, and even though it was not such as we were used to, being mostly rice and vegetable, for the first time in months our bellies were full.

After we had eaten, Saldhana commanded his men to go into the houses and fields beyond and take such things as we would need to ensure the survival of the people of Colombo. Rice we took, and fruits and vegetables, pepper, oil and honey, not in great quantity because the village did not have a large stock of these things. After the goods had been brought together, Saldhana commanded that all the cattle belonging to the village be slaughtered and set the casados to salt the meat thereof, so that it would not be spoiled before our return to Colombo. Hearing of this the head man pleaded with Saldhana to spare their livestock, for they had no other means of tilling their fields. Whereupon Saldhana became enraged and put the head man into captivity inside his own house together with all his family, placing a guard at the door.

After the cattle had been slaughtered and we had transported the victuals to the Santa Cristabel, making two journeys, Saldhana summoned the village before him and had the head man and his family, who altogether comprised five people, brought forth. Upon seeing the assembled villagers, the head man threw himself at Saldhana's feet, begging forgiveness for whatever wrong he had done, and saying that if any punishment was due, it should be inflicted upon him and not upon his family. Despite the man's anguish, Saldhana commanded that they all be bound and given fifteen lashes each, even the head man's wife and daughter who was hardly more than a girl. When the sentence had been carried out and they were left suspended from the branches to which they had been tethered, their backs bleeding and raw from the stripes they had received, Saldhana ran through each of them with his sword, saying let that be an example to all who followed the Chingala King and that this was his revenge for the loss of his company, outside the Fort of Colombo.

We set sail soon thereafter, and during the next two days put into more villages, where again after we had loaded the Santa Cristabel with such victuals as were available, Saldhana inflicted cruel tortures upon the head men and their families before putting them to death.

On the evening of the third day we called at a village of the Chaliyars, who are people of low caste and are despised by the Chingala for whom they have no great friendship. They work only in the cinnamon gardens and are not permitted to live or trade elsewhere.

Being friendly to us they gave us great welcome with food and coconut brandy and told us because of the wars they had not been able to harvest the cinnamon. This was of great distress to me, because cinnamon was an important item of our trade.

That night Saldhana's own men complained that while

they had nearly filled a whole ship with victuals, they had not themselves had a spoil of any kind whatsoever. Fearing that they would become restive, Saldhana promised them a sack the next day, but even though all the next afternoon, we left the ships and advanced along the coast, burning villages and taking for ourselves such things as we could find, there was little more than food.

As by now the Santa Cristabel was fully laden, Saldhana commanded that it should return to Colombo while we sailed further south to harry the enemy and find more prizes, for it had been told to Saldhana by the Chaliyar that the towns of the south were more prosperous and there was also a Pagode of great richness.

THE SURFEIT

The next day we parted company from the Santa Cristabel and sailed south. Our first raid that morning had yielded no greater profit than before and the men were muttering amongst themselves, so that Saldhana decided to abandon the ravaging of villages and make haste to the south.

The towns to the south were held by the Chingala and the Moors, and fortified with tranqueiras[1] so that they could not be successfully attacked by our small troop. We also wished to avoid Gale which was one of Raju's chief towns, guarded by many men. So Saldhana put out to sea wishing to arrive by stealth, so that the people not being warned, would not hide their treasures. The place we sailed away from was Anubigara[2] and the next day we crossed the Equator.

We sailed for two days after that without ever sighting land. The small supply of food we had kept for ourselves from the last onslaught was consumed, but that was no great hardship, for we were able to obtain a great plenty of fish, such as albacoretta and bonito, all of twelve to fifteen pounds, also dolphin, all these being very delicate sea fish tasting almost like pike. These fish were good to eat fried

1 Fort or stockade.
2 I have not been able to identify this place.

lightly in their own fat and laid in vinegar.

During this portion of the voyage we were reasonably content and wanted for little and the men were made quite expectant by the surfeit they had been promised.

On the third evening having covered the greater part of our journey, just as we set about towards land, there threw up a thunder storm accompanied by a cross wind, so fierce, that I believed our ship was well-nigh lost. The arache who had remained with us became at this point greatly frightened, saying that this storm was a curse sent upon us by the god of the Pagode, who learning of the insult about to be done to him, had begun to chastise us. The arache's fears made Saldhana all the more determined to reach the Pagode, and when the tempest was past set our course again to the north-east towards the land.

Soon after sunset we cast anchor in a small bay about half a league to the east of the Pagode and went ashore without incident. As the sea around these parts is continuously high and thunder storms work up frequently, it had not been thought possible for a ship to reach land. We therefore marched unopposed to the Pagode, reaching it shortly thereafter.

At the gate to the Pagode, we were resisted by a band of guards, but they were ill trained and unable to take the force of our blows and shot, and soon they took themselves inland[1] leaving eight of their number, dead. We broke open the gate and proceeded to enter the gardens of the Pagode, without encountering any further resistance.

Alarmed by the sound of the conflict there were gathered together in the Pagode two priests and the women who ministered to the Pagode. Upon sight of the women our troop with the exception of Barracho Domingos and the arache who had received a wounding during our battle with the guards, were seized with madness, and fell upon the women like animals, two or three to each, tearing the clothes off them and holding them to the floor, with much

1 The manuscript has "desprezáram." This is presumably an error for "despejeram," meaning "withdrew." The guard obviously went inland.

screaming and shouting, enjoying them forcibly against their will, having first killed the two priests before the very eyes of the women.

At the sight of this I began to realise that though Christians, our people were more ill-conducted than the heathens, who if they did not spare property or life, are not wont to break out against the honour of women and that it is a great disgrace in that pagans should be more civilized than Christians in this.

Knowing well that after each man had satisfied himself to the full, the women would be killed also, I approached one who having been enjoyed by Saldhana and his lieutenant lay as if in a stupor, for she had not known any man before. And taking her at knife point outside the door of the inner Pagode, as if I meant to enjoy her privately, I escorted her to the gate of the Pagode, where I gave her my doublet and sent her towards the town some two leagues hence. Another woman I dispatched also in like fashion before my strategy was discovered and the soldiers fell upon me and brought me to Saldhana, who being relieved of his appetite, was proceeding to plunder the Pagode.

Saldhana did not wish to punish me because he was afraid that the Captain-General, knowing my family, might hold him in fief. At the same time he did not want me to report upon his vile and un-Christian actions. For these reasons and on account of wishing to proceed with the sack of the Pagode, before the guards and the women raised the alarm in the town, he ordered the soldiers to bind me hand and foot and place me in a corner of the Pagode where afterwards they leashed and brought the women also, so that if any of them were so disposed later, they might again enjoy them.

They then began to destroy the idols of clay and wood and copper, first taking out any precious stones and things that were valuable. A troop was dispatched to the cells wherein they found much ivory, fine clothes, copper, pepper, sandalwood, jewels, precious stones, wax, all of which they collected together for transport to Colombo. The ornamental doors of the chapels they broke down and burnt and took from the roof those projections that were made in the form of snakes and made of gold. The carvings they defaced where they could and upturned the pots with flowers and herbs so that the whole place was covered with earth and blood. There were two golden idols which were of such dimension as not to make for easy transport. So having defaced them with blows Saldhana ordered them to be taken to the sea and cast therein. The silver pedestal upon which rested the jade column, he took for himself, and having stripped the jade of its ornaments, he not realising its worth ordered it to be cast into the sea also.

Replete with their plunder which filled their caixes de liberdade[1] many times over, they went forth and brought into the Pagode, cattle, whom they slaughtered. Upon seeing this the women began to wail and beat their heads upon the ground with great force, for what was now being done was far worse than what they had suffered at the hands of Saldhana's men, killing of cattle being the most unclean thing possible and for the purification of which great ceremonies are required and which would prevent the Pagode being used for their worship again.

Having taken as much prize as they could carry, and their appetites and passions being sated, they took the women outside and killed them so that there would be no witnesses to the shameful things they had done. I believed that my end too had come and commended my soul to my Saviour, though I could not find it in my heart to forgive Saldhana his evil. The soldiers did not return however and soon afterwards I smelt the flame as they put the Pagode to fire and set off charges underneath the platform.

Knowing now that Saldhana wished my death to appear accidental, and knowing they wished to leave me to my fate, I rolled towards the flames for it had not yet reached the inside of the Pagode, and pushed my hands towards them, burning flesh at the same time as cord. Being free though in great pain I was trapped in the inferno, with

1 Liberty chests. Most Portuguese soldiers had these to carry away their spoils.

walls and pillars crumbling around me. With great fear I sought a gap in the flames and having obtained it, leapt through it to the pond they keep for purifying themselves before worship.

My company having departed some while I set off inland, hoping to find some person who would take pity on me. But as my map had been left on the Santa Maria I had no thought of which direction to turn and set off away from the ship, for if Saldhana knew of my fortune, he would surely now have put me to death and risked the wrath of the Captain-General.

I had hardly gone a quarter of a league when I was confronted by a large crowd of people, armed with spears and bows and other primitive implements, who had on hearing of what transpired at their Pagode and now seeing it aflame, come to defend their Pagode and help preserve it. Upon seeing me they fell upon me with many blows and took me captive back to the Pagode where after some considerable time, they extinguished the flames.

When they saw the result of the sack they wished to put me to death and again gave me many blows before leading me back to their town so that I could be shown to their chief.

Their chief was a wise and elderly man who had ruled them for many years. He was enraged at the sacrilege that had been committed and decided that I should be put to death in the manner of being torn apart between two trees which is a horrible and painful punishment because quite often the trees do not spring apart strongly enough and the sentence has to be carried out many times before the prisoner dies, all the while suffering great pain of torn and dislocated limbs.

However my store of good fortune had not yet been expended, for the woman whom I had the previous night rescued was brought forth so that she could witness how one of those who had violated their Pagode would be punished. Despite the blood on my face and the state of my wounds she recognised me and rushing to the chief absolved me from blame, showing him the doublet I had given her to cover her nakedness.

Whereupon they freed me from my bondage and took me away from the place of execution to their chief's house where they bathed my wounds and gave me good food and sustenance until I was completely whole, for this woman was a relation to the chief. Afterwards she came and ministered to me and taught me aught of their language and customs.

For many months after I was whole, I waited for the landing of a ship but it did not happen. While I was no longer a prisoner in the town, it was not possible for me to make my way to Colombo, for there were in between the lands of Raju who would put to death any stranger found in his Kingdom. So I stayed in the town and made a living by knitting caps. Despairing of ever seeing my home land again I took the woman to whom I had given the doublet to wife, as she was now not able to live in a Pagode and she had been exceeding kind to me. Afterwards I lived as one of them though still practising my religion in private and remaining faithful to Christ.

34

LINDSAY AND ELMER WERE DOWN in the bar, looking serious. Lindsay said, "The manuscript is a forgery. I've little doubt of that."

"A forgery! But Dirkian—" If the manuscript was a forgery, then I just might have lost Barney. If it was a forgery, the Moroccan police would only be the start of my problems. "It reads true," I said, "It must be true. Even Diaz wanted to buy it back."

Lindsay said, "Let's keep it short. I've got a headache and I don't really want to think about that damned manuscript any more."

I sat down and stared moodily at the imitation coconut thatch over the bar and the row of glistening bottles.

"Firstly," Lindsay held out a forefinger, "the diaries are historically inaccurate. Saldhana took a great risk in putting out to sea in a small craft to avoid Galle. Now while Galle might have been held by the Sinhalese thirty years previously, it was not held by them at the time of the siege, about 1582.

"Secondly," another extended finger, "there is no historical record of the temple. Thirdly, if the temple had existed as described, it would have been a temple dedicated to Vishnu, not Siva. Sivaism came late to Ceylon. Fourthly, at the time there was no close relationship with China. That came earlier, about the fourth century, and later, about the fifteenth." She paused and looked at me. "There's also the question of the voyage."

Lindsay reached into her satchel and unrolled a large black and white photocopy of a map. It was headed, *"Nieuwe Kaart van het eyland Ceylon, op gefteit, door Francois Valentyn."* "According to Diaz, they left a place called Anubigara and crossed the equator." She pointed to the map. "This is a Dutch map, probably printed about a hundred years after Diaz's voyage. The names of the coastal towns are however identical to those used by Portuguese historians of the period. Anubigara does not appear on it."

"Now," she said, "About the equator. Ceylon is six degrees north of the equator. If Diaz crossed it and sailed south, the only land he could have reached was the Maldive Islands, somewhere around Gan. He wouldn't have found a Hindu temple on Gan. The Maldives are Moslem."

"In any case," Elmer said, "Diaz could never have got there in two days. A modern steam ship takes a day and Diaz would have taken at least a week.

"Diaz says they only sailed for two days," Lindsay said.

I sat back and watched the smoke hovering above us, trying to face the reality of the manuscript being a forgery and wondering what the hell I was going to do about Barney, about the Moroccan police and about Hassan.

Lindsay said, "You look upset."

"I am," I said.

Elmer asked, "Why don't you check our sources? Who knows? You might come up with something."

Like a historian's nightmare, I thought and said, "Why the hell not."

35

I ARRANGED CIGARETTES, ASHTRAY, LIGHTER, a fresh bottle of Haig, soda syphon and glasses where I could get at them without effort. I locked the door and placed a chair against it. I checked the safety on the Webley and placed it underneath my pillow. Then I settled down to read.

I read for hours. I read till my eyes seemed filled with sand, and my brain was numb from the sonorous convoluted prose. I learned a lot about the Portuguese in Ceylon.

It was a story of treachery and violence, of greed and tremendous courage. The Ceylonese were truly unfortunate, in that their first experience of Western colonisation, should have been at the hands of the Portuguese. The Portuguese had built their empire upon superior sea power and a desperate soldiery. Short of manpower, short of the administrative capacity of the typical English civil servant, suffering from an ever increasing need for wealth and religious converts, they spread the tentacles of their empire far and wide. Too far, and too wide. Their colonies were peopled with adventurers as well as *fidalgos*. They cared little for the people they colonised, except to convert them to Catholicism. Their main concern with the lands was what they yielded.

The policy of fire and sword and blazing cross survived, till other nations built bigger and more powerful ships, till other nations became capable of engaging in the East Indies trade. Then the Portuguese empire, weakened from within and without, collapsed.

All of which was interesting, but threw little light on the authenticity of the Diaz diary. As far as I could see, Lindsay and Elmer had covered the ground thoroughly. After hours of research, I had found nothing to support me, everything to support Lindsay. After hours of reading, I even began to hope for a visit from Barney and his mercenaries.

I put the books away and got out of bed. The Scotch I noted with surprise was still unopened, and that I remedied immediately.

After a lot of remedying I went back to bed and picked up de Couto again. Turning pages at random, I found something that Lindsay hadn't checked. It was two hundred pages before the section she had referenced, thirty years prior to the period we were concerned with, page one hundred and seventy, 1554 AD, as they say in the most learned of footnotes.

In that year, a predecessor of Raja Singha had ravaged the south-western coastal towns and exterminated the Christians and their churches on a wholesale basis. He had also ended the Portuguese settlement of Galle.

I skimmed through the book, looking for further references to Galle. It was on page four hundred and four that I found it. The Portuguese did not build another Fort in Galle till 1595. So if Diaz had passed Galle in the 1580's, it could still have been in Sinhalese hands. Beautiful, I thought, hopeful. Brilliant. I went through the books quickly again. But luck, like lightning, doesn't often strike twice in the same place.

I fell asleep more hopeful, now more concerned about Diaz' navigational problems. If Diaz wasn't a sailor, he wouldn't have known he was crossing the equator, unless someone had told him. If he was a sailor, he wouldn't have made such an elementary mistake.

Which led to another question, I hadn't thought of earlier. If the diary was a forgery, would the forger himself have made such a pointless and simple mistake?

* * *

I woke up early the next morning, with blurred memories of sieges and plunder, of sailing ships and navigational charts.

Lindsay and Elmer were walking slowly along the front of the esplanade. It seemed as if I was not the only one who'd had a fitful night.

Lindsay had been thinking about the map. There was, she said, an exhibition of mediaeval maps at the Colombo Museum.

We went there as soon as it opened, wandering around the poorly illuminated map room, with light reflecting off the glass frames, making detailed study virtually impossible. After a while I found the map. Anubigara was on it, as large as life and the equator thick as a man's finger. The only trouble was that at the time Diaz had sailed, that particular map had been thirteen hundred years old.

* * *

There was only one thing to do, Lindsay said, unrolling her black and white photocopied map. Find the site.

"Sure," I said, "and Troy, and Atlantis, and Pompeii as well."

"Why not?" Lindsay asked.

Why not indeed. There are many ways of searching for the site of an ancient temple. One could engage a team of people to survey the area and start probing into unnatural mounds and crevices. One could take specialist aerial photographs and pin-point possible sites. Or engage a team of experts to go and dig. Or simply dig. Or look.

We had no resources, not much time, and little money. We had no option but to look.

Lindsay's idea was perfectly simple. We would drive down to a point where she estimated Diaz had landed. Then we would walk along the coast, a matter of a few miles, and hope. It was better than sitting in Colombo, worrying. So we took our two hundred year old map, and went.

The day turned out to be blazing hot, and in order to keep to the coast, we found we often had to leave the road and walk along the beach. Thin, fine, golden, gritty sand got into our shoes. We removed them and the soft soles of our feet were baked by the hot beach and the even hotter macadam. Inquisitive children followed us everywhere. Helpful villagers offered to direct us back to civilisation. Elmer got sunburnt across the shoulders.

We sweated and thirsted and roasted, and felt it would be easier to shrivel up and die. And found nothing.

In the early evening, we set off back to Colombo, footsore, tired and despondent. Elmer drove, while I caressed blistered feet and Lindsay sat behind us, staring gloomily out of the window. Palm trees and beaches and railway lines scudded by, together with tiny gleaming bays and the dark hulks of fishing canoes. The way I felt I hoped I would never see sun or sea or sand again.

Then Lindsay said, "Do you see that?"

I turned and looked back. "It's a temple," I said.

"Is that all?" she asked.

I looked harder. There was a little dagoba rising above a cluster of palm trees. There was nothing remarkable about that. One saw little dagobas everywhere and this one didn't look particularly special.

"What's so great about it?" I asked.

Lindsay shouted to Elmer to stop the car. We climbed out and she led us to the railway line. "Look," she said, "There's a man going to the temple. He's holding his clothes over his head and walking into the sea."

The temple was on a tiny island about thirty yards from shore. I still didn't see anything worth stopping for.

"He's got to get to the temple some way," I explained. "Perhaps he hasn't got a boat."

"Why do you think anyone would build a temple there?"

At the time all I could think of was gallons of cold beer and sleep in an air conditioned room. "I don't know," I said. "Perhaps it was an auspicious place."

Lindsay led us onto the beach. My feet curled with anguish. "Let me show you something else," she said.

The salt and the heat began to dehydrate me.

"See those rocks?" Lindsay asked pointing along the beach to where a clump of rocks showed up a slight embankment. They were not a natural formation and had obviously been placed there.

"The purpose of those rocks," Lindsay said, "Is to prevent soil erosion. Each year the sea encroaches on the land. You don't notice it but each year this coastline gets smaller and smaller. Those rocks have been placed there to help slow the process down." Without warning she flung her arms round Elmer and me. "Just think," she cried, "What could have happened in five hundred years!"

I thought. Five hundred years without even the primitive protection of strategically placed rock. Five hundred years of steady constant erosion. Why, even that island must have once been part of the mainland.

Elmer said, "If I follow you ma'am you're saying that the site of the pagode is away from the land and under the sea?"

"Right bazza," Lindsay cried. "You'd better get your diving boots on."

36

THE NEXT DAY I PURCHASED admiralty charts and looked. The next day I also resolved the problem of Rubeiro Diaz's map.

The admiralty charts showed that the sea bed along our part of the coast, sloped gradually. At a quarter of a mile it was not more than thirty feet deep. Which not only substantiated Lindsay's theory of erosion, but also made the whole lunatic idea possible.

Diving at under thirty feet we wouldn't need a team of divers, because we wouldn't have to spend time decompressing. Decompression only became necessary at depths in excess of thirty feet, when divers had to pause in their ascent to rid their bodies of accumulated nitrogen. Working at under thirty feet also meant that we could use scuba. Scuba was easily available, portable and cheap.

The man who sold me the admiralty charts had the slightly frantic, slightly frenzied air of an expert. I only mentioned my interest in cartography, when he was smiling all over me, showing me maps to explain that atlases did not attain their current day accuracy until after 1700. Before that, he said, half the world was unexplored and little known and looked as if he had personally contributed to the end of that state of affairs. Even in the middle of the sixteenth century, he told me, the basis of popular atlases was Ptolemy's *Geography,* Ptolemy's maps were completed about 150 A.D. and updated to take into account the discoveries of the new world. For example, the Strasbourg edition of Ptolemy published in 1530 had twenty modern maps and the Basel edition, printed in 1545, thirty-two. Ceylon was not however one of the updated maps. He showed me, taking the backing off a print of Ptolemy's map of Ceylon, that I had seen earlier in the Museum.

It was part of the Basel edition, squid shaped, yellow and pink and blue, with a hand drawn range of mountains running down the centre of the island. There was a galleon in one corner, not drawn to scale and a flotilla of little islands. There was also a pink and white equator cutting across the lower sixth of the island.

I thanked the expert, and left. Rubeiro Diaz had not been a sailor. He had been an intellectual who could read and write and was going perhaps on his second sea journey. What could be more natural than that he should take with him his atlas so that he could know where he went.

* * *

Lindsay said, "I'll buy that. I'll recommend the manuscript to the Reede Museum."

I said, "That's fine." Now I only had Harvid and Barney to worry about.

Elmer said, "Have you thought, that there really is a fortune lying under thirty foot of water."

I thought about it and said, "Well?"

Lindsay said, "Fantastic! I've dived all around the Barrier Reef, but diving for treasure, wow!"

Elmer smiled softly. "One for all, all for one," he said. "Let's go."

* * *

I spent the rest of the day organising the hire of diving equipment, snorkels, masks, fins, knives, weight belts, regulators, a dozen American type scubas holding seventy-two cubic feet of air and painted a bright yellow. Elmer disappeared somewhere and returned with two sweating coolies and a tired looking Bauer Utilus compressor, six spare filter units and enough compressor oil to run a battleship. Lindsay swopped the Peugeot for a Volkswagen Kombi, shod on locally made Kelani tyres, two of which were rather worn.

We left early that evening. Our destination was Matara, a hundred miles south of Colombo, hardly six miles from the spot Lindsay had picked as the probable site of the temple. She'd picked a spur of rock jutting out into the sea which she'd noticed on our trek. It was within a league of a deeper bay, where Diaz could have anchored and was close enough to the site of the other Vishnuite temple, which the Portuguese had also sacked. In any case, if she proved to be wrong, we had ten days to find the right stretch of water.

Matara was a small, shabby town dominated by a single towering rampart. The Rest House huddled underneath it, looking over the narrow, empty streets of the Fort with its gloomy Dutch architecture and drooping banyan trees, and on the other side, faced the sea. It would never have been elected the most swinging town of the year. We were its only visitors.

Our rooms were particularly large, big enough to store all our equipment in, sheer height and width making the wood framed beds under the mosquito nets look diminutive amongst all that bare floor. The rooms led off to open verandahs and the sea breeze made up for the fact that it wasn't air conditioned.

It was all very quiet, very peaceful, idyllic. I felt, as I had done that afternoon in Galle, that quietude could be its own reward.

* * *

The next morning we left early, covering the six miles or so to the site in hardly any time at all. We stopped at a small, rocky inlet, fringed with a narrow strand of beach and lined by tall swaying palms. The spur that Lindsay had picked, jutted into the sea like a long finger.

We decided to follow the spur of rock as far as it went, and then sweep on either side of it. The dinghy would be anchored at a central point to give us a bearing and we would take turns sitting in it. It was a simple, primitive method of searching, but we had neither the time nor the money for much else.

We'd changed in the Volkswagen and I'd finished inflating the dinghy when we hit trouble. Trouble in the shape of a horde of natives, running along the beach towards us, bare bodied, brightly coloured sarongs hoisted above their knees, and carrying knives that made my Grisbi look like a toothpick. They surrounded the Volkswagen and us, in a shouting, gesticulating mass. We pantomimed incomprehension and wondered what to do.

There was no way of getting the Volkswagen out without running over some of them and inciting them to further violence. There was no way in which we could understand them or they us. I was jerked out of a horrible nightmare in which I was being slashed to ribbons by a vicious knife, by an elderly man who thrust his way through the crowd and stared at me through the single lens of his gold rimmed bi-focals and said, "You must not fish here."

He was a short, weedy character with beetle stained teeth and a face that looked as if it stayed up over candlelight, studying workshop manuals.

I said, "We aren't going to fish."

He translated and came back at me. "If you aren't going to fish, why are you going to the water?"

"For fun."

There was a roar of disbelief, and much waving of knives. Someone began to prod exploratively at the dinghy.

"Leave us alone," Lindsay said. "We don't mean you any harm."

He didn't bother to translate that. He simply said, "Don't stay. Not unless you want to get dynamited."

The crowd had grown more silent. They had also grown more restive. The man was still prodding the dinghy.

"You mean they dynamite fish around here?" I asked One Lens.

"Yes, sir," he said. "And if you don't do what they say, they'll drop some on you."

It seemed as good a reason as any for kissing goodbye to a fortune.

Elmer said, "Tell me, sir, what would these good people lose, if we fished here?"

The translation brought rapid discussion and an equally rapid shaking of heads. The dinghy prodder returned to the fold.

The knives I noticed, were lowered.

The translator summarised the conference. "They say, sir, that you must not fish here. That you will frighten away the fish."

"How many fish, sir?" Elmer asked. "And how much?"

More discussion. A few heads nodding this time. Even a couple of smiles.

"Tell them," Elmer said, "I will give then six hundred rupees if they will let me fish in their waters."

The heads moved vehemently. The dinghy prodder returned to the attack. The smiles turned to raucous laughter.

The translator said, "They say you can do it for seven hundred and fifty."

Elmer reached for his wallet. A group leader appeared and took charge of the money. He pointed along the bay apparently showing us where we could dive, or the area of his domain, I wasn't sure which.

All that I knew was that this payment halved our diving time to five days. For all our sakes, I hoped Lindsay was right.

37

WE ONLY HAD ONE HALF of a wet suit and no one the right size for it. I'd contented myself with an old T shirt and cotton shorts. I was pleased to see that Lindsay had done the same, even though hers said, "Make Love Not War." Fat chance of either.

The fact that she hadn't displayed herself in a bikini, meant three things. That she had dived before, and I mean really dived, not just ducking her head under water and looking at the pretty fishes. It meant she wasn't going to turn all feminine on me if she saw a moray eel or a shark and that she intended to do her share of work and be treated like one of the fellers. Well, if I had a choice, I'd . . . Stop drooling, Maasten. The young lady has made it quite clear you don't have a choice anyway.

After we'd gone a few yards in the dinghy, I dropped over the side into the warmest clearest water I'd ever dived in. Below me the spur of rock was like a lunar landscape, dark and black, teeming with fish and coral. I kept kicking so that Elmer wouldn't have to make all the locomotive effort, and saw Lindsay's long white body flash down, parallel to me. We moved over an outcrop of stagshorn coral, beautiful violet tipped flaring tendrils, watched a school of brilliant red parrot fish dart into a crevice trailing tiny white shreds of excreted coral, watched a silvery blue gourami dart across the face of the rock. Lying face down, supported by the water, the sun warm on our backs, moving effortlessly, I felt a new sense of freedom, of elation and the mundane problems of smuggling and robberies and sunken fortunes seemed a long, long way away.

All of thirty yards away. Elmer parked where the spur of rock ended and the real work began. For the first couple of hours Lindsay and I quartered the area methodically, hovering over pale cream sand and rock, over yellow and brown striped angel fish and scurrying squid. It was a very pleasant way to find a fortune.

Five hundred years was a long time, I thought, to look for something under the sea. Hell, five years was long enough. Everything that sinks to the bottom of the sea, gets silted up, flattened, with time it takes on an overgrowth of sand and coral and if it has cavities it becomes a home for fish to breed and live in. In time it assumes the form of, and becomes indistinguishable from, its marine habitat, and you could swim over it for a thousand years and never know it was there.

Unless you were lucky. Unless you were out just after a monsoon and found the rain had swept the sand away, or a wayward current had left an unusual shape on the pale cream sea bed. If you felt lucky enough, or mad enough, it was worth-while spending a few days of your life looking for a jade phallus, two and a half foot long and thick as the neck of a man, and to look for two life size statues made of gold. With the prices of West African jade masks being what they were, I reckoned that little lot was worth all of one hundred thousand pounds. Even if we had to sell in a hurry.

That day we weren't lucky. We dived or rather lay, face down on the water, looking at the pale cream sand and sandstone rock, looking at flat, brown organic brain coral and large green cabbage patches, watching white pectoralled butterfly fish and stubby, cigar-like sea slugs. But not the minutest trace of a ruined temple.

We returned exhausted, but exhilarated. Sea and sun does that for you. Four days to go and the chance of a fortune slip-ping away every hour, didn't seem all that momentous. Not if you had been hooked by the sea.

It was only when we got back to the rest house, that the day was spoilt. Inspector Harvid was there.

He was seated on the verandah facing the sea, bare feet raised up onto the extended arm of the chair. His gangster's tie was yanked half way down his chest and he had a bottle of Lion Lager and two glasses on a stool beside him.

He sat up as I entered. "Good evening Mr. Maasten, what a pleasant surprise." He said it in the tone of a man used to pleasant surprises.

I said good evening and busied myself with unloading the VW. Harvid made no move to help. After I had finished unloading, and after Elmer and Lindsay had gone to their rooms, I went over to him.

"I was waiting to hear from you," he said and poured beer into the glasses. It tasted as flat as it looked, so it had probably been standing there all afternoon. I sighed. Even Police Inspectors were having to watch their expenses.

"You'll hear from me, when I've something to say."

"That is a shame," Harvid said. "I thought we had an arrangement. When I heard that you had checked out of the hotel and come down here, my first thought was that you were with Goldman." He shrugged the heavy shoulders. "But I am disappointed. No Goldman, no information, nothing. So I've come to talk to you."

A brooding silence fell between us, while I waited for him to talk to me. At last Harvid said, "Interpol have asked us to trace you. I understand the Moroccan police are interested."

It was nice and slow and casual, like a six inch sliver of steel between my ribs.

Harvid said, "There's also the question of this man, Ponsonby. He drank too much, fell out of a hotel window and died. You knew him, didn't you?"

Again the question that brooked no denial. "How did he die?" I asked. "Was it an accident, did he commit suicide, or what?" It was as good a performance as I could give under the circumstances.

Harvid looked at me gravely. "I was hoping you could tell me that."

"I didn't know Ponsonby very well. We met in Morocco."

"In what connection?"

Art dealing was out. Air Chartel was out too. "We met through a mutual acquaintance," I said, and that was in a sense true. "Stavros Dirkian."

"Stavros Dirkian," Harvid repeated thoughtfully. "Tell me why I should know that name."

"He was in Ceylon during the rebellion. He hired a boat, I think from Latif, and was sailing around here."

"I remember," Harvid said. "The Galle police searched that boat for arms about five days after Dirkian had left Ceylon. Communications aren't very good here, at the best of times. I suppose then, it was much worse." He looked across the verandah, at the sea. "There was something else. Diaz and his daughter. They each drove down from Colombo to pick up Dirkian. Very noble, a three hour drive through a riot torn country to fulfil their obligations to a customer. At least that's what Diaz said."

"Diaz isn't concerned in arms smuggling?"

"He isn't. I checked him out myself. What was Ponsonby's connection with Dirkian?"

"I think Dirkian let him down on a deal."

"What deal?"

"He never told me. Perhaps it was arms."

"And Goldman?"

"He was involved, too."

"What about you?"

"I never did business with Dirkian," I said.

Harvid asked, "What's your involvement in all this, Mr. Maasten?"

"You," I said. "I was here buying art for the Reede Museum, remember.

Harvid gave me a thin smile. "But you are involved, Mr. Maasten. Tell me what you think of all this. Arms, Ponsonby's death, Goldman?"

I made a great show of thinking. Even Rodin would have been impressed. "I think Dirkian was an arms smuggler and that during the rebellion he was forced to abandon a shipment of arms. It's quite easy to do, if the goods are properly wrapped."

Harvid looked at me, strangely.

I went on, without the expertise, "Goldman was associated with Dirkian, and the dagoba robbery was to pay for the arms which hadn't been delivered. Goldman is now looking for the arms."

"Go on," Harvid said in a soft voice.

"This is only a theory, mind you, but Ponsonby paid for those arms, and he came here looking for them, too."

"And Goldman pushed Ponsonby out of a hotel window?"

I shrugged.

"Where are the arms?"

"I think they're off the coast, near here."

"And you're looking for them?"

"Pretending to look. As long as Goldman thinks I know where they are, he'll follow me here. Heaven knows, I left an obvious enough trail."

Harvid sat, looking thoughtful. I hated to do this to someone like Harvid, but it was the only way. If I told him the whole truth and nothing but, he'd have no option but to hold me for Interpol and the Moroccan police. This way at least both of us could be temporarily happy.

Harvid continued looking thoughtful and asked, "What does Goldman want with the arms?"

"It's obvious," I said, and left the obvious conclusion to him. "They can't have capital tied up under the sea."

"You wouldn't know, if they had a customer waiting?"

"That is also possible," I said, with a show of reluctance.

Harvid was looking abstracted now. "You have a gun?"

"Where would I get a gun from?" I asked. "And what would I do with it?"

'I hear a mutual friend of ours met with an accident. He needed three stitches and he didn't do it shaving."

"I'm surprised. I've always found the local razor blades rather lethal."

"Our friend doesn't look so pretty," Harvid said, "And he resents that. He's not the sort of man to carry grudges lightly."

"Thanks for the warning," I said.

Harvid was telling me this to show how much he knew, and all the while, was thinking what to do about the arms.

Harvid sighed. "Unauthorised possession of weapons is a serious offence," he said. "Especially since the insurgency. Now if I were sure of Goldman . . ."

"You're sure of him," I said as confidently as I could.

"And the arms, and his contacts here."

"I can only do my best."

Harvid sighed again. "Communications in this country are getting worse," he said. "I suppose I could give it three more days. In three days they are considering me for promotion to Assistant Superintendent."

And then you'll be able to afford two decent beers, I thought, instead of one flat one.

Harvid stood up and yanked his tie up to his shirt collar.

"While you're diving, if you find anything that is valuable and over a hundred years old, remember it cannot be exported without a permit."

"Thanks for telling me," I said. "My only problem is knowing what's old and what's valuable."

* * *

That night I told Lindsay and Elmer about Latif and Diaz and Harvid and showed them the Webley. "From now on," I said, "whoever is in the boat keeps this."

"You don't expect—" Lindsay began.

"I do," I said. "I've deliberately left a trail for Goldman and he should be sniffing at it, about now. If he does show up he isn't going to be friendly."

"Why didn't you tell us before you left?" Elmer asked.

'There was no profit in worrying you unnecessarily. We've all had a great day, not worrying about anything. Let's keep it like that, and just be prepared."

Lindsay looked down at her plate. "I'm sorry, Nicholas," she said. "I didn't realise that going to the police would cause so many problems."

"It always does," I said. "But don't worry. Just make it up to me."

She gave me a mischievous grin. "One day," she said, "I just might."

But not that night.

* * *

The next morning was much the same. Sun, sea, fish and

coral. But no temple.

The afternoon was better. Lindsay diving ten yards beyond the mooring point towards the centre of the inlet, came up arms waving like a fan dancer, her cries thin and shrill against the wide expanse of sea and sky. Underneath her face mask she had a grin a mile wide and she was pointing excitedly downwards.

I snorkeled down and flattened out over the sea bed, feeling the pressure build in my ears, closing around my body, feeling the water grow a shade colder. Lying below me on the sea bed were broken bits of masonry. I drifted over them, the thud of my heart beat filling my ears. They looked like stone pilasters, and on one of them there was a definite carving of a peacock. Then it was time to go up.

We spent the next two hours using scuba and bringing up stones from the sea. Fragments of pillars with carved peacocks, a frieze of arms and tendrils, what looked like the lower part of a loin cloth and torso, a smiling face with streaming hair.

But no Siva. No Parvati. No jade phallus, but the masonry at least was something.

The next day was much the same. Lindsay took the centre of the inlet, and I stayed near the rock. Currents are funny things. Sometimes they can sweep solid objects for miles. For all we knew, the statues had been swept out to sea and were now somewhere between the southern tip of Ceylon and the South Pole.

But seriously, that was unlikely. I reckoned that while odd bits and pieces had been swept around, the bulk of the Temple was buried under the sand by the rock.

Yet all we found that day was more stone, and different fish and Elmer got stung by a coral. There were definitely no deities and definitely no fortune.

On the way back we had a flat tyre. Consequently we arrived at the rest house late, tense and ravenous. We left the unloading of the Volkswagen till after we'd eaten, then we got the gear out and parked the VW as usual under the lighted porch. I gave Lindsay a hand with the stones she'd added to her collection.

Her room was as large as mine, with the same diminutive twin single beds and the same off white mosquito net. In a row, by the door were the previous day's stones. I squatted and laid today's additions beside them. From behind me, Lindsay gasped. "Nicholas, I think a couple of the stones are missing!"

"You're sure," standing up fast.

"Yes. The streaky haired one with the smiling face. That's gone. And the one with the fan tail of the peacock."

I looked slowly around the room. Lindsay dropped her aqualung by the head of the bed and said, "I can't understand it."

I couldn't understand it either. I mean a few pounds of stone aren't something you casually pick up and walk away with like a packet of cigarettes.

"Who's got the gun?" I asked.

"Elmer."

At that moment the aqualung clattered to the floor. I jumped six feet and came down with my knife in my hand.

Lindsay looked very white, and as the lung rolled along the floor she gave a tiny laugh. "We're as ratty as hell," she said.

"What's that?" I asked pointing to a stream of water trickling out from underneath her pillow.

"I don't know," she said.

I waved her behind me and advanced towards the bed, knife fully extended. Arm still outstretched I stuck the knife into the pillow and lifted it away. Underneath the pillow lay a burst bag of paper thin plastic and amongst its remains was a small, speckled, cone shaped object, with a thin point, and two diagonal brown bands.

"It's a shell!" Lindsay cried delightedly, pushing past my extended arm. "A lovely shell! Now who—"

I dropped the knife and grabbed her. Instinctively she struggled. I jammed my knee into her back, forcing her upright. Then recovering my balance I flung her around, away from the bed.

She turned to face me, eyes blazing. "What the hell!" she cried. "Keep your—"

I stood between her and the bed. "Don't touch that shell," I said. I wished I had a cigarette, and realised I'd gone a whole day without smoking. "It's got a sting that can kill you."

"That little thing!" She moved towards the bed.

"That little thing," I said, "is a species of cone shell and it has a sting that protrudes far beyond the shell. It is very, very nasty."

"You're serious!" she said and stopped. Lindsay watched as I eased the shell to the floor with my knife, then picked up one of the stones and used it as a hammer.

"You'd better get the gun from Elmer," I said. "Unless you'd like me to stay and protect you."

She gave me a weak smile. "Perhaps tonight, the gun," she said.

"OK," I grinned. I reckoned she really believed in fates worse than death.

* * *

I hefted my own scuba along the verandah, went into my room and stopped, and let the scuba down quietly inside the door. My room was empty, but I had an uneasy feeling that there was someone there. And there was a smell. A strong smell of tobacco smoke. Caporal tobacco. Gauloise.

I eased the knife out of its sheath again and moved across the floor to the shabby grey door of the bathroom. There was no covering on the bare cement, and my progress must have been as audible as a herd of buffalo. I made the bathroom door, and heard a soft, distinct movement. I gently rested my hand on the knob and even more gently, twisted it.

The door opened with a creak. The light in the bathroom was on and there was a slight, tousle haired figure crouching in front of the mirror.

"Come on in," Cindy said. "I was just prettying myself for you."

15—TPF * *

38

SHE'D DONE MORE THAN THAT. She'd used my room as if it were her own. She'd used my bath and a floppy pair of jeans and a pale, green smock hung from the hook by the door. She was wearing an off white, high chested, short sleeved dress that fell to about half way down her thighs. "How are you Nicholas?" she asked. "Why don't you put that knife away."

I sheathed the knife and stood aside to let her into the bedroom. "What are you doing here?"

She stood in the centre of the room with her back to me. Then she turned, brushing an invisible curl away from her face. "I was on my way to Tissa," she said. "One of our cars has broken down and I was going to bring the passengers back."

"And you stopped here," I said, "just like that."

"Just like that," she said and giggled.

And perhaps someone gave you a textile cone shell, I thought, and you just happened to lose it under Lindsay's pillow.

"What do you know about shells?" I asked. "Nasty, vicious shells that sting."

Cindy laughed hesitantly, took out a Gauloise and placed it between her full lips. She waited for me to light it.

I went over to her and grabbed her by the shoulders. "What kind of game are you playing?" I asked. "Don't you know those things can kill?"

She stared sullenly at my chest and took the cigarette from my mouth. "They can't," she said. "And it was only a joke."

"Stop joking, then," I said, "and tell me what you're doing

here."

She lifted her shoulders and sighed. "I told you," thrusting her chin out at me. "If you really want to know, I stopped here for dinner. I saw your name in the register and decided to say hello."

"In my room?"

"I didn't want you coming in and going out again."

Like where, I thought. Matara was one of those towns where when you got home, you stayed home.

"I've got my own room," she said. "If you'd like me to go."

"And the shell," I said. "Tell me about that."

"I bought it from a boy who brought it to the rest house."

"But why Lindsay, for God's sake!"

She lowered her head. "Sunil told me," she said, "about her and you. And I thought, if she was ill . . . perhaps . . . we could go diving, like you said."

"You vicious little bitch," I said.

"I'm sorry, Nicholas. I didn't mean to hurt her. Honestly, I didn't. I just thought you would come back to Colombo and then go away and we wouldn't meet and—"

"Leave it," I said, and released her.

We stared at each other. "Tell me," I said, "about the day you went down to Galle to pick up Dirkian and Claude."

"There's nothing to tell. I simply drove down to Galle and brought Dirkian back to Colombo."

"Harvid thinks you were very brave."

"Oh Harvid!" she cried. "That man! He looks under every palm tree for plots to overthrow the government. After we brought Dirkian back, they questioned my father and me for two days. Harvid thought Dirkian was smuggling arms."

"Was he?"

"I told you they were diving."

"What happened to Claude?"

"He left, before the rebellion started. He had to go back to his architect's business in Italy."

"Tell me more about Claude," I said.

"There's nothing to tell."

"How did you get on with him?"

She hesitated. "Alright."

"I mean did you like him?"

"Stop it!" She cried. "Stop it! Of course I liked Claude! I liked him very much! Is that what you wanted to know?"

"Yes," I said. "Where's Claude now?"

Her face clouded. "I don't know."

I asked, "Why did you run away from me at the hospital?"

She said, "I didn't know why you'd come. I thought you had done Sunil harm."

I shook my head. "I wouldn't do that."

"I know now," she said. "Sunil fell off a train."

"Is that what he said?"

She nodded. "And he said to thank you for the bread."

"When did you start smoking French cigarettes?"

She looked at the cigarette between her fingers. "A client gave them to me."

"Who?"

"I don't know. A French couple, I picked up at the airport."

"You're sure they were a couple?"

"Of course. They came in on an UTA flight and I dropped them at the Taprobane. The next day I took them shopping. Why?"

"No reason," I said.

She said, "If you want me to go, I'll go," and moved towards the door. Slowly.

I hesitated. As Lindsay had so correctly analysed, the first time we'd met, I was confused. "OK," I said. "Wait."

She turned. Her lips trembled into a smile. Suddenly, without realising it, we were both moving across the room, hands reaching for each other, mouths searching, pressing against each other as though our lives depended upon it. And I was still confused.

When we broke away, she turned and raised her hands to the back of her neck. "Undo me," she said.

My fingers slipped on the hooks and then she was easing the dress over her head, standing slim and erect and practically naked. I unhooked the bra and felt her breasts surge free. Then I turned her around and ran my hands slowly down her smooth body.

She was lovely. Petite and lovely with skin like marble. Wide shoulders and perfect round apples of breasts, the nipples standing dark and pointed against the pale coffee of her skin. Small waist, large hip bones jutting away from the flat stomach, legs that were straight and soft, seemingly covered with puppy fat, beautiful dimpled knees.

Her hands touched the top of my shorts. I never heard my shirt fall to the ground. My ears were full of a tripping, thudding sound, my body aching with desire.

Arms round each other, lips locked in warm moistness, I moved her to the bed, stooping over her as she sat, moving her backwards and sideways, rolling the thin wisp of panties from under the back of her upraised thighs.

Mouth closed over mouth again, and I could feel her body spread out against me, soft, yet firm, smooth, cool, stark. An arm came round pressing my back, a hand pressed my head into her face. I felt her begin to move with me, gently, easily, slowly at first, guiding me with an arm, I felt darkness closing around us, darkness and the cool liquid sea, I was drifting, floating, aware of light and sensation, of warm moistness and of Cindy stretched below me, her body straining upwards, movement, rhythm, soft delicious, lubricous, great yawning chasms of desire, moving together, faster, faster, her eyes screwing shut, sweat starting, binding us in a moist curtain, desperate, desperate, now, Cindy tearing her mouth away, her fingers kneading my back, her nails scarring, her body moving under me, and twisting, twisting, and a great thunder clap like bomb bursts.

For a long while after, I lay on her, face buried in the pillow by her cheek, listening to the soft murmur of the sea, feeling the steady, quieting throb of my heart. Spent. Months, years later, Cindy moved from underneath. I heard the scrape of a match, smelt cigarette smoke.

"Want one?"

"I'm trying to give it up."

A long hiss of breath. "That was lovely, Nicky, darling," she said.

I turned and looked at her, arms cradling the curly tousled head, her body dark against the white sheet, knees bent, smoking.

"You taste of salt," she said.

I kept looking at her, resting on one elbow. "I'll have a shower soon. And we'll do it again."

"Yes," she said. "Please."

* * *

It was a long and glorious night, warm, beautiful, moving slowly into delightful nothingness. Once she pulled me tightly to her. "Don't leave me," she murmured from warm sleep. "Please don't leave me, darling, never, ever."

The way Claude had, I thought, holding her, thinking that there had been riots and no public transport, thinking of Claude and Dirkian putting into Galle and that anything might have happened to them there. I thought of Cindy driving down to fetch them, ignoring the fact that anything could have happened to her too, and Diaz following, hoping to protect everyone with his Webley. I thought of Cindy getting to Galle and finding there was only Dirkian.

I kissed her, feeling the dampness against her cheek.

"Don't go, please don't go," she muttered.

I held her close, trying to keep away the pain, trying to bring forgetfulness. The trouble with life, I thought, was that nothing ever lasted and you never, ever knew.

In the morning she was gone. All that was left was the depression on the pillow, a lipsticked cross on my bathroom mirror and a pleasant, relaxed, loved feeling throughout my entire body.

39

THAT DAY I FELT I HAD TO BE LUCKY. That day I felt nothing else could happen.

I looked at Lindsay, sitting all curled up in the side of the dinghy, Lindsay looking carefree and abandoned, her salt straightened hair tied in a tight knot at the back of her head, the face mask glinting under her neck, I looked at Lindsay lying on bent elbows, bent knees raised on the inflated curves of the dinghy, thighs slapping flat against the rubber. I had a delicious vision of Cindy and the thought of pleasure past sent a strong flame of desire licking right through me. Again. Desire for Lindsay. Not Cindy. Confused as ever.

I tore my eyes away and looked over the flat, rippling sea. About two miles out to the right, a regular effluorescence of breakers marked a reef, fronting the deep bay in which Diaz had anchored. I leaned forward over the side and went in, temporarily confounding confusion. I let the boat drag, streaming, cool, and as the Moon Crater rock face flowed below me, I knew that today we were going to be lucky.

It happened quite late that morning. I'd been diving on the further side of the spur, away from the inlet. It happened as I was making my way back, and thinking it was time for lunch.

A school of Moorish idols darted underneath me, yellow and brown and triangular heading for the inlet side of the rock. I followed them round it and came face to face with a lost, baby grouper, all bulbous eyes and meditative gills, thick negroid lips and grey and brown camouflage. We stopped, suspended in mid water and eyed each other, both equally interested.

Then with a heavy twist of its flatulent body it was off and pressure closed in on me with a soft muffled bang.

My body shot forwards, upwards. I glimpsed vicious, jagged rock. My face mask tore away. My eyes stung with salt and felt as if they would pop. Water streamed into my nose and the sea bed flashed below me in an endless stream of multi coloured fish. A glimpse of light through a heavy curtain, more rock, more whirling fish. And then my head erupted through the water, damp hair streaming in front of my eyes. I spat out my mouthpiece and breathed deep, hoping I'd had reflexes enough to exhale as I was flung upwards.

Ten yards in front of me, the dinghy floated, one side of it wrinkled like a collapsed bladder. A deep black glittering blob in the centre of the bay, told me Lindsay was alright. But no sign of Elmer.

Kicking hard I raced for the dinghy, seeing the light silvery splash as Lindsay cut through the water to it, too.

The sea below me was unbelievable. Gone was the smooth, calm, pale cream sand, the placidly swimming schools of fish. Below me was a maelstrom of whirling and twisting sand, and through the viscous cloud, I could see that the sea bed was littered with thousands of wriggling, silvery, mangled bodies. The sea above was worse.

It was filling up with boats and humans, bumping dangerously over the spur, shouting, laughing, diving into the water with great silvery splashes. Bastards, I thought, swimming desperately, bastards. That was no way to kill fish. Or people.

The dinghy was listing heavily when I reached it. Elmer lay huddled on the twisting floor, a lump half the size of a squash ball, striped by a mottled band of red, lifting up his sandy crew cut. I put an arm round the boat and started dragging it to the shore. Loaded with Elmer and the spare scubas, with air hissing out of the gash on its side, the boat felt like a ton of water-logged sponge. My arm ached with the strain, and for all my desperate kicking, we hardly seemed to move at all.

I cursed, turned on my side and yanked. The boat lurched after me, and hissed. I faced the shore, thrust my head down and kicked. Kicked like I'd never kicked before. No time now to look at the carnage in the sea bed. Just look at the beach, look at the tiny rock strewn strand of yellow and the dusty, biscuit coloured VW.

Lindsay's head emerged beside me, streaming. The boat jolted, dipped, moved a little lighter.

"Push it," I panted. "If it sinks, grab Elmer." Aqualungs were expendable.

One of the sides had already collapsed. Water was swirling in and the dinghy wallowed heavily. I could feel the wet drag of its soggy rubber against my flashing heels and I turned and yanked again. And again. And again, till I was able to turn round and stand on the sea bed, dragging the collapsing dinghy after me till I felt it scrape along the bottom.

I bent, kicked off my flippers and hurled them onto the sand. Then I stooped down and picked up Elmer. He was only little, and he was only wearing shorts and T-shirt, but he felt like three hundredweights of blanket. My weakness, or his limpness. Lindsay swung our sodden clothes over her shoulder, picked up the lungs and dragged them after her onto the beach. The dinghy sank with a sucking, gurgling sound, spreading out flat and yellow under the restless sea.

I laid Elmer down in the long, thin shadow of the VW. His eyes were still closed and there was a thin stream of froth bubbling out of his mouth. Mysteriously, his glasses were still on his face, intact. I hoped to hell he hadn't drowned when we were dragging the dinghy ashore. I grabbed his wrist and held it up. The pulse was still there, throbbing slowly, persistently. But there.

Lindsay handed me a glass of orange juice and a damp shirt which I placed under Elmer's head. It seemed an eternity before he opened his eyes and said, "What happened, sir?"

"You got mugged," I said grimly. "And someone dropped a load of dynamite in the bay."

The inlet was still full of fishing craft, and swooping, whooping bodies.

Elmer closed his eyes.

"How do you feel?"

"My head hurts," he said.

I fed him orange juice.

Later when he could sit up, we placed him in the back of the transport and drove back to the rest house. By the time we got there he was able to take a genuine interest in things, but I insisted that he went to bed, and sent for a doctor.

Elmer still didn't know what had happened. He'd been sitting in the dinghy, looking over the inlet, keeping an eye for sharks and intruders and trouble. He'd felt a tug on the side of the dinghy behind him. Before he could turn, his head had exploded. And that was all he knew; except that the Webley had slipped from his grasp to the bottom of the sea.

40

THE DOCTOR CAME AND SAID he'd always thought diving was a dangerous sport. He dressed Elmer's wound and said if he wouldn't go to hospital, could he try to do nothing for two days. That left me with a whole, long afternoon, seven unused scuba and the fading possibility of finding a fortune under the sea.

"I'm going back," I said to Lindsay. "I'm going to finish what we started."

She put down the book she was reading, and stood up. "I'll come too," she said.

An extra pair of eyes would be useful, I thought. Perhaps even an extra pair of hands. "OK," I said, "But this time it's going to be different. We don't go into the water together." I explained that the sea was full of dead and mangled fish. "It will attract sharks," I said, "and even though they don't normally eat divers, I'd like to know if one of them is sitting on my tail."

"Only sharks?" Lindsay asked.

"Or predatory humans," I said.

"Right on," she said, walking towards the transport. "What do I warn you with?"

"You could try blasting the horn," I said. "Or drive the Volkswagen into the sea."

She reached out and squeezed my shoulder tightly. Then she opened the door and stepped up into the driver's cab.

*   *   *

When we got there, the inlet was deserted. No ships, no boats. No one. Lindsay parked the transport at the water's edge. "We'll take turns," she said. She meant it too.

I turned and looked at her. I felt sure she knew that it was not only the statues I was after. "OK," I said. "When my air runs out."

Once more the squeeze on the shoulder, suddenly the moist full lips pressing against mine. Then I was walking across the beach and stepping backwards into the water. I kept going till the water was slapping round the weight belt at my waist. Lindsay was standing on the footboard of the VW looking out. We waved and I turned round and swam out along the spur of rock.

The sea bed below was almost normal. It was murkier than yesterday, full of tiny swirling grains of white sand. Here and there the shadows of waves rippled over silver corpses of fish. The beautiful violet tipped stagshorn coral was no longer there and part of the cabbage coral had shattered like a broken plate. A few fish swam frantically, darting into the shelter of the rock.

I reached the end of the spur and stopped, letting the gentle waves brush lightly against me. I had come back that afternoon to finish what we'd started. And dynamite wasn't going to stop me. Whoever dropped it. This time I would be ready and waiting. Brave thoughts in a pliant sea.

I moved out to where the dinghy had been moored. And as I drew closer I saw that here, things had changed. The whole sea bed looked like a bombed, abandoned village, no fish, no gentle slope of sand, only irregular churned up hills and the black ridges of valleys.

I switched the air on, tested with two swift sucks and swooped down, moving freely, lightly, without sound, or weight. At fifteen feet my ears began to hurt and I cleared them, blowing my nose and going on down. The hills and valleys had been caused by the shovelling of sand, thrown out by the explosion. I patted them, prodded them. They were soft, malleable, concealing only more sand.

I moved away out of the inlet, around to the front of the spur. Here the sea bed was more churned up, revealing protruding stone pillars, mounds of flattened rubble. I swam over it looking, my ears filling with the steady rush of my breathing, in . . . out . . . in . . . out, a sturdy, reassuring sound, confirmation that I was still alive, though surrounded by water. The human body is a wonderful thing. You spend years breathing and never noticing it. You could live a lifetime without noticing it, till it stops or you have to do it a special way.

I knew I could stay under for around forty-five minutes, so I took my time hovering and looking. I ceased thinking about breathing and moved around the humps. This was probably where the temple had stood, roofless, stone pillars pointing at the sky. It had probably stood there for years, abandoned, desolate, covered with thicket and creepers and each year, the sea had drawn closer and closer washing over the platform, swirling over the umbrella of cobras, eroding away the stone from the pillar. Till one day the sea had taken it.

I was so busy hovering and looking that I didn't see the upraised arm till the top of my head touched it. I backed away, startled. I lifted my chin and looked. It looked like an arm, bent double, poking out of the sand. It was a shadowy, dark brown, the colour of bark in autumn and it was covered with a scaly encrustation. Behind it was another arm without hand or fingers. The whoosh whoosh of my breathing accelerated. I could hear my heart tripping with excitement. I flung myself to the sea bed and began to scrape away sand.

Sand curled away from my fingers in muddy twisted wisps, sand whirled around the hole that appeared in the middle of the cloud. I reached through the hole and touched. Solid, hard, scaly. I tore away the sand and looked. A breastplate, part of a torso. The Siva was there, under thirty feet of water and two of sand.

I'd spent nearly fifteen minutes under and I decided not to stay with the Siva any longer. There was no hope of my excavating it, and even if I did, no hope of taking it back to the shore with me. I decided to look for the Parvati and the jade. If the Siva was there, they must be nearby, and heaven knew, they might be easier to transport.

It was then I saw the scuba lying abandoned on the sea bed. It was bent over at an angle, with a large dent across its middle. The regulator had been torn off and tattered yellow strips of plastic harness floated from it. I dived down and took a closer look.

The scuba was full of water and the dent had nearly chopped it in half. Most of the paint had flaked off and the body was corroded, but not corroded enough to prevent me reading the stencilled lettering about the mouth of the scuba. It read, C S RI.

I moved away looking. So Claude Cesari had met with an accident while diving, and drowned. And Dirkian, already suspected of arms smuggling, hadn't dared report it to the authorities. He'd sailed back to Galle, driven to Colombo and flown away. Except Diaz had guessed, or known. Hence the photograph in Dirkian's safe, hence the regular payments to Diaz's bank account in Switzerland.

I combed the area for about ten minutes and moved on without finding any other traces of Claude Cesari. Human flesh does not last as long under water as metal or bronze.

The Parvati was only a few yards away, lying on its side, only its ankles embedded in sand. The beautiful face was discoloured, corroded, the perfect round breasts pockmarked with holes. I lingered over it and decided it too could wait. I moved to find the jade.

It was the jade I really wanted. Unlike the statues it wouldn't have been affected by its long immersion and if it wasn't buried in the sand, it was probably light enough to take back with me.

I swam over it twice, before I saw it. It looked like a shadow on the sea bed. Stiff and immobile, a single column whose green matched that of the sea. It was only when I realised that the shadow was impervious to the movement of the water that I went down to it. And touched it. And swam around it and saw the places where it has been chipped and the holes where the sapphires had been set. And decided to take it back with me.

Getting my hands underneath it was the most difficult part, that and raising it the first few inches. After the first few inches all I had to do was hang on to it. It was smooth as polished aluminium and I had to roll it onto my forearms and hold it in front of me like a baby. And then I had to move very slowly. If I became unbalanced or moved hurriedly the column would drop into the water, and if that happened, I might never roll it back onto my forearms again.

Moving slowly through the water, the column seemed to weigh about ten pounds. Deliberately I swam at about fifteen feet, hoping that the pressure of the water would keep it at that weight, until I reached the shore. I passed over the mooring site and moved against the rock, looking down at the rapidly smoothing sea bed, looking ahead trying to see it rise shallowly to the beach. One of the problems of wearing a face mask is that while you can see perfectly well ahead of you, and below you, you have no side vision at all. And no rear vision either.

So when the diver streaked out at me from the back and from the right, I never saw him. Not, that is, until the tip of his flippers puffed sand in front of my face. I twisted my head and turned my body and felt the column go, saw the masked figure leaning over me with an outstretched arm holding a knife.

Instinctively I kicked sideways. My legs locked against a solid knee and then his body dropped on top of me, feather-light, but only at first. His weight soon crushed me, pressing me to the bottom and as we fell I twisted round to face him and reached out for the knife. My head bounced against the sea bed, then the scuba cut into my body. His face mask knocked mine, sending a sharp ridge of pain across my face and bouncing my head onto the sand, again.

Still holding on to his knife arm I brought a knee up slowly, but our legs only tangled. I stared into magnified blue eyes, a clean shaven round face. I stared at floating strands of dark brown hair and a high pale forehead. I bounced against the bottom again, pulled up my legs, quickly this time, curved and rolled. I had leverage and I had the initiative and once I got him moving he was weightless.

I did a complete roll, landing astride him, pinning his knife arm to the sand. There was no power, no convenient edge for the quick dash of the wrist. Before he could spin me round I reached across and prised away the little finger of his knife hand.

The man reached up, tugging at my face mask. Water gurgled and the sound of my breathing was like an express train in a tunnel. Christ! At this rate I'd only have five minutes left! I twisted the finger back against the sand. I felt his body arch underneath me and whipped my wrist round. Extra bubbles gurgled from the mouthpiece, and as his finger snapped, the knife came free.

My face mask sprang back with a jar that should have ended my consumption of toothpaste for the foreseeable future. Not that the foreseeable future was all that long. I rolled away with the pain and he helped me with a push and a kick. I dragged round on the sea bed, momentarily confused, and then he launched himself at me. My midriff folded around his head. I moved upwards and cannoned against rock with a clang of metal. I kicked off from the rock bank and wrenched his face mask. He bounced me against the rock again, his mask now filling with water. I came off the rock, knees bent, protruding, jabbed him in the stomach, dived, slipped through his flailing legs and turned round.

He was facing the rock, adjusting his face mask. I floated up to him, grasped the thick curly hair and bashed his face into the rock. His head wriggled in my grasp, broke free, turned. A crack across the glass of the face mask, a small red stream across the nose.

He cartwheeled and tried to make for my legs. I tilted forward and leant on him. Sucking great lungfuls of air, I pushed him downwards. Hold on to him for fifteen seconds, I thought, and then let him go. But at the last moment he struggled and I pushed him further down. He landed face first on a wooden spur topped by a row of sea urchins that looked like black and spiky oranges.

I left him there and streaked to the surface. In those last few seconds there hadn't been any air coming through, and I thought if my assailant was any good at diving, he shouldn't be in any serious trouble. In pain yes, but no trouble.

My head broke the surface and I breathed in a great lungful of air. The horn of the VW was bleeping faintly, far away. And Lindsay was running into the water wearing a lung. I waved. She pointed. A split second later I heard the weight belt whizz through the air and five pounds of lead caught me behind the ear.

41

THE WORLD WAS ROCKING UNDER MY PROSTRATE BODY, rising and falling in a continuous dizzy rhythm. My body felt cold, fingers and toes like icicles. There was a steady, wet thrumming sound that mingled with the steady dry roaring in the middle of my skull. I opened my eyes. A sharp blinding stiletto of pain stabbed through my eye balls. I shut my eyes. Hurriedly.

I lay there and let the world rock around me. My head felt fuzzy, tired, my tongue dry and salty and swollen. I let the world get on with it. I was out for the duration.

Gradually the pain passed and let me feel. I felt my body moving, my body was moving with the world. The world was rocking and my body was rocking with it.

Something hard and bunched pressed into the small of my back, and there was a strange pain along my triceps. I tried to lift my body and found it was resting on my hands. And my hands were bound so tightly together that the ends of my fingers were tingling.

My legs were bound too, and my body kept moving. I imagined the best thing I could do, was to open my eyes. Or try to. I did it, slowly. No pain this time, at least not as bad as before. A ribbed wooden ceiling edged with white paint stretched above my upturned face. As I looked, the ceiling moved and I moved with it. I was lying on the floor of someone's boat.

I dropped my head to the left and looked at a row of green lockers underneath one of those long, bench type seats that never have enough room for your back or your legs. To my right were feet. Bronzed, bare, sandalled feet. Two pairs of them. And legs. Two pairs. Hairy. One pair smooth with skin like marble, straight and faintly podgy, the colour of pale coffee with beautiful dimpled knees.

Barney asked, "How do you feel man?"

I twisted and looked up at him, his bearded face flat against the ribbed ceiling. The pain stabbed again, and I shut my eyes. "How do you think? Bloody awful." My voice was a good imitation of a frog trying for bass.

Barney said, "You know you killed Karl?"

Karl? Karl who? Karl what? Who killed Karl. I remembered the man with the bulbous blue eyes and the smooth, round face, the man with the gun in Galle.

"I only urged him into some sea urchins. Couldn't he swim?"

"He drowned man, drowned. That was bad."

"Next time," I said, "Use a pro."

"We did man, we did." He pointed over his shoulder to Maurice, bearded and lachrymose.

Memory came slowly. I remembered that last lungful of air, the whizz of the belt. I remembered Lindsay coming into the water. And something else.

"You think you can sit up now?" Barney asked, "I want to talk to you."

"I'm thinking," I said. Yes there had been something else. Lindsay turning back from the water. Running across the beach back towards the Volkswagen. Good girl, I thought. Good, sensible girl who believed in fates worse than death.

Hands lifted me up and set me down on the bunk. I rested my head against a pane of vibrating glass that set off sympathetic rhythms underneath my brain. I moved away and tried to look at them. There were three of them in the cabin. Barney, Maurice, Cindy. The cabin itself was hardly large enough for them to stand in, flanked by glass windows, bordered by the built in bunk. To the left there was a small corridor, cabins on either side, a small stairway to a rear deck. To the right, a raised platform, a helm and Pierre's white trousered legs and a V shaped windscreen. I looked back at the rear deck. Strapped to it were two large, shrouded shapes. Our end of the shroud was open, revealing scaly, green brown metal, pitted with a couple of holes.

Barney said, "We got the statues."

I said, "You'll have to declare them to customs when you go ashore. That's the law."

We were moving steadily, surrounded by open sea. I wondered where they were taking me. And what for?

"It was a nasty trick," Barney said. "Telling the police about us."

"You too," I said.

"I thought you were for us, man, I really did." Barney leaned forward, hands on knees. "Tell me, Nicky baby, what exactly did you tell the police?"

"Nothing," I said. "She did all the talking. I wasn't even there."

"Did you say anything about . . . Thailand?"

"I don't know what she said. In any case, what about Thailand?"

Barney stood up and sighed. "You're a bloody fool, Nicky. Getting caught up in the middle like this."

I started to shake my head to show that I didn't know what I was getting caught in the middle of. I stopped. Head shaking was going to be strictly prohibited for some time.

Barney thrust a flaming cigarette into my mouth.

"I'm giving it up," I said. "Gives you cancer."

Maurice said, "If I were you, I wouldn't worry about that. Cancer is a lingering disease." And he laughed.

Barney said, "Latif would like to see you, after we've had our little chat." He paused to let that sink in. "But I like you, Nicky. Honestly, I do. So I've persuaded Maurice and Pierre that if you are a good boy, we'll drop you off quietly, and everything will be dead cool."

Including me, I thought, unless they used dynamite. "I don't even *know* what we've got to talk about," I said.

"Enough," Barney said. "Out there, Nicky baby, we've got the statues. Now why don't you be a nice guy and tell us where you stashed the manuscript."

There was no point in saying what manuscript, because they already knew I had it. So I said, "I've forgotten. One clout on the head and I get amnesia. Had it since a child."

Barney said, "You should have accepted Diaz's offer, you know. You could have made a profit."

"We all make mistakes," I said. "In any case what are you going on about the manuscript for? You've got the statues."

"That manuscript is worth money," Barney said. "That's why." He lit a cigarette. "You know that tart of yours started a whole heap of trouble. She cost us a packet of money when she forced us to abandon the other job. She caused Diaz a lot of trouble too. Because we'd lost money we had to remind him that we'd bought a manuscript from him before and he couldn't deliver it. You see, if we hadn't lost so much, we wouldn't have to bother Diaz or anybody."

"Who is we, Barney? The three of you?"

"There's more than the three of us, Nicky. Far more than three. In fact I even thought of asking you to join us. You've got experience, and you've got some brains. We could use you."

"For what?"

"Much the same sort of thing you did in Africa. Only it's better organised and better paid. And we run the show."

Barney couldn't possibly have any idea of what I'd done in Africa, but I was getting a very clear idea of what he was doing in Ceylon and Thailand. It was what I had expected. A gang of ex-mercenaries deciding that organised crime was more profitable than disorganised war. And a lot safer. With wars, people were always shooting at you.

Dirkian had been involved with them too. He had organised the Thai robbery for them, and when he had kept more than his fair share they'd tried to get it back, by robbing him of the Greek vase. He had come out shooting, and they had shot back. That was all there was to it.

Ponsonby had found out about Dirkian's visits to Thailand and he had somehow connected that with Dirkian and the robbery.

"I wouldn't join you," I said. "You're nothing without Dirkian. Dirkian would never have let you kill Ponsonby."

"Hey man, Ponsonby was trying blackmail."

"He committed suicide," Maurice said. "He ran short of money and when we wouldn't give him any, he jumped from his hotel window."

"I don't like violence," I said.

"Neither do I, Nicky baby, neither do I. But sometimes it's necessary." And to prove that point, he stubbed his cigarette into the middle of my naked chest.

I forced back the scream as the raw and searing pain crescendoed. My head bounced against the glass and started quite a different pain.

From behind Barney, Cindy cried, "Tell him Nicholas for God's sake, tell him! What do a few scraps of old paper matter?"

"That's the idea," Barney said. "The little girl is right," and he flung an arm around her and smiled. Cindy simply stood there, rigid.

I grinned insouciantly at them. Those wads of old paper did matter. That wad of old paper was important, and not only because it could fetch Elmer and Lindsay and me, three thousand pounds. It was important because I was the only one present who knew where it was. Once they knew where it was, I would be as useless to them as a bull's udder. Meanwhile, I thought of Lindsay running to the Volkswagen. Time was what I needed. Time was on my side. Barney came up and squatted in front of me. "Alright, Nicky baby, tell Uncle Barney all."

I told Barney what he could do with all, his mother, his sister and Auntie Barney as well.

Time, I thought. All I needed was more time. Spin it out, prolong it, anything to gain time. Lindsay had seen me being kidnapped. She had gone for help. And sooner or later, she'd find us. Sooner I hoped, than later.

"Pierre used to be a boxer," Barney said. "He's dying to get some practice."

I said nothing. It was a good way of conserving strength.

"Come on, Nicky. Tell me where the manuscript is."

"Tell me about the dynamite," I said.

"That was for the girl. She knows too much, and talks too much. It would have looked liked an accident, and the fishermen would have been blamed."

"You're stupid," I said. "And that's another reason I won't work with you."

Barney looked at Maurice and Maurice called Pierre in a

soft, low voice.

Pierre came down from the bridge, clad only in a vest and white slacks, wiping his hands on the seat of his pants. He was a callous looking bastard, with well rounded shoulders and wide, scarred hands that looked as solid as elm. Fortunately for me, he lacked imagination. But he made up for it with a kind of innate brutality.

He began by cuffing me lightly about the head and sticking punches into my ribs and stomach. I couldn't do much to avoid the blows, except roll, and relax, and try to absorb them as much as was possible. Then it became a little more serious. Taps around the eyes, jabs up against the nose, hard vicious slaps to the face. Finally he really began to beat me up, slowly, systematically, methodically, the punches really telling, forcing me up against the back of the bunk, raising deep blue bruises on my face and body. I sagged and rolled, and gasped.

One of the advantages of being beaten over the head is that it limits the amount of punishment you can take afterwards. After a while Pierre's blows ceased to come through. My mind felt separated, packed in cotton wool, the cabin and Pierre and Barney and wide eyed Cindy receded and receded, diminishing to a tiny, far away circle, and just before the comforting blackness came I thought of Lindsay running across the beach.

Thinking that time was still on my side.

I was wrong.

42

THERE WAS A RIGID BAR of pain across my back and a throbbing in my head that felt like dentists' drills gouging out pieces of soggy brain. My mouth was dry and full of salty tongue, my body felt as if it had been trodden on by an elephant wearing clogs. I was lying on my side curled up on a narrow bunk, my hands and feet still bound. A crack of yellow light seeped underneath a door and I rolled gently. I was in one of the aft cabins and the boat seemed to have stopped.

The cabin was quite small, with hardly enough room to change a shirt in. There was a narrow bunk opposite me, a tiny porthole above. The only sound was the steady chugging of the engine and the slurp of water against the side.

I rolled onto my back and forced myself to sit up. Outside the sea was dark and empty. We were in the middle of nowhere and waiting. For what? I stared at the black ripples of foamless waves. Far out there was a speck of light, another boat. I lay back on the bunk and tried to think with what was left of my head. They were waiting for Lindsay. They had tried to get her twice and failed, and this afternoon I'd been second choice. Lindsay was in that boat, and Lindsay was the one they owed something to. She'd sabotaged their plan to rob a dagoba, she knew too much about them, and she could be made to talk more easily than I could.

I had another chilling thought. Whether Lindsay came or not, I was soon going to be dead. Dead as Dirkian, dead as Ponsonby. I knew more about them than Lindsay did, and as long as one of us was free, none of them would be safe.

I lay in the dark and thought about dying and wrestled with my bonds, feebly.

The ropes were damp with sweat and tightly bound. Even if I didn't feel as though I'd been through a concrete mixer, I couldn't have done very much about them. Except lie on my back and stare at the thin darkness filtering through the porthole and think about dying.

The cabin door creaked. A quiet click, a brush of light, a low voice whispering, "Nicky?" Cindy's voice.

"Over here."

I felt her stand over me.

"I've brought a knife. Let me cut you free." Her hands explored my back, a knife sawed at my bound wrists. "I'm sorry for what has happened," Cindy said. "They made me do it. Find you, I mean. Otherwise they were going to do to my father, like they did to Sunil, and he's too old for that."

"You could have told the police."

"My father owes them money, for something he sold them before. He is not a bad man, Nicholas. You must believe that. He is just dishonest."

And not averse to a little blackmail on the side. I took the knife from her and began cutting the ropes around my ankles. Blood was surging into my hands, making the ends of my fingers tingle so that I could hardly move the knife. "Here. You cut them."

"There's something else I must tell you. About yesterday."

The ropes came off my legs, letting through the tingling and the numbness. Desperately I began to rub them. Yesterday was a million light years away. Last night was a million light years away too.

"They wanted me to check how many of you were there, and if you had found anything, diving. They wanted me to bring something back. I gave them the stones and they got quite excited, as if the stones were gold."

"It was Maurice who gave me the shell. And they promised not to hurt you. Barney said it was a question of business and that you would understand. He said he'd known you a long time and you'd once robbed a vase for him and that you needed help to bring up the treasure anyway, and they would work with you. He said the others, the American and the girl would cheat you."

I sat there, feeling the blood flow into tortured limbs. "What are we going to do now?"

She said, "If you can swim, go over the side and get away." She began to rub my wrists. "They didn't force me to sleep with you. I did that because I wanted to. You must believe that."

"Why are we stopped here?" I asked.

"They're waiting for your friend," she said. "Once they've sunk their boat and got all of you, they think it will be easier to make one of you tell them where the manuscript is. They want the girl, especially. Whether she talks or not, Pierre says they're going to do to her what they did to the women terrorists in Algeria."

I thought grimly about Lindsay and bits of broken glass, of the necks of bottles and of hand held dynamos, of the things they could do to her with a simple piece of wire. Outside the porthole, the speck of light had grown to a swiftly moving rectangle. My hands and feet still tingled with a million pin-pricks a million times a second. There was no way I could warn them, there was nothing I could bloody well do, except sit there and watch.

"Afterwards they're meeting up with one of Latif's boats. They're going on to India and Latif will take this boat back and get the manuscript for them. They've promised you to Latif."

I waited for the numbness to ease, for the blood to flow into my arms and legs. I waited for what seemed an eternity.

"We'd better hurry," Cindy said.

I swung my legs off the bed and said, "Okay, let's go," and staggered, sharp blinding pain shooting up my legs all the way to my head. Cindy caught me and we stood there for a few moments, while I got my breath and balance back and waited for the pain to go away. Then I tried a few cautious steps, took a deep breath, did a few deep knee bends and said, "I'm ready."

Featherlight Cindy slipped the catch. Light flooded in, light obstructed by the heavy figure of Barney Goldman, and reflecting off the two inch barrelled Colt Detective Special he held in his hand. He jabbed the gun into her stomach and snarled, "So that's where you got to, my lovely," and pushed her back into the room.

I caught Cindy and moved her back, to one side. Barney stepped over the raised edge of the doorway and came into the cabin. "You treacherous little bitch," he said and turned to me and smiled. "I don't know how you do it, Nicky baby, but tonight we're going to find out."

Three of us in that cabin made quite a crowd. Barney smelt of alcohol and sweat. He said, "So," and slapped Cindy viciously across the face. Her head jolted against my shoulder and bounced upright, her hair whipped my cheek. She whimpered, bit back the cry of pain, and stood there erect. I stood there too.

"That's for the present," Barney said. "Afterwards we've got plans for you." He moved closer to her, peering into her face for a reaction. Then I moved. He was holding his gun right handed, slightly in front of his waist, like the amateur he was. Barney Goldman should have stayed with selling guns instead of trying to use them. My left hand swooped from in front of my shoulder, grasped the back of his gun hand and swung it across his body. At the same time I brought my right hand across, palm slightly cupped, fingers extended. The extended fingers jammed into the cold, squishy wetness of his eyes.

Barney's head rocked back and by then I was swinging my hand again, turning it sideways, chopping with the fleshy edge of it right across his windpipe.

Barney gasped once and ran out of air. The gun came free. He staggered back. I moved forward swinging my fist, large knuckles upwards and outwards. All my weight was behind that blow, all my weight, and all my frustration and resentment at having been chased, cheated, tied up and hit over the head. The blow slammed into Barney's solar plexus in a steep arc, flesh and cartilage folded around the knuckles with a jar that nearly dislocated my shoulder. Barney lifted off, bounced his head against the cabin wall and crashed down over the bunk to the floor, his eyes already glassy, his mouth a rigid, soundless O.

I moved the gun into my right hand and looked through the porthole. I could see the boat clearly now, a twenty foot motor cruiser, much sleeker than our ancient houseboat. It was travelling quickly, stern low in the water, its cabin throwing yellow squares of light on the sea and foam peeling white from its bows. As it drew nearer a searchlight on its foredeck came on. Fools, I thought, they were only making the target easier.

I hefted the gun in my hands. "I'm going out," I said to Cindy. "You'd better stay here." The gun felt nice in my hand. Comforting. I raised it to the light from the porthole and looked at it. It was a nice gun alright. But it only had one bullet.

One bullet for two people. I edged slowly into the corridor, thinking I had to do something. The main cabin was brightly lit and I went towards it on bare feet, pressing my body to the wall.

Pierre and Maurice were there, kneeling on the seats, looking through the window at the approaching boat. They both wore wet suits. A scuba and harness lay on the seat between them. Beside them were two Uzi machine pistols and a box of grenades, the new smooth variety.

There was a movement behind me, a breath of air on my cheek. I turned to look at Cindy. I pointed urgently to the ladder and the open hatch at the rear of the corridor. She looked confused, pointing to the galley and the rack of spear guns on the bulkhead. I made another gesture. She had no doubt this time that I wanted her up and out.

I heard the sound of the approaching boat quite clearly, lower now than the chug of our own engines. Gently, as if I was unleashing a hair trigger, I loosed the latch that held open the door between the corridor and the main cabin. Holding the door in my left hand, I stepped towards the cabin.

In the last split second, the door creaked. Pierre turned, eyes widening in amazement as he recognised me, hands streaking for the Uzi. I fired between them, slammed the door shut and was blown backwards. My ears filled with a great cracking sound as the .38 slug ripped through the scuba and air trapped at two thousand two hundred and fifty pounds per square inch exploded out of the metal casing. The engine coughed and went silent, and in the stillness there was an awful moaning sound.

The lights flickered and I dragged myself along the corridor towards the cabin. Slowly, tiredly, I dragged myself up against the wall. The cabin door was buckled open and I had a glimpse of tattered green cushions and slivers of glass, of jagged bodies crumpled on bloodstained boards. Then I heard the high-pitched shriek of a bullet ricocheting, and fell.

I turned round. Barney was lying across the ledge of the aft cabin, a tiny pistol in his hand, blood trickling down his face and a desperate searching look about his wavering arm. The arm found me and stopped. I waited, too tired to move, too late, too tired and too shocked from the explosion to even think of moving.

Then there was a twang and the chunky sound of metal sticking into wood. The gun clattered to the floor and Barney was staring at his wrist transfixed to the door by a harpoon from the gun Cindy held.

Cindy came slowly down the steps, eyes wide, mouth gaping, the harpoon gun held in nerveless hands.

"Cindy," I shouted. "Wait there."

Automatically she stopped.

Blood was trickling out of one of Barney's eyes and he was staring disbelievingly at his crucified wrist. He tore his gaze away from the wrist and looked up at me.

"Barney love," I said, "The boat's sinking and you're bleeding to death. You can die both ways, for all I care."

"Nicholas man, please."

I heard footsteps thud on the planking above our heads. I heard Lindsay's voice crying, "Nicky, Nicky."

"The two temple guards," I said to Barney. "Dirkian, Ponsonby. You're going to die very slowly."

I turned and walked towards Cindy.

"Nicky!" Barney cried after me. "Nicky!"

I turned back. "You killed Dirkian?"

"Yes."

"Ponsonby?"

"Yes."

"And the temple robbery?"

"Yes, man, yes."

"Who is behind it and where is he?"

Barney shook his head.

"Tell me where Dupre is, the person who set up the Thailand job with Dirkian."

"In Spain," Barney said and muttered out an addess.

I turned away from him. "Goodbye Barney," I said, over

my shoulder. "I'll see you in about twenty years," I went towards the end of the corridor where Elmer, Lindsay and Harvid were crowding around Cindy.

I felt very tired and very old. "I'm sorry it wasn't arms," I said to Harvid, "but he should tell you enough to secure your promotion."

I went up the ladder onto the deck. The air tasted cool and fresh and beautiful.

I stood there a long time staring at the restless sea and the shadows on the water.

43

It was eleven o'clock when I woke up. Cindy lay beside me, battered and bruised, sound asleep. I leaned over and kissed her lightly on the forehead. Then I went out. Outside, it was another scorching day.

Elmer and Lindsay were on the far verandah.

I drank some coffee and asked, "Are the scuba still in the VW?"

"Yes," Lindsay said, "Why?"

"I dropped something," I said.

My body was still aching and stiff and the ride in the VW didn't make it any better. Lindsay parked at the water's edge and helped me sling on the aqua lung. Then I walked backwards into the water and said I wouldn't be long.

I set off the way I had done the previous afternoon. Only after fifteen yards, I went under and hovered over the sea bed. I made for the mooring point and turned back. And did it once more, looking down from above. And once more, crawling along the sea bed. All I found was a shell. The columnar immobile shadow, a shade greener than the sea, had gone, as if it had never been there.

When we got back to the rest house, Cindy had gone too. She'd left a note pinned to my pillow. "I love you Nicholas Maasten," it said, "but for the present, twenty-four hours with you is enough."

*   *   *

Harvid was waiting for us at the hotel in Colombo. "We can all have beer," he said. "Today I have been promoted and have also received commendations from the Moroccan and the Thai police." He turned to me. "You're a dangerous person, Mr. Maasten, but I like you. I won't spoil my day by having you arrested."

That was decent of him. After all he'd made three arrests last night. "What happened to the bronzes Goldman recovered?" I asked. "We're entitled to a reward."

"Yes," Elmer interjected. "Treasure trove and all that."

"An unfortunate thing happened to those bronzes," Harvid said. "They'd been so long in the sea that on being exposed to air, they wasted away." Harvid smiled at me. "Have another beer, Mr. Maasten."

I raised the foaming glass and grinned at him. "Cheers," I said.

Harvid said, "But I have arranged for two other bronzes to be shipped to you. I think you would describe them as interesting fakes."

Harvid raised his glass. "Ticky-tock," he said, smiling.

* * *

The plane wheeled over the palm-fringed bay banking slightly, easing slowly upwards. From the seat between us, Elmer said, "I'm sorry it hasn't been as profitable as I expected, but we did have fun."

My body ached as I unfastened the seat belt. "Speak for yourself," I said.

Elmer said, "I might be able to push up the price of the manuscript, by a thousand say, for authentication."

Lindsay steadfastly pretended not to hear.

"It still doesn't leave us with much profit," he said.

I reached into my pocket. "Put this in the kitty," I said and handed him the shell.

He looked at it and said, "Why sir, it's a sea shell."

"Look at the spirals," I said. "They're left-handed."

Lindsay leaned across interested. "What is significant about that?"

"They're very rare. *Turbinella purum* is what they're called. The sacred chank. I think you'll find it'll add over a thousand pounds to our profit."

Elmer kept the shell in his lap and sat back in his seat, looking thoughtful. I looked across the cabin, towards the porthole. Below me were palms and beaches and sea and somewhere underneath that resplendent blue sea was my jade phallus. And somewhere below me, was Cindy.

Someday, I promised myself, I would return. Someday soon.